HOW TO BE A BADASS WITCH

HOW TO BE A BADASS WITCH

HOW TO BE A BADASS WITCH™ BOOK ONE

MICHAEL ANDERLE

LMBPN Publishing
PMB 196, 2540 South Maryland Pkwy
Las Vegas, NV 89109

First US edition, November 2020
Version 1.02, January 2021
ebook ISBN: 978-1-64971-336-0
Print ISBN: 978-1-64971-449-7

To Family, Friends and
Those Who Love
To Read.
May We All Enjoy Grace
To Live The Life We Are
Called.

CHAPTER ONE

"Blergh." Kera MacDonagh poked her head out of the tangle of covers, looking for the source of the beeping in her immediate vicinity. The clock near her bed showed the time 11:42 am. That was well before the alarm she had set, which meant the culprit was her phone. Wild flailing in the blankets produced nothing and she flopped over to reach blindly around on the floor for her phone. "Ughhhhh."

Her fumbling produced the damned thing, currently displaying her mother's contact information. Kera dropped her head back onto the pillow with a groan as she answered. "He—" She cleared her throat. "Hello?"

"Hello, Kera, it's your mother." Her mother's voice had the sort of impeccable diction and unidentifiable accent practiced by news anchors.

"Oh, good." Kera forced herself to sit up and began wiping sleep crusts out of the corners of her eyes. "For a second there, I was afraid someone had stolen your phone and called me from it."

"Yes, dear." There was a little sigh. "I had a few spare minutes, so I thought I would call you."

Kera, who had been slouching as she rubbed her face and smoothed her hair, sat up a bit straighter. A sigh instead of a joke? Her mother, a devoted philanthropist, had *a few spare minutes?*

"I'm, uh…" She shoved herself out of bed and curled her toes under on the cold concrete, wincing. Her Spidey senses were tingling. "I'm good. Thanks for calling! Great to hear your voice, but I know you're super busy, so—"

"*Wonderful.*" Her mother studiously ignored the implicit request to hang up. "So, how are things going?"

Kera rolled her eyes heavenward. Her mother had a specific question for her, but it would be useless to ask her to cut to the chase. The woman would lead with side questions, maneuver Kera into a verbal trap of some sort, and then pounce. There would be no speeding this up.

"Things are good," she said finally. "You know, work. The usual."

The second the words came out of her mouth, she cursed herself. There was no going back, however.

"Wonderful," her mother said again. "You know, it *just* occurred to me that today is the two-month anniversary of your graduation."

"Here we go," Kera muttered.

It was too early for this shit.

"With your grades, companies should be tripping over each other to hire you." Her mother's tone was sweet and cheerful. "And, as we all know, Los Angeles is host to twenty-three of the fifty-seven Fortune 500 companies in California, all of whom need computer science graduates."

"The only people who know that are the ones who read about Los Angeles on Wikipedia." Kera rubbed her face. "Look, Mom, I really appreciate you trying to help me get a job, but the fact is—"

"You haven't gotten a job offer and not told me, have you?"

As a matter of fact, she had gotten a few calls from recruiters, but Kera knew that if she admitted it, her chances of getting out of this conversation alive were slim to none.

"I haven't been *looking* for jobs like that," she said honestly.

"Why is that, honey?" The tone was still sweet, but there was a warning there.

"Because as I've told you *several* times, I have no interest in working with AI developed for customer service robots." Kera, having been raised by this woman, was able to give as good as she got. "I'd rather be a waitress-slash-bartender, and do you know why? Because when there's idiocy on the other side of the bar, there's a reason behind it, compared to the idiocy of the AI, which is usually *technically* logical but stems from a missing comma or some ridiculous parameter that management insisted on even though they don't understand AI."

Mrs. MacDonagh sighed, and Kera braced herself.

Sure enough, the lecture that came next could have filled out a bullshit bingo card in record time. "Kera, you can't just waste your abilities and potential working on your motorcycle and slinging drinks." Her mother's tone was crisp, which was a sure sign that she was angry. The angrier she got, the more formal she became. "I understand that it *seems* like good money when you're getting tips, but trust me, a stable job with good benefits is worth far more in the long run. Have you considered the raises? Have you considered the health insurance and the retirement investment matching?"

"Mom—"

"When things go south—and they *will* eventually since *everyone* has bad luck sometimes—you will want stability, and—"

"*Mom.*"

"No, listen to me, Kera." She could see her mother drumming her fingers on the kitchen counter. "You always wanted to do something that made a difference."

Kera clenched her free hand and fervently wished she was holding something she could throw at the wall.

"Be honest with yourself, dear." Her mother's tone had gotten slightly gentler. "I know that an entry-level job in IT doesn't seem like a dream come true, but the ten-year trajectory it puts you on is *very* different from the one you're on right now. What are you going to do, buy the bar?"

Kera was sighing when an idea struck her. "Maybe," she said. "Maybe I will. Maybe I'll buy the bar, start a chain, and let people open franchises. I'll rake in the profits while other people do the dirty work, and then we can talk about whether I'd be better off in a cubicle, getting harassed about semicolons."

There was silence.

Kera sighed. "Mom. Please. I know all the people who ended up in those jobs. They're not happy, and I wouldn't be, either."

"So, you're still in touch with some of the young men you studied with?"

Kera, sensing that the subject was changing into yet another dangerous area, immediately began evasive maneuvers. "I have to go, but you bring up some good points. I'd love to talk about them another time. How does five weeks from Thursday look for you?"

"Whatever happened to that nice running back you were dating?" her mother asked, determinedly ignoring Kera's rapid-fire goodbye. "Michael."

Kera sighed. "That was sophomore year."

"And?"

"And he is now married, with a baby on the way, living in the suburbs and teaching high school football."

"Well, strike that option, then."

"You think?"

"Darling, if you're attracted to…" Her mother cleared her throat. "Well, please know that if you're worried about shocking us, we aren't going to disapprove."

"Mom. I haven't had a boyfriend in a while, so you're asking if I'm a lesbian?"

"I just didn't want you to be afraid of telling us," her mother said. "If you were."

"I'm not. Mom, can we talk about something else?"

"Kera, you're awfully squeamish. You always were apt to stick your fingers in your ears when it came to talking about sex."

"Because you tried to give me the talk by telling me where Rob and I came from!" Kera waved her free hand. "Oh, God, and I worked so hard to suppress those memories. When will someone come up with brain bleach? It would make a billion dollars on the open market."

"There you go," her mother said smugly. "Now you have a goal —one that isn't bartending, but also isn't one of the cubicle jobs you so hate."

"Sure. I'll get right on it, thanks."

"Mmm. I have to go, sweetie. Have a good day. Try not to lose the ability to learn. Grab a business book, learn an extra craft, but do *something* with your life."

"Goodbye, overprotective maternal figure with a goddess complex."

"I can't help it," her mother asserted. "Our family—and that means you, too—has had special genes for generations. I'm just making sure you find a productive way of—"

"Wasn't this the point where you were supposed to hang up?"

"Not without having the last word," the elder MacDonagh pointed out. "Goodbye, baby."

Something on the other end clicked and the call ended, the screen returning to Kera's list of contacts.

"Ugh, mothers."

It wasn't even noon, after all. There was no reason for her to be awake at the current hour, but her mother had not only woken her up, but she had also robbed Kera of the ability to go back to sleep.

After all, there was nothing more frustrating than ruminating on the fact that college was a gigantic con and life after it was a glorified hamster wheel.

Not that Kera disliked her job, of course, and she had *loved* her degree. She had taken to learning the internal logic of how things worked, how to measure them, and how to troubleshoot them like a fish to water.

She just hadn't figured out what to do next. Working as a bartender wasn't really changing the world—which, unfortunately, was something she *did* want to do.

Except that it seemed insufferably juvenile as a goal.

Kera groaned and looked back at the bed, but she knew she wasn't going to be able to sleep. With a sigh, she headed off to take a shower. Now she had to come up with something to do for the next three hours that wasn't going to make her feel like an abject failure.

She picked her phone back up and stared at it for a moment before opening the reading app she used. She navigated to the store and hesitated.

What the hell should she search for?

"How to become a slumlord for bars?" she said aloud. She grinned. "How to…how to… Okay, start there." She began typing. "How to…"

She blinked. Suggested results had already popped up, and one of them didn't look like the others. She double-tapped it, frowning. It was a joke book; it had to be.

After all…

No, there was no way anyone thought that was real. On impulse, Kera clicked the Buy Now button, then rolled her eyes at herself.

"Good job, MacDonagh. You're trying not to feel like a failure, and what's the first book you download? Something written by a crazy person. Still, as far as How To Be guides go, I *do* like the idea of *How to Be A Bad Ass Witch*."

CHAPTER TWO

<u>Six weeks earlier</u>

"James? The council is assembled if you would like to begin." The voice was smooth and cultured, with just the faintest hint of French roundness to the vowels. Footsteps sounded, and another figure came to the window. "What are you watching?"

James P. Lovecraft nodded at the scene outside the windows. Beyond the rolled-aside crimson curtains and blue-tinted glass planes that opened out on the mansion's property, the rolling hills and fields of upstate New York were blanketed with pure white snow. Icicles hung from the evergreen boughs and gnarled branches of the surrounding trees.

"Festive, don't you think?" He looked at his companion. "And appropriate for a meeting of the council."

"Snow," Mother LeBlanc said with a shudder, "is *never* appropriate."

He smiled at her. Her age was a mystery. At first glance, she looked no older than twenty-five or so, a beautiful woman with smooth mahogany skin and a perpetual broad, pleasant smile of relaxed bemusement. Her long box-braided hair added to the effect.

The dress she always wore, however, was ... strange. It seemed to have been woven from dozens of square feet of multicolored silk and velvet. It had no particular shape, yet it somehow emphasized the curves of her body as she moved or when it settled around her. Its bright hues appeared to have changed each time one looked. It was almost miraculous but sufficiently bizarre that people who first met her took some time to overcome their slight discomfort at its implied mysteries.

James knew it was likely a holdover from the New Orleans voodoo tradition from whence the woman came. Though she'd moved on to mainstream thaumaturgy, the magic of old Louisiana still held secrets that were obscure to the other members of the council.

For example, in addition to the dress's sheer ponderous massiveness, it also had the curious ability to disguise the presence of whatever else LeBlanc might be hiding within its folds.

James recalled an incident five years ago when she'd pulled something—he couldn't recall what—out of her sleeve unexpectedly. He'd quipped that she could likely cook an entire meal with the contents of her dress.

Without missing a beat, she had promptly reached into the garment's many billows and produced an iron pot, a sharp kitchen knife, an onion, a bag of spices, a ladle, and, finally, a live chicken, which squawked and scattered loose feathers across the floor. She held the unfortunate fowl over the side table and slammed the knife into its neck, allowing the bug-eyed head to roll into a corner before gutting and plucking the rest. Meat, diced onions, water, and spices had all gone into the pot, which she took into the kitchen.

When the soup was done, she'd brought it back for them all to partake of, and that was that. He'd never again questioned or commented on Mother LeBlanc's wardrobe.

It helped that the soup had been delicious, though he wouldn't have dared mention it if it weren't.

"Are you ready?" she asked him.

He nodded and adjusted his glasses, clearing his throat as he did so. He was a trim man who appeared to be somewhere in his mid-thirties, with high cheekbones and a narrow jaw. People were generally unsurprised to discover he was descended from old English aristocracy.

The two of them entered the mansion's dining room, and James nodded to the other master thaumaturges gathered around the ancient oak table.

They were ready, though they did not yet know it, to hear his plan to save their profession.

He took his seat partway down the table from Mother LeBlanc at the head. She cleared her throat and looked at the assembled council. "Ladies and gentlemen, welcome once again to the annual meeting of the High Congress of Thaumaturgy." She gave a wry smile. "We appreciate you showing up only two weeks before Christmas; it's a busy time of year, but at the last vote, everyone agreed to maintain the traditional date." One eyebrow lifted conspiratorially. "So, no complaining."

A few people chuckled drily. James figured that if anyone were going to protest, it would be Mary Mitchell two seats down from him, but she remained silent.

"This is an important meeting. As you know, recruitment remains at an all-time low, and we have been unable to fill the vacancies left in our congress." LeBlanc gestured with a slim dark hand at the three chairs that sat empty around the table.

Everyone looked around uncomfortably. Those who currently sat on the congress called themselves the Twelve for obvious reasons, but the round table had been meant to accommodate fifteen. The other three seats had been empty for far too long.

Mary Mitchell raised a hand. "We *did* decide not to promote anyone else to the triumvirate position," she said. "And we're functioning just fine without a leader. Is it truly *necessary* to replace those seats, or is it only centuries-old force of habit?"

James had to admit that she had a point, but as usual, she was missing the big picture. Lady Mary Carter Mitchell was a slim, thin-faced woman, who combined an old-fashioned primness and sense of propriety with a highly modern impatience. She disliked meetings, procedures, and oversights, preferring to rush through such things as quickly as possible so she could return to her lifelong hobby—the study and manipulation of plants.

They were almost at the point for James to segue to his own plans, but before he could, Damian Diaz spoke.

"High Witch Templeton," he said, in his booming, theatrical way, "was not only our head bureaucrat. A proper coven *requires* thirteen members." He gave a wry smile, "Yes, she had an unfortunate tendency to be busy somewhere else whenever any of us reached out to her for help," there was a round of chuckles around the table, "but she never shirked her duty when it came to larger-scale spells, which there are now no way for us to perform should we need to. We should fill the thirteenth position, at least, or better yet, all three of the empty seats."

"Yes," James said at once, seeing a natural segue, "and that is why it's imperative that we seek new recruits. Mother LeBlanc and I are in agreement on this."

"In the past five years, we have found no students," LeBlanc told them. Though the fact was well-known, it was not often spoken aloud, and many at the table looked away. She continued, "In the past two years, we have found no candidates for training. Within two or three generations, unless we turn things around, our discipline might disappear entirely, and, with it, our ability to guide events for the good of humanity."

The thaumaturges around the table looked at one another, then most of them ended up gazing at Lauren Jones. Round-faced and ginger-haired, she was the sort of person who perpetually looked younger than she was. On even brief acquaintance, however, it became clear that she could command the attention of any audience. As the best teacher among the Twelve, she had been particularly worried about their lack of recruits.

Now she turned her brown eyes on James, though she thought for a long while before she spoke.

"It has weighed on me," she admitted. "We say we have stepped back from human affairs due to the increasing interconnectedness of the world, because even a small intervention is more likely to be noticed, because interventions are less likely to be necessary, but I wonder. I wonder if we have stepped back because we feel powerless. And I wonder if our abdication of our duty means that someday we will be needed, and we will not be there."

There was silence. Even James, who had come prepared to argue for expanding their ranks, had not thought such dire things. Over the millennia, thaumaturges had intervened rarely but impactfully, aiding scientists who attempted to cure diseases, helping isolated groups of soldiers who might turn the tide of a battle, and sometimes turning wildfires or storms away from highly populated areas.

As the interconnectedness of the world grew, the number of isolated groups cut off from human aid shrank, as did chances to intervene without someone noticing.

And now, without thirteen members in the coven, there were many spells that could not be done at all, even if there was a need and they could do so without revealing themselves.

James nodded quietly and swallowed.

Lauren did not let him recover from her bombshell. "We all agree that this is an urgent need," she said. She did not spare a glance for Mary Mitchell, and her tone suggested she would brook no argument. "Tell us what your plan is." She gave a small smile. "I assume you have one."

James hid his own smile as he turned to LeBlanc. "Madam, with your leave? My idea might take several minutes to explain."

Though not formally their leader, she served as their spokeswoman and held some degree of authority over how the discussion would proceed. Since his idea was unorthodox in the extreme, he needed every iota of respectability he could garner.

The two of them had planned this in advance, and everyone knew she would say yes from the way she hesitated, drawing out the moment. If she were planning to say no, she would have said so instantly. Still, James found himself waiting anxiously for her assessment.

She smiled. "Yes, Mr. Lovecraft," she pronounced. "Make your pitch."

"Excellent." James sat up a little straighter in his chair. "Society is changing around us; each day, it's a new world out there." His background in advertising had taught him the value of dramatic, attention-grabbing statements. "If we are not only to thrive but even *exist* in the decades to come, we must rebuild our ranks. We need a proper coven again, and we need apprentices to carry on our legacies."

Mary and the other more conservative members narrowed their eyes at this. Old, stuffy, and absorbed in their own affairs, they were less than amicable to the prospect of having to accommodate newcomers.

James, however, was not prepared to stand by and watch thaumaturgy die out. "I propose a solution that is at once new and old: *publishing*. In this unprecedented age of literacy *and* with the recent advances in e-reading devices, a grimoire could be easily distributed."

"Write a new grimoire?" Mary Mitchell objected. "*That* is your grand plan?" She looked at the others, contempt plain on her face. "We cannot even find new recruits, and you want to rewrite our grimoire?"

"No." James took a deep breath. This was the place where his idea was the most unorthodox. "My plan is to release the grimoire to *potential* recruits. To self-publish it in the hope that some of those who find it have the will and talent to practice the spells."

There was a long silence. Damian looked shellshocked, Lauren was sitting back in her chair with her eyes focused on the middle distance, and Mary was fuming. The others wore expressions of disbelief.

Only Mother LeBlanc seemed calm. Her half-smile adorned her face as usual, and she leaned lightly on one arm, watching the others.

"You mean," Mary asked finally, "give out our secrets to the *entire world?*"

Everyone looked at James.

"Yes," James said simply.

His calm acceptance made Mary look like she was about to have an aneurysm. She glanced around at the rest of the table for support, but no one seemed to know what to say.

"For those who cannot use magic, the book will seem like nothing more than a novelty." The voice was a surprise. Even James swung his head around in shock.

He had not expected Mother LeBlanc to weigh in.

"But some *will*," Mary snapped. "For God's sake, will *none* of you say how insane this proposition is?"

"I have concerns," Damian admitted. "While my knowledge of the …social internet is not good, I cannot imagine how you mean to track who has downloaded the book and who has not. Are you able to do such a thing?"

LeBlanc looked at James curiously. She did not yet know about this piece of his plan.

"A good question," James said. "I have created a method by which I will be able to find new thaumaturges. In fact, it's sitting in front of you right now."

The Twelve leaned forward. The heavy silver bowl in front of them was filled with water, and, now that they were looking, a map of the United States lay at the bottom.

"Watch," James told them. He activated the spell that would utilize the scrying bowl and a golden dot appeared over upstate New York, along with smaller ones in several other areas of the country. "We are able to scry for thaumaturges."

"You have to know what you're scrying for," Mary Mitchell objected.

"We are scrying for magic," James told her. He was proud of this invention. It had taken weeks of thought to come up with a way he could find the new recruits once they had tried the spells. "As we know, manifesting and drawing upon magic happens after the art is being consistently practiced. This will not show us potential recruits—it can't—but it *will* show us those who begin using magic after the book has been released."

There was a moment of silence. Damian was smiling now, as was Lauren.

Mary wasn't. "When has *anyone* become a great thaumaturge simply by reading a printed tome?"

"It *is* unorthodox." James suspected she was using tradition as a pretext to avoid having to deal with the work that would go into processing new recruits, but he held back from disagreeing with anyone just yet. He had learned to take the opinions of the others into account, and the other attendees were still contemplating her words.

"I must agree with Ms. Mitchell," Lauren said. Her tone was regretful but firm, and her earlier smile was gone. "Magic is only mastered through a long apprenticeship of hands-on practice guided by a master. This would be like trying to learn martial arts from a book without ever sparring with a real-life opponent, or trying to learn to drive by reading a manual but never getting behind the wheel with someone who's done it before."

Others nodded, but no one spoke.

Seeing his opening, James cleared his throat and adjusted his glasses. There was truth, however unwelcome, in what they said, but he had considered the problem while coming up with the idea.

"Lauren and Ms. Mitchell bring up a good point," he said. "Thaumaturgy is an art beyond words, relying as it does on the proper understanding of magical forces. We have all had apprentices, and we have seen that all minds understand language differently—and, therefore, must find unique ways to conceptualize the forces with which they work."

Everyone nodded now, even Mary, who had a look of triumph on her face.

She wasn't going to like what was coming next, James thought.

He worked to keep his face straight and shrugged. "A book that has only a few ways to describe each concept will not reach *every* prospective student. We *will* fail to reach those whose understanding would have been gained by using different language or in-person instruction."

"If we will miss so many," Mary riposted back at once, "the plan is fundamentally flawed."

James tried not to smile at his triumph. She had set him up perfectly to hit a home run.

"However," he said gravely, "at this time, we are finding *no* candidates. Finding *any* allows us to begin growing our ranks again, and with more thaumaturges out in the world, we will have a better chance of reaching the others. But we must start somewhere."

Mary fell silent. She was indeed quite unhappy with him, but she could not refute his point. In addition, the others were now paying more attention.

"The idea is to rope them in," James said. "Lay out the basics so they are drawn in the direction of traditional instruction methods."

Nods went around the table.

"We will make it difficult to see who has published the book," James continued. "That will make it easy for us to find them before *they* find *us*. My background in advertising, meanwhile, will help me with the branding and so on that will allow the book to reach the widest possible distribution."

Damian snorted. "I have to say, I'll be amused to watch you try to advertise thaumaturgy to today's youth."

"We haven't agreed to this yet," Mary Mitchell snapped.

"Ms. Mitchell makes a very good point," Mother LeBlanc said gravely. "James has presented his idea but has also agreed to abide by the decision of this Congress. We should now put it to a vote."

James sat back in his chair, his heart beating fast. He trusted Mother LeBlanc's instinct on when to have the vote, but it was still very sudden. He had been working on this idea for months, and now…

Now, it was going to happen.

Or not.

Mother LeBlanc waited as calmly as if she had no stake in the matter.

"Aye," Lauren said after a moment.

"Aye," Damian agreed with a nod.

James's heart leaped. Four more and this was in the bag.

"You'll make me say it?" Mary asked them. "This is a ridiculous idea. Nay."

"Aye," Carter Brooks weighed in, his voice deep.

"Aye," Rosa Sanchez agreed.

"Aye."

Every head swung around. James had not expected Mother LeBlanc to indicate her preference at this point. She inclined her head to him. "Your plan is well-thought-out, and our need is great."

After that, the matter was as good as settled. There was one other nay, somewhat of a surprise, but the rest agreed. Mary

Mitchell left soon after, her face set in a scowl, and James tried not to worry what might come of that.

"Don't take it personally," Carter advised him. The older man nodded and clapped James on the shoulder. "A new era calls for new techniques. It is uncomfortable for all of us, but it is necessary."

"Agreed," Lauren added. She smiled at James as she slipped out the door.

"How close are you to publishing?" Damian inquired.

"Very," James admitted. "I collected the grimoire materials just in case. It's surprisingly easy to publish an e-book. Creating a bestseller is more difficult, but I'm looking forward to *that* challenge."

"Yes, and to get back to my question, how *are* you going to advertise it?" Damian was laughing.

"You don't think *Being A Noble and Solemne Studie of Thaumaturgy* will appeal to the youth of today?" Rosa teased.

The others laughed and looked at James, who hesitated. He knew this last idea was going to be just as uncomfortable for them as the rest of it.

"Actually," he said, "I, uh…I came up with a title, too. I want to call it *How to Be a Badass Witch*."

CHAPTER THREE

<u>Present Day</u>

Kera yawned. A scalding shower had helped her wake up, as had two cups of ridiculously strong coffee, but she was still feeling the lack of sleep.

Thanks a lot, Mom.

She padded into the main part of her living area, combing her still-wet hair with her fingers. When searching for apartments, she had found a converted warehouse. Judging by the bare-bones nature of the bathroom, this place had been meant to be used as a workshop of some kind, allowing someone to clean off engine grease or sawdust before heading home, but Kera had seen the potential in it.

The bathroom and shower were separate from the rest, but otherwise, her home was all one big open space, which was fine with her. She'd cleaned things up and brought in a handful of furnishings, though most were as bare-bones as the bathroom: wooden pallets to go under her futon, a serviceable butcher block table that had been hellish to get up here, a work stool that was too high for the table, and an office chair that was too low.

On the side of the warehouse pierced by huge double doors were her motorcycle and a pile of used workout equipment she'd gotten as an insanely good deal but hadn't yet put up. Kera stared at that area for a moment and tried to come up with the energy to hang up the punching bag and clean the weights.

"Maybe I'll be a better person tomorrow," she muttered finally and headed for the fridge, where she pulled out a pre-packaged salad and an iced mocha.

She settled into the office chair and looked around as she ate. Choosing this apartment had been one of the first things that was entirely her own selection, and working at the bar had been another.

Her mother didn't approve of either.

Kera ate quickly, keeping an eye on the time. It was 3:09 when she finished, which meant she had time to do an oil change on her motorcycle, Zee. She threw away the packaging from her food and got out the oversized grease-covered t-shirt she wore for motorcycle repairs.

Zee was a 2017 Kawasaki Z900 and by far her most prized possession. After the classic Z1000, Kawasaki had downgraded to the somewhat half-assed Z800. It was a good enough bike, but it had been rushed to market, in her opinion. Plus, why would they count down rather than up?

She wasn't the only one who'd had reservations, and Kawasaki had plugged the gap between the two with the Z900, intended as a replacement for both. It was a relatively no-frills model compared to recent high-end motorbikes, with things like electronic aids being kept to a minimum.

As far as she was concerned, the Z900 was a bike for people who appreciated the history and tradition of bikes. It wasn't for short-term trend-chasers.

In keeping with the model's focus on the basics, Kera had opted for the black-on-black version. It wasn't as striking as the ones with the green accents, but flashy colors weren't necessary. The ride was the important thing.

And at that, it excelled. Smooth to ride at lower speeds. Nice and easy for driving around town, but capable of revving its way up to something far more ferocious on the freeway or the back road in the boondocks.

Zee was five years old and she took good care of him, as well he deserved. Right now, he needed an oil change. That was a quick enough job.

"Don't worry, Zee," she said in a soft voice, "today's the day. I promised you wouldn't have to wait any longer." Over the years, nearly everyone she met had rolled their eyes at her habit of speaking to inanimate objects.

Kera didn't care. In her experience, things worked better when you spoke to them. She regularly thanked her alarm clock, her microwave, and Zee, to name a few things. She thanked her phone less often, but that was because it was what her mother used to get in touch with her.

She knelt next to Zee with a smile and set the motorcycle up for the task, spreading out the necessary tools, the oil, and towels and rags. All of those were stored in a large wooden box, which kept the area reasonably neat. Given that she lived in a warehouse, she wasn't worried about making a mess or spilling a drop of oil, but as her father liked to say, you should do something correctly or not do it at all.

It was a maxim Kera took to heart.

She had only owned Zee for about two and a half months. He wasn't new; she'd bought him used, but he was new to her, and she was still learning his individual quirks.

Prior to that, she'd had a 2009 model. It had only cost her a fairly reasonable $4,500, but she'd had to fix the damn thing up. Repair work was a fun way to spend her time, but it ate up a certain amount of time and money. There was always the temptation to get in over one's head or do an ill-advised upgrade.

Finally, right before she'd finished college, Kera had sold the ancient thing at a profit, her maintenance and improvement skills paying off in a big way.

And lo, the Z900 had become attainable, so she had attained it. She knew it would give her massive torque and power on the 110 while also providing a more...*civilized*...riding experience in the thick of downtown LA.

The best of both worlds.

A drop of oil splashed on the bike's hull.

"Aww," she exclaimed, picking up one of her emergency rags to wipe it off. "Sorry, Zee. Here, let's get you cleaned up."

Zee, of course, said nothing, but she liked to think he enjoyed being clean.

Soon, the task was done. She stood and admired her handi-work, then took off the work shirt and gave her hands a thorough cleaning. She still had time to leave for work a good ten minutes early, which would continue her streak of zero late days. Her boss Cevin was strict about coming in on time, and so far, Kera was the only one who'd managed to do so every shift.

In fact, she had enough time to stop and see Mr. Kim on the way in. She pulled a white button-down shirt over her tank top and denim shorts and added a leather jacket and leather pants on top of that. She often ran into people who thought leather was merely a fashion statement, but it provided better protection against abrasions during falls than most other materials. That was why bikers had adopted it.

And why it was particularly stupid that so many had dispensed with it.

She opened one of the tall wooden doors, swung a leg over Zee, and fired him up. He responded instantly, and she smiled at the smooth roar. He was running well again.

She pulled the motorcycle out of the warehouse, closed and locked it behind her, and drove into Los Angeles, the city that had become her home.

The day was grayish and damp. It wasn't the sort of weather people usually associated with Southern California, but a certain amount of rain was expected in the winter. Kera didn't mind. It kept things interesting, for one thing.

For another, no matter how gloomy the weather got here, it couldn't touch the bone-chilling cold of the northeast, where Kera had been born. She'd take that trade all day long.

She wove her bike through traffic, noting with approval how smooth a ride it gave at the restrictive speeds within the city. Only one motorist honked at her. She was driving sensibly, but there was always *some* asshole who had to lean on the horn.

The convenience store was approximately halfway between Kera's warehouse-apartment and the Mermaid. It lay tucked between an oil change place and a comics shop. Kera didn't have much need for the former, but she'd thought about checking out the latter sometime.

What held her back was that she had a sneaking suspicion the guys at the comics shop were going to form the same impressions of her as the guys in college.

She parked in the corner of the lot and took her helmet with her into the convenience store.

As usual, Mr. Kim was behind the counter. He was an older gentleman of Korean descent, better-dressed than his job technically required, with a full head of graying hair.

"Hello, Kera," he called.

"Good morning, Mr. Kim!" Kera waved back, then checked herself. "Or good afternoon. Morning for me, though!"

"Yes, you keep very late hours." She came in often enough that he knew a little bit about her, including her job. "How are you doing today?"

"I'm great," Kera told him. She plucked a bag of trail mix off a shelf, then headed to the line of coolers against the far wall. "I just got Zee cleaned out. You know, like when someone drinks a high-fiber smoothie or something. Anyway, how are you?"

"You have some strange ideas of what to put through motor-cycles," Mr. Kim quipped. "I got that tea you like."

"Thanks!" She opened the cooler and reached for a can of lightly sweetened green tea. This brand had quickly become her favorite, and the Kims had started ordering it regularly for her.

At the register, she laid out her purchase and watched Mr. Kim punch in the numbers from memory. He winced slightly and caught her worried frown.

"My arthritis is flaring up again. Such a pointless condition, but that's life."

Kera smiled sympathetically. "Yeah, one of those things. What flares up, though, must flare back down, right? So wait it out, and it will get better again."

He grumbled something about how he wasn't so sure anymore, but the twinkle of amusement in his eyes suggested it was only for show. She paid him, waved goodbye, and headed back outside, where Zee waited for her.

Pauline Smith stood before a white dry-erase board she'd set up within a small office in downtown Los Angeles. Her hair, almost a white-blonde, had been dyed a darker golden color. Her nails were immaculately painted with black polish, the sort of touch a trend-conscious, younger professional might add to an outfit. You would only see the unusually pale blue eyes if you looked closely enough to realize she was wearing brown contacts. Her figure, currently encased in a tailored suit, showed a combination of natural slimness and strenuous dieting.

Everything about her public image was carefully chosen and executed to perfection, and she was prepared to pull off the same thing with her newest venture.

She looked around the room with a perfect smile. "Everyone knows that Los Angeles is currently in the midst of a crime wave," she said. "This violence is regrettable, and we will do everything in our power to eradicate it."

No one spoke yet. There was Johnny, slender, bronze-skinned, and black-haired; Sven, broad and pale and grim-eyed, with reddish hair; and Lia, a trim young Korean-American woman with an impassive face and wavy black hair that reached her waist. All of them, like Pauline, were in their mid-twenties and none too far removed from well-respected institutes of higher learning. All three of them also wore tailored suits.

"It is absolutely necessary," Pauline said, "to create happiness and motivation in the population so that peace can be achieved. There must be a sense of allegiance, access to a good life, an appreciation of the social order."

Johnny opened his mouth to speak but closed it when Sven kicked him under the table. He had been born and raised in Los Angeles, left for business school in Austin, and signed on with Pauline after Lia had sought him out two weeks ago.

He also had zero idea what was going on. This didn't sound anything like the job he'd been led to believe he would be doing.

"Unfortunately, people cannot always be trusted to make good decisions," Pauline said simply. "It is a sad fact, but one we must embrace in order to move forward. What we must harness is our potential clients' desire for self-betterment. We will project that image ourselves, so we'll rise naturally to the top of the ecosystem."

Johnny stole a glance at Sven and Lia, both of whom were nodding. He nodded as well, making a mental note to speak to Sven at the earliest opportunity. He just hoped he could get out of this meeting without embarrassing himself.

"Our goal is to bring stability to downtown Los Angeles," Pauline said. "We will need to reach out to business owners and community leaders and grow mutually beneficial relationships. Mr. Jensen, Mr. Torrez, this will be your role in the organization."

Johnny plastered a smile on his face and nodded. Please let her not realize he was completely out of his depth. He'd gone to UT Austin, for fuck's sake. He'd graduated near the top of his class. He still had recruiters calling him at all hours for ridiculously boring jobs.

He was going to call some of them back just as soon as he was out of this clusterfuck.

"These relationships are crucial for us to understand the lay of the land," Pauline said. "We *must* be aware of the terrain in which we navigate. This allows us to plan out our strategy in advance and adapt quickly in the smaller details." She nodded at Lia, who had raised one slim hand. "Yes, Lia?"

"Do you have preliminary timelines?" Lia asked her.

Timelines for what? Johnny wanted to scream.

"A good question. I was coming to that. I simply wanted to ensure that everyone was on the same page. Mr. Torrez, Mr. Jensen, any questions?"

Johnny shook his head emphatically.

"Excellent." Pauline smiled. "Now, as per Ms. Min's insightful question, our goal is to control ninety percent of supply within three to five years. However, this long-term goal *only* manifests if we lay the groundwork now. That is why our next steps are so important. Ms. Min, for our next meeting, please bring me dossiers on all suppliers who have sustained increased or decreased market share in the past quarter. Mr. Torrez, Mr. Jensen, I would like you each to identify six business owners or community leaders with whom you will begin networking. Is everyone clear?"

Johnny nodded again.

"As you will learn, I prefer short meetings," Pauline said crisply. "I will see you all tomorrow at 10 o'clock. Do not be late."

Johnny stood, buttoned his suit jacket, and nodded to Lia and Pauline before following Sven quickly out of the room. The two of them had been acquainted in high school, and he would rather ask Sven about this shit than Lia.

"Yo, Carrot Top." He snapped his fingers at Sven.

"Mr. Torrez." Pauline stood in the doorway behind him. "Public image is deeply important. Please maintain professionalism at all times."

"Yes, ma'am." Johnny gave her a nod.

There was a faint flicker on Pauline's face at the word "ma'am," but she nodded in return and went back into the meeting room.

Johnny caught up with Sven a moment later. "What the hell was that?" he demanded under his breath.

"Not here," Sven said, also *sotto voce*.

"She wasn't making any sense!" Smart as a whip, Johnny had been educated on the dime of several family members and a lot of grants, but he had never outgrown the common sense his rancher grandparents passed down to him. When it came to business, he preferred plain talk, not whatever the flavor of the week in corporate America was.

It was one of the reasons he wasn't keen to take any of the jobs the recruiters were calling him for.

"Not *here*," Sven muttered again. Louder, he added, "Let's go grab lunch. You wanted to show me your new car, right?"

"Uh, sure." Johnny led the way to his brand-new Mustang Cobra.

Or new to Johnny. The last Cobras having been manufactured in 2004, but it was only *lightly* used, not a scratch on it, and the hint of pearl in the torch-red paint job glimmered in the noonday light. A quick press of the remote fob and both men climbed in.

Once inside, he looked at Sven. "So? What the hell was that shit about?"

"Drive," Sven said. "I'll explain as you do."

Johnny sighed. "What do you want for lunch?"

"Tacos."

"Right."

Sven only spoke once the Cobra was gliding down the street past palm trees that seemed to droop in the thick, mild air. LA's smog was nowhere near as bad as it had been a few decades ago, but it was far from nonexistent.

"All right. I recommended you and Lia brought you on, right?"

"Right, but what *she* said was—"

"We'll get to that," Sven interrupted. "First thing you gotta know is about Pauline. That's not her name."

"Really?" Johnny had seen a lot of people give themselves new names, but none of them had chosen a new one quite as boring as Pauline Smith.

"Yep. It's actually Polina…Testre? Testrovsky? Tchaikovsky? No, not that. Something like that, though."

"Sounds Russian," Johnny commented.

Sven stared at him for a long moment. "That's the *point*," he said finally. "It *is* Russian. *She's* Russian."

"Okay." Johnny waited to take a left, and, a moment later, did a double-take at Sven. "Wait, seriously?"

"Mmhmm." Sven nodded.

"So, all that stuff about making peace and people not necessarily choosing the best path on their own…" Johnny drummed his fingers on the steering wheel.

"Mmhmm."

"Okay, so when Lia brought me on…"

Sven leaned back in his seat and waited, a smile playing around his lips.

"She was talking about the same thing Pauline is talking about."

"Yep," Sven said.

"So, those documents I got about our KPI, A/B Testing, B2B, B2C, churn rate, conversion rate, cost per acquisition…"

"Mmhmm." Sven was grinning now. He looked out the

window at a pair of women with artfully blown-out hair and long tanned legs.

Johnny was too caught up in digesting this new information to spare much attention for them. LA was full of beautiful women, but things like this didn't happen too often. If he took the information he'd been given in that meeting and translated it out of business-school corporate bullshit-speak, that meant…

"What a pile of self-serving horseshit." He shook his head. "Does she believe it?"

"I've found that with the Russian mob, it's best not to ask."

"You got me recruited by the fucking Russian mob?"

"Not precisely, but I think it's safe to assume she's got ties." Sven shrugged. "Look, you and I both knew we were not going to come back from business school and go on the straight and narrow, right?"

Johnny wanted to object, but he cracked a grin. "Yeah, you're right." He sighed as he pulled into the drive-thru of his favorite taco place. "On the other hand, did you ever think you were going to use your world-class MBA to sell meth to tweakers?"

CHAPTER FOUR

The problem, Christian thought, wasn't so much that he was yet another anonymous employee in a cubicle, wearing a white, collared shirt and drinking passable coffee under the glare of fluorescent lights.

It was that he had another forty years of this ahead of him.

He sighed and rubbed his eyes. He'd been staring at the screen for two long hours, and he really, really needed a break. The calendar next to his computer had a nice picture of a tree, but also a lot of work notes and scribbled due dates.

He leaned back in his chair and craned his neck to look down the aisle between the rows of cubicles. He wasn't one of the lucky ones who got a view of the city, but he could see the windows if he leaned the right way.

Except for right now, when a small group of middle managers was blocking the view while they talked and gestured emphatically about…something.

Honestly, he didn't care. That was part of his problem. He turned his head back to his computer and sighed again. His current project was a report on a strange quirk at the intersection of banking regulations and technology that meant the company would save a significant amount of interest by moving their money through one more shell account before the checks hit the final debited account.

He was good at this. It was one of the reasons he'd been hired, and also one of the reasons he kept getting incremental raises and turning down repeated entreaties to move into management.

He hadn't anticipated how mind-numbing this job was going to be and how much of a trap career progression was.

As their floor supervisor strode off to supervise someone else, one of the employees who'd been standing by the window strolled over to Chris's cubicle and leaned against its makeshift doorway.

"Good afternoon," he drawled, then took a swig from a coffee mug.

Christian swiveled his chair around. "Hey." His eyes narrowed slightly. "Still working on the money movement report. You know, just in case you came here to draft me for another project."

Ted cracked his neck and smiled. His full name was Theodore, but he only used that when he was trying to impress chicks with his upper-crust background and estimable breeding. Born and raised on the east coast, Ted had attended one of the multitude of private schools with English-sounding names and liked to complain about things like the lack of good intramural lacrosse leagues in LA. Fittingly, he worked in Human Resources, far from the ho-hum existence of the cubicle drones.

For all that, Ted was one of Chris's favorite people. Unlike most of the other managers, he didn't take the rules and regulations of the office too seriously, just like he didn't take his own background too seriously. His sense of humor made him one of the best people in the company to work with.

"Of course," Ted said. "You're busy, you've got too much on your plate already, et cetera, et cetera." He gave an easy grin and sipped more coffee. "Not why I came."

"No?"

"No. I saw you the other day coming out of the Mermaid." Ted raised an eyebrow. "You know, that bar and grill in Little Tokyo?"

Chris blinked. "Yes. Yes, I *do* know. I was…there."

"Right. Have to say, that doesn't really seem like your kind of place."

"Just trying something new." Chris took a sip of his own coffee to keep from meeting Ted's eyes. He wasn't a great liar.

"Oh, didn't I mention?" Ted sounded excessively casual. "That was the *second* time I saw you there."

Chris heaved a sigh. "Fine," he said. He knew it was pointless to lie. Ted would simply pester him until he got the information he'd come for. "I heard one of my college classmates was working there, so I went in a couple of times. I'm…working up my nerve."

He sat and waited for the litany of jokes and innuendos he was certain were coming.

Ted's eyes widened with excitement. "Working up your nerve to…ask her out, you mean?" He was practically vibrating with energy.

Chris attempted not to cringe and only half-succeeded. "Let's not get carried away. I'm going to start by sitting at the bar."

Some men might have thought that was a joke, but Ted knew Chris well enough to understand it wasn't. "Oh, it's like that, huh? So, you haven't even said 'hi' to her yet, I take it?" He drained his coffee.

"Yeah," Chris grumbled, "that'd be a no. Come on, you know me."

Ted glanced around to make sure no one with authority was watching him waste time, then he slipped into the cubicle and pulled over the secondary chair. He leaned his elbows on his knees and got a faraway look, trying to figure out how to begin his lecture.

"Okay," Ted began finally as if discussing tactics during a football huddle. "It's like this, my man. You *have* to go up to her and say 'hi.' That's always the first step. That way, if nothing else, you'll find out if she remembers you from college, right?"

"I guess." Chris grimaced.

"What? What's that look?"

"Okay, say she remembers me." Chris put his cup on the desk and leaned in as well. "Does that do me *any* good?" Though some girls had on occasion thought he was cute, he knew he was not the type who easily and automatically drew women's eyes to him. He wasn't classically attractive, and Kera *was.* Blonde hair, the figure to go with a cheerleading scholarship, and the down-to-earth vibe of the classic Girl Next Door.

Even if she remembered Chris from college, there was what seemed like an insurmountable gap between that and her wanting to date him.

"You ever heard the term, 'necessary but not sufficient?'" Ted asked. He sat up a little to throw his coffee cup into one of the trash bins at the end of the cubicle row. "Hole in ooooone."

Chris resisted the urge to sink his head into his hands. Ted was the kind of person Kera might go for. Ted, with the breeding and the money and the athletic skill. In fact, he was pretty sure Kera had come from the east somewhere too.

"Chris."

"No, I haven't heard that term."

"It describes preconditions for a certain outcome."

"Is this going to be HR bullshit?"

"No, thank you *very* much," Ted said with great dignity. "It is *economics* bullshit."

"Oh, well, then. Carry on." Chris waved a hand.

"So, here's the thing." Ted held out his hands as if he were about to illustrate a football play. "Sure, her remembering you isn't going to be enough to make her end up as your wife."

"Wife?"

Ted waved his hands. "Keep your voice down, and whatever. Girlfriend. So no, her remembering you—or getting to know you—isn't sufficient, right? But it *is* necessary. In other words, you are *never* going to go out with her if you don't at least say hello."

He had a point. Chris didn't like that.

"So, say hi," Ted said finally. "Offer to buy her a drink. Better yet, buy a lot of drinks, tip well, and, er..." He waved his hand in a circle.

Chris stared at his friend. "You want me to get sloshed in front of her? Is that *really* your suggestion?"

Ted considered. "Mmm, I was thinking of how to loosen your inhibitions to talk to her, and I didn't think of the potential downside of loosening up too much. I always forget you're a lightweight."

Chris waited for a moment, then started to pivot back to his report, only for Ted to grab the arm of the chair and spin him around again.

"Got it!" Ted was grinning. "How about *this*? The Mermaid isn't far. You start going there once a week, and I'll go with you. We can do this together."

"You'd go drinking with me just to help me get up my nerve?" Chris raised an eyebrow. Ted had never given him any reason to question his friendship, but the whole thing bemused Chris. What was a blueblood on the C-suite track doing slumming it with one of the geeky IT guys?

"Come on." Ted raised an eyebrow right back. "Like we aren't hanging out every week anyway? And," he added, drawing the word out, "you'd be buying. Consider it my consulting fee for aiding you."

Chris rubbed his eyes. "I'm going to regret this, aren't I?"

Ted ran his tongue around his mouth as he thought it over. "Yeah, probably," he admitted.

"Thank you for your honesty," Chris said gravely. A smile tugged at the corner of his mouth. "I accept your premise, however. I will never go on a date with this woman if I can't say hi to her, and you might just badger me into doing it. At least your plan has a *chance* of working."

"What was your plan previously?" Ted inquired.

"If you *must* know, I was hoping for a miracle."

"A good Plan B." Ted stood up and slapped him on the back. In a jovial tone, he replied, "We'll keep that one in our back pocket. In the meantime, see you at five o'clock!"

"Right." Chris spun back to his computer before realizing what Ted had said. "Wait, what? Five *tonight?*"

But Ted was already gone—and looking down, Chris saw that he had a coffee stain on his shirt.

"Crap," he mumbled. If he was going to the Mermaid tonight, he was going to need to get a new shirt on the way to the bar.

Unlike Ted, he didn't think there was much he could do to increase his chances with his former classmate, but he was pretty sure a coffee stain on his shirt would decrease them.

James greatly preferred being at the estate when he and Mother LeBlanc were the only two in residence. Cramming all the other thaumaturgists in at the table made things too crowded and complicated. Without them present, the chamber could breathe. The tapestries, dating back to the fourteenth century, stood out better.

Plus, he had the entire council chamber to himself as a study.

Currently, he had his computer set up there and was clicking the refresh button on his sales tracker with dogged determination. "Come on, come on, come on...oooh." He perked up. "Maybe if I switch browsers?"

"Who are you—" The door behind him creaked open.

James turned around to look at Madam LeBlanc, who was peering around the empty council room. "Just talking to myself."

"Yes, I see that." She came over to the table, her dress rustling. "What are you looking at?"

"Sales for the book." He pointed at the sales dashboard, where a bar graph showed the prior days and the number of sales.

"Do they get sent to you each..." She paused, considering. "Year? Quarter?"

James grinned at her. "Keep going."

She smiled back. "Each *month*?"

He savored the moment before saying, "Each *hour*."

"*Hour*?" Her brown eyes widened. "You mean to tell me, you can learn how many people have purchased your book each hour of the day?"

"That's the one." He smiled and leaned back in his chair with his hands laced behind his head.

"I see." She stood up straight again and wrapped her shawl more tightly around her. Though the house was toasty by James's standards, she had never gotten used to upstate New York's bitter winters and seemed able to feel the outside temperature even from inside the house.

James went back to opening a new browser. He logged in, checking his phone for the two-step verification—and stabbing each number in with annoyance—before leaping out of his chair with a whoop.

"Oh, yeah, baby! Oh, yeah! That's right!"

Behind him, Madam LeBlanc cleared her throat.

"They tried to freeze the results," James said, pivoting toward her with a giant smile on his face. "Their cookies tried to hang things up, didn't they? But it *didn't work*. I have multiple browsers, baby. I have the *power*!"

Her mouth twitched. "James."

"Yes?" He started dancing in place, grooving his hips.

"James, you remember when we spoke to the council, yes?"

"Uh-huh." He began doing hip thrusts.

"And there was the business about how we would keep tabs

on magic users, and how we would prioritize which we would get to first, and how we would handle things once we met them?"

"You got it, baby."

"All that requires work," Madam LeBlanc said mildly.

James only nodded as he transitioned into the twist.

"Work that we are presently not doing because you are focusing on your hourly sales reports." She checked her watch. "In the middle of an hour."

James slowly stopped dancing and stared at her. He cleared his throat.

"How much can the numbers change in an hour?" LeBlanc asked him.

"Well, it's not really about that."

"No?"

"See…" He sat down in his office chair and scratched his neck. "See, it's like this."

"Let me guess: you have a button that sometimes provides new numbers, therefore you must click it indefinitely."

"That's it! Yes!" He came out of his chair again. "High five."

"James, get hold of yourself." She gave him what would have been a withering glance if it weren't for the humor dancing behind her eyes. "Would I be correct in assuming that you wish to show the other council members how successful your idea is?"

"That's part of it," James admitted.

LeBlanc smiled slightly. "In that case, I must remind you that Lady Mitchell is, to speak plainly, an idiot. You do not need to jump so quickly to secure her good opinion simply because she doubts you." She reached into the pleated folds of her legendary garment and pulled out a curved wooden pipe, already lit and smoking. She took a puff, and the coals glowed orange while filling the space around her with aromatic fumes.

James sighed. She was right, of course, but the point rankled. He settled back into his chair and tried to look dignified. "For what it's worth, I would *also* like to make this a bestseller."

"For the money?" She raised an eyebrow and blew out a puff of smoke. "James, we have more money than we could ever possibly use."

"No, not for the money. Because my background is in advertising and I want to *win* this thing."

"Ah." She smiled slightly; the smooth tobacco had relaxed her somewhat. "Well, as long as you're clear on your motivations."

"Exactly. I'm going to start taking out ads on the Amazon site soon. I'm trying to figure out all the intricacies of—"

"James, remember our true goal: more recruits." She leaned over to put her hand on his, a rare gesture from her. "Enough of us to *help* if the world needs us."

"Yes," James agreed.

"Why don't we get some lunch?" LeBlanc asked sensibly. "We can come back after to check the scrying map. James. *James.* Come along; you need to eat."

"But…" James trailed after her, looking over his shoulder at the computer. "But…but the clicky button."

CHAPTER FIVE

Little Tokyo was liberally dotted with restaurants, some on the ground floor of the many apartment buildings, others on corners or in strip malls.

The Mermaid, tucked away between two larger buildings, catered to a different crowd. It often didn't open until 3PM and was filled with everyone from construction workers and bikers to the white-collar cubicle denizens who went elsewhere for lunch. Its menu reflected that, showcasing a mix between standard delicious bar fare and inventive cocktails whipped up by the various bartenders.

Kera pulled Zee into an alcove in the alley. Her bike wouldn't be visible from the street, but she would be able to see it out of the back hall. There hadn't been any thefts recently, but she was protective and liked to be able to peek at it over the course of her shift. Leaving it locked up in place, she trotted across the pavement and used her security code to let herself in through the Mermaid's employee entrance.

Beyond the door lay a storage area where trash was staged before being taken out to the dumpster, as well as the usual assortment of fire extinguishers and supply boxes. It led into a narrow rear hall that forked toward both the staff's break area and the kitchens and the bar proper.

Kera rounded a corner and almost bumped into Cevin, her manager. He was olive-skinned, with large, bony hands, and though he was tall, he perpetually stood in a stooped posture. He had a wide variety of shirts but only one blue tie.

Or possibly a bunch of identical ties. She wasn't sure.

"Hi, Seven," she greeted him with a cheeky smile. He had made a big deal when she was hired, of the fact that his name might be spelled with a C but it should be pronounced as if it were spelled with a K.

"Still on that, huh?" He shook his head, his mouth in a bunched-up squiggly line.

"Aww, you make such a fun face every time I do it."

"Mmhmm. Well, how about this?" He paused at his office door and looked back at her. "I will give you one and only one reminder that I can schedule you for the entirety of every upcoming weekend."

Kera clamped her mouth shut. "Okay, Cevin like Kevin-with-a-K, got it." She gave him a hurried thumbs-up and pushed open the door to the break room with her hip. She had told her mother she was fine with being a barmaid, and she wasn't lying.

But she liked having her weekends to herself.

Cevin stayed where he was but called after her, "What do you need weekends off for anyway? It's not like you have a boyfriend or anything."

"It's personal," Kera called back as she set the bag of the provisions from Mr. Kim's store on the break room table. The door was swinging back and forth between them. "Besides, do I need a boyfriend to take time off work? *And,*" she added, warming to the theme, "aren't businesses not supposed to pry into their employees' personal lives? Don't go all corporate-stalker on me. I work here to avoid problems like that."

The supervisor snorted loudly and came to hold the door

open. "How can it be stalking when you told me about it on your last shift?" He lifted one eyebrow. "I believe that was the same discussion where you said your mother was probably going to call you *today* because it was the two-month anniversary of your graduation from college. You were complaining that she would pester you about, and I quote, 'all that motherly stuff—you know, job, boyfriend, apartment.'"

Kera looked over her shoulder with a multi-purpose glare that suggested he wasn't supposed to remember these things and also that the call had been just as infuriating as expected. "She should know," she said, holding up an index finger, "the old adage: ask me no questions, and I'll tell you no lies."

Cevin smiled and shook his head as he headed to his office. Kera went over to the row of lockers on one side of the room. She took off her leathers and folded them carefully, placed them at the bottom of her locker, and put her backpack on top of them.

She still had seven minutes until she was required to clock in. To pass the time, she pulled out her phone and opened her reader app.

"Right. Time to further smarten myself and get Mom off my case. Mostly the second one. New books…there it is. *How to Be a Bad Ass Witch.* Not what I had in mind when I searched for *craft*, har-har, but I might just get Mom to succumb to apoplexy if I tell her I've taken her suggestion and become a witch."

She skimmed the table of contents, and her curiosity was piqued. She had expected her first sleepy perusal to be wrong, but the book did not appear to be about Wicca or any other witchcraft-oriented religion.

Without overly grand pronouncements or self-important talk about harmony and resonance, it seemed to be speaking entirely seriously about the practical applications of magic. It was, as far as Kera could tell, a twenty-first-century update on an old-fashioned grimoire.

One item in particular jumped out—a chapter beginning on

page sixty-four entitled, "How to Erase Something You Can't Stop Thinking About."

"Well, *well*," Kera murmured. According to this book, the key to inventing honest-to-gosh brain bleach was magic.

That, she admitted, made as much sense as any other solution she could think of. If nothing else, the book would be an excellent peek into historical ideas about magic and technology. Her mind had danced around the question of memory removal off and on for months, especially since she'd woken up today and remembered her mother's birds and bees talk, but Kera hadn't come up with an answer. She doubted that any ingestible formula could accomplish it. Maybe surgery.

But magic? That might be easier.

Not that she was seriously considering it. She snickered as she closed the app on her phone and got ready to clock in.

"Hey, Kera."

"Hi." Kera looked over her shoulder as Stephanie came in.

A few years older than Kera was, Stephanie was one of the longtime employees of the Mermaid. Whereas Kera tended to stay behind the bar, Stephanie primarily worked as a waitress.

Now, she smiled as she added her stuff to the break room table. "So, did your mom end up calling?"

"Ugh. Yes." Kera stretched her arms, neck, and shoulders. "The whole shebang, with a disco remix. 'You're not doing enough with your life, sweetie, and please come home from that *awful* city now that you're done with school.' About what you'd expect."

The other woman shook her head with an empathetic smile. "That's too bad. I get it, but you know it's only because she cares. My family's lived in LA since forever, so I can't speak to the 'come home' stuff, but I get the rest. Both my parents are always telling me, 'Stephanie, you need to work in an office, one that's open nine to five.' As if *that* makes a difference in how good the pay is."

Kera snickered. "Right, right. You're not a successful, responsible adult if you wake up after the sun rises or are still at work after it sets. Makes perfect sense." She checked her phone. "Shall we?"

Stephanie nodded and, talking about what kind of business they expected for the night, the pair strolled out of the breakroom and clocked in.

The bar wasn't busy at this relatively early hour, with only half a dozen or so patrons lounging around, so both women began to set up for the night ahead. Stephanie went to see how things were looking in the kitchen, and Kera examined how well-stocked the bar was. When a quick check showed everything in order, she grabbed a tray and headed out to clear the empty glasses and damp napkins that were already on the tables.

Kera opened the board separating the bar from the main floor and made haste toward the first table.

As she walked by one of the booths, a slender Latino man sitting there caught her in his gaze, getting a perfunctory smile in return. She was in Work Mode now: polite, focused on her tasks, and emotionally checked out.

Which meant she didn't notice that the man was watching her every move.

Johnny Torrez reclined in his corner booth. It kept him out of the way while giving him a good clear view of the rest of the bar and the Mermaid's customers.

Who, ideally, needed to become *his* customers. And Pauline's.

Based on what he'd seen so far, the Mermaid's clientele ought to provide an excellent potential market. An *emerging* market, as the business-school assholes liked to put it, one that was brimming with untapped lucrative potential.

He had fallen out of that way of speaking as soon as he came back to LA, but the meeting with Pauline was bringing it all back.

The people here were clientele instead of marks, and the people bringing the drugs in would be shipping agents instead of mules.

Behind the language, it was the same thing. Pauline was going for white-collar workers on the fast track to management jobs. If you changed the clothes and the language, they were the same people who were the top marks for other drug pushers: young, upwardly mobile, and eager to spend the money they assumed they would soon have.

Once they were hooked, they could *always* be counted on to find the money for the products Johnny would bring them.

No, not "hooked." Loyal. Loyal customers. And while he would never have thought he could get business school assholes hooked on meth, Pauline seemed sure of herself. It was all, as Johnny's teachers would have said, in the product positioning.

He snickered to himself.

One of the girls behind the counter slid out and walked past him, seemingly on target to clear a table of some leftover glasses and so forth. Johnny's eyes went to her immediately. Her bright gold hair was tied up in a high ponytail, and a few strands of it fell over her face in a slightly careless way that only made her look better. She had high cheekbones, full lips, and a rounded chin.

Unfortunately, she seemed engrossed in her work and hadn't paid him any heed.

So far.

It gave him more time to watch her. Her body didn't stand out, yet everything about it appealed to Johnny, who prided himself on having a connoisseur's gaze. She was in good shape, well-proportioned but not too tall, with enough curves to command appreciative notice. The white button-down shirt she wore suggested perky medium-sized breasts, though he couldn't see the details.

As the girl bent over to clear the table, Johnny leaned a tad farther out of his seat to watch. Unfortunately, her denim shorts came halfway down her thighs, long enough that he couldn't get much of a view. Looked like she had a good enough ass for his taste, though.

He had plenty of time to win her over. She had just come in, after all. *She's not going home anytime soon, is she?*

He grabbed his cocktail and took it up to the bar. When he leisurely sat on a stool, the blonde finally noticed him.

She looked up from the table she was wiping down and gave him a distant smile. "Another drink?"

"Nah," he responded, "I'll finish this one and call it good. I got shit to do this evening. I'll be free, though, by…say, two in the morning?"

The girl nodded in a vague, noncommittal way. "Okay."

"Oh." Johnny grinned. "So you *do* want to go out. I mean, I figured. I know a couple of all-night places within a block or two of here, and there's always tomorrow. Lots more opportunities then."

The bartender blinked at him for a second, then her face settled into a bland smile. "I'm busy, sorry." She turned to check on another drinker, an old fat sad-sack of a guy. To Johnny's eye, he had no business in a place like this but probably figured he could catch an early drink before the night crowd streamed in.

When the girl turned back to head behind the bar, Johnny introduced himself. "Johnny. And you must be…" he squinted at her name tag, "Kera. Nice to meet you. I can tell you're single, so you can't be *that* busy."

"Busy enough," she said simply, not looking up from where she was putting something into the computer. "Which is why I'm trying to keep things nice and simple. I'd rather not complicate things."

Johnny had heard these excuses before. He leaned forward on the bar and kept his gaze locked on her. "Then how about something *uncomplicated?*" he suggested smoothly. "No strings attached." His voice dropped lower and became smoother.

"Something you can tell your girlfriends about." This one was a Goody Two-Shoes, he could just tell.

Goody Two-Shoes white girls liked to play around with guys like him.

Guys like him didn't mind that.

This one stopped what she was doing and looked him dead in the eyes. "No, thanks," she said flatly. She wasn't angry, not yet. A young woman who looked like her probably got hit on about as often as she ate, drank, or yawned.

He lingered for another five minutes, giving her four of them to cool off before he attempted to make conversation one last time.

"So, how long have you worked here?" He turned his glass between his fingers and tried not to let his gaze drift down to her chest. "I have seen this place before, but this is my first time stopping in. Has a nice reputation."

"The kitchen's good." She barely looked up as she slid him a menu. "You should take a look."

He could tell he wasn't getting any farther with her and that only luck or extraordinary persistence would do the job. She was too aloof and professional to give much away, but she'd put her walls up. It was useless.

With a quiet sigh of frustration, he put his glass down on the counter's surface and folded a couple of crumpled bills neatly under the bottom of the glass.

He was always precise.

By this point, more customers had begun to filter in, and another bartender was gearing up for duty, a brunette. The daylight was almost spent, and people were getting out of work.

Johnny was well aware that if he stuck around for longer, he might encounter more potential buyers, but the experience with Bartender Chick had left a sour taste in his mouth. Besides, Pauline had specifically told them that today was only a scouting mission to scope out places where they ought to focus their future efforts.

He might as well try someplace else.

He spared a last glance behind the bar, where the ponytailed bartender continued to sling drinks and exchange light banter with her customers, as well as the waitress who worked the tables.

Blondes. Cute blondes with perky tits were a dime a dozen in this city, but every one of them thought they were God's gift to the world. Johnny shook his head and headed out with a muttered curse under his breath.

Dime a dozen, he told himself again. He shouldn't let this one get under his skin.

Someone opened the door just as he reached it, and two men stepped in—office workers, to judge by their shirts and ties. One guy looked like he *might* belong in a place like this. The other was a total geek.

Not missing a beat, Johnny pivoted sideways and effectively slipped around and behind the pair as they moved, catching the door as they trudged past it and disappearing outside before they were even aware of him.

He stood on the pavement and took his sunglasses out of his jacket pocket. The sky had faded to reddish-purple, so it wasn't like he *needed* them; it was the principle of the thing. After all, as Pauline had said, they needed to position themselves.

He slid into the Cobra and turned the key. Onward.

Sven better not have done better than he had, or the man was getting punched.

CHAPTER SIX

Christian took a deep breath as he stared at the door leading into the Mermaid. He had on a new shirt, a plain t-shirt he had spent far too much time picking out. He'd also been chewing gum to get rid of his coffee breath, which meant that his mouth now tasted like a minty hellscape and beer was going to be a torturous experience.

He was not ready for this.

Ted was by his side, which made him feel marginally better, but Christian couldn't stop thinking that Ted didn't really get this. Sure, the HR guy got shot down all the time, but he had the magical combination of looks, confidence, and money.

Unlike Christian, Ted didn't start every conversational attempt with the utter certainty that the woman would have to be crazy to go out with him.

Christian could not tell if this was going to end well or with the two of them going down in flames.

Ted, of course, was oblivious to Christian's worries. He gestured at the door with a flourish. "After you."

Christian sighed as he opened the door, then stepped back as a slender man pushed past them. After a single moment of intense scrutiny during which Christian sensed the man was assessing everything from his badge to his haircut, the slender man pulled out a pair of sunglasses and went on his way.

Christian breathed a minor sigh of relief. Getting into a confrontation was the last thing he needed right now. *It wasn't going to turn into a fight*, he reminded himself. *You're just jumpy.*

Still, as soon as he got into the bar, he made a beeline for the farthest, darkest corner booth.

A hand clamped around his arm. "Ohhhh, no, you don't," Ted said firmly. "Not this time. We're going to stand here a minute and pretend we're trying to decide where to sit."

"Why?" Christian asked faintly.

"First, because that's not what we're actually scouting for, and I want to know what I'm working with here. Second—and this is important—so she has a chance to see you."

"That's what I was trying to avoid," Christian muttered.

"I know. That's why you brought me." Ted flashed him a smile. "So, which one is the girl you mentioned?"

Christian swallowed. "Uh…" He gestured subtly with his head. "Over there. The, uh, the bartender."

"Brunette?"

"Nope. The, uh, the blonde."

Ted considered her for a moment, hands in his pockets. Finally, he sucked his teeth and said, "I hate to admit it, but we might have to go with Plan B."

"What?" Christian had expected ridiculous pick-up lines and overly ambitious strategies. He had expected Ted to tell him to go get a makeover and come back. He hadn't expected Ted just to give up.

"I'm so sorry," Ted said. He did sound regretful. "First, let me congratulate you on your taste in women, because *damn*. However, I must inform you that that woman is…how shall I say this nicely…way out of your league. Like, *so* far out of your league. Like, there's out of your league, there's way out of your league, there's a few miles of gray space, and then there's her."

There was a moment of silence.

"You could have stopped at 'out of your league,'" Christian told him finally.

"If I could have, I would have," Ted said whimsically. "Christian, my friend, do you know how I keep getting women to go out with me?"

"I have zero idea. That was why I brought you along."

Ted cleared his throat, then took Christian by the shoulder and guided him away from the open floor space toward the booth Christian had first made for.

"I thought you said she needed to be able to see us?" Christian asked.

"I no longer think that's in your best interest."

"Ouch."

Ted grinned. "Look, man, like I said, I get women to go out with me because I don't aim out of my league. Now, you? Your league extends farther than you think it does. Seriously. You've got a good job and a good face. Wouldn't hurt you to lift a bit, but you've got something to work with. But what you're aiming for right now is a supermodel who is, for reasons unknown, slumming it with us mere mortals in a random bar. The only guys she's going to go for are the hot, rich, Beverly Hills types."

Christian felt the first spark of hope. Normally, he thought Ted knew way more about women than he did, but in this case, he happened to know that Ted's guesses weren't infallible.

"Kera's not like that," he asserted. "I've never been attracted to stuck-up girls, no matter how hot they are. Kera is nice."

"And you know this because?" Ted arched an eyebrow.

"I told you she was a classmate, didn't I? We were in a study group together."

Ted looked deeply skeptical. "For what class?"

"Algorithm Design and Analysis," Christian answered promptly. Seeing Ted's blank look, he grinned. "Nerd stuff."

"Okay, so when you said classmate…" Ted looked between Christian and Kera. "You meant she majored in Computer Science? That girl, the one who looks like she should be in the Industry?"

"I hope to God you mean Hollywood."

Ted waved a hand. "Whatever. She got the same degree you did. She's one of you genius types? Please tell me she's not. Tell me she sucked at it. I can't take any more bombshells today."

"She did not suck at it." Chris had to admit he was enjoying this evening immensely. "She mentioned a few times she thought she should have gone into engineering because she's better with things she can touch and hold than she is with theoretical concepts, but she was really good at CompSci stuff." He frowned. "I think she was working on a motorcycle? Like, fixing one up."

Ted gave a groan and flopped his head on the table.

Christian waited, his mouth twitching.

"Okay." Ted still had his forehead on the wood. "But do you see how it makes sense that she would be some sort of…oh." He picked his head up. "Maybe she's a terminator."

"She is not a terminator."

"So you say." Ted shook his head. "I'm going to need a few drinks."

"We agreed I wasn't going to get sloshed."

"They're not for you, they're for me." Ted sighed. "I'm increasingly convinced that I need to get my nerve up before I shoulder the responsibility of tossing you into all this. Also, if I get sloshed, it makes you look better by comparison. Two birds."

Christian began to laugh. "Okay, okay."

"And remember our deal. Drinks are on you."

"Oh, absolutely." Christian grinned at him. "I'm more than willing to pay just for the privilege of seeing you get drunk off your ass."

Johnny and Sven reconvened at one of the multiple clubs downtown, complete with blue-tinted lighting and pounding music. By this point, they'd both done enough successful reconnaissance to be able to claim their night's work was done, and this establishment was a place to relax more than one to case.

These people might be their clientele someday, but not yet.

"What about those two?" Sven nodded at a young East Asian couple who were chatting to each other over martinis at the bar.

Johnny gave them only a quick glance. Both were wearing the sort of street style that had become more popular since K-Pop took off in the US, but he knew immediately that neither of them was the kind of mark Pauline was looking for.

"I'd say B-minus," Sven said.

"Nope." Johnny preferred to do these things pass-fail. "Too straight-laced. They're the type that balance their checkbook before coming out to see how many drinks they're going to buy. You want to talk B-minus? Neither of them would dare get a B-minus in math, that's how Goody Two-Shoes they are."

Sven looked at him as he took a sip of his drink. "Don't you think that's a bit…I don't know, racist?"

"Yeah, sure, Whitey's gonna lecture the barrio kid on fuckin' racism. Sounds good." Johnny drained his drink.

Sven frowned as he flagged the waitress down and ordered refills for them both. He sat in silence for a moment.

"So, what the fuck happened to you tonight?" he said finally.

"Keep your nose out of it."

"Nah." Sven waited as the waitress set down the new drinks. When she was gone, he said, "I brought you on. You go sideways, that's on me, too."

"I'm not gonna get you popped in the head." Johnny looked over and saw Sven's expression. The other man wasn't going to give up on this until he knew what was going on. Tersely, he explained what had happened at the Mermaid—specifically, his failure to make any headway with the blonde.

It didn't help his mood when Sven laughed and waved a hand.

"It's no big deal, man. Look around." He gestured at the club. "There's gotta be five, ten women hotter than her just at the bar."

Johnny knew it was true, which should help.

It didn't, though. He was still pissed. "She wasn't even playing for it," he muttered.

"Ohhhhh." Sven nodded. "Every guy wants to be the one who turns one of those into a slut for a night."

"Exactly." Johnny clinked his glass against Sven's. "Is there anything better than a good white girl going bad for a night? Eh, I don't suppose you'd know. No one fucks you to get back at their parents."

Sven grinned good-naturedly. "I'll take your word for it. I—" Both of their phones buzzed, and Sven broke off to take his out of his pocket. "Shit."

Johnny pulled out his phone in a hurry and looked at the text from Lia.

The project just got moved up. We need to move into our second phase of marketing ASAP. Do you have potential target markets?

Johnny rolled his eyes. "Do you remember what the second phase was? I had zoned out by then."

"It was in the briefing packet," Sven reminded him.

"Name me one legit business that has briefing packets. If I wanted that shit, I'd have gone corporate." Johnny shook his head. "So, what do we do now? Go start making connections with bars?"

"That's the one. I've got five. You?"

"Four." It might have been five if he hadn't spent his time at the Mermaid trying to hit on the blonde, but Johnny wasn't going to bring that up.

"I'll reply for both of us." Sven started typing.

Johnny watched the conversation unfold and shook his head. Anything in writing probably should be coded, but they were using encrypted messaging. In his opinion, Pauline was wasting time that would be better spent doing business.

In the end, once all the business gibberish was decoded, their night's directive was clear: go back to all of their bars and make offers. With supply coming in that night, Lia was hoping that distribution could begin the next day.

In Johnny's experience, some people got weird if you didn't have a sample on you, but he'd talked his way out of that before. He downed some of the ice water instead of the rest of his drink and stood up, pulling out his sunglasses.

"Oh, and Johnny?"

"Yeah?"

"Don't go back for that blonde, okay?" Sven looked serious. "The other thing about white chicks is that they call the cops when you come on too strong."

Johnny shrugged. Sven had a point.

"And—man, everyone gets turned down sometimes. Don't let it get to you."

"Right." The man sounded like a fucking PBS special.

Johnny threaded his way through the crush of people, hardly noticing the beautiful women he brushed past. He took his keys out of his pocket and sped up, then swung into his Cobra and considered his options.

He could go back to the Mermaid now.

No. He'd be responsible and save dessert for last. With a cold smile, he backed out of his spot and pulled into traffic with a roar of the engine.

***

James put the final touches on one of his ads and rubbed his eyes, which were stinging. He had been trained in marketing back when ads were printed in newspapers and magazines. As his type of work adapted to the internet, he had left his day job for his position on the council.

Diving into the constant iteration and churn of digital marketing had been incredibly fun. He enjoyed the late nights and the huge mugs of coffee. He also enjoyed tweaking text, tracking down new fonts, and adjusting colors by the tiniest margins.

It was also sucking up all his time. As with the sales, advertising results came back in close to real-time, so James found himself pushing off his next meal, his next shower, his next cup of coffee "just for a few minutes" while he adjusted an ad's audience or tag line or…

That was probably why he smelled.

He took a sniff under one of his arms and cringed. He needed to get out of here before LeBlanc came in and saw him like this. She might be very progressive in some ways, but her opinions on hygiene and grooming were rigid.

He stood up and winced. His muscles weren't used to moving. That was probably a bad sign.

As he was working on standing up straight, a bloom of light caught his eye. His eyes jerked over to the scrying pool, causing a crick in his neck to send shooting pains through his shoulder.

"Ow, ow, ow." He hunched the shoulder up as he stared. "Come on. Come back. I know I saw you."

Nothing. He maneuvered around his chair and went to the middle of the table to stare at the scrying bowl. He really had to use the bathroom, and he was becoming aware that he was ravenously hungry in addition to being exhausted, but he couldn't have looked away now if the Kool-Aid man had come busting through the wall.

"Come on," James murmured. "Come on, baby."

As if it had only needed to be sweet-talked, the bloom of light came again, golden-bright in the day's fading light.

James caught his breath and began to laugh, a rusty sound that sent him into a coughing fit. He was pounding on his chest, still laughing, when the bloom flickered out, but he knew what he'd seen. It was somewhere along the eastern seaboard; he'd guess in either South Carolina or Georgia.

"LeBlanc!" he called before remembering the current state of his appearance.

Crap.

She didn't answer—she rarely raised her voice—but he heard her footsteps.

Crap. Well, he was happy enough that he almost didn't care.

Another bloom of light popped up. This one was farther south, firmly in Florida. James gave another whoop. He could hardly believe it. Two.

Two. They had been waiting for days, and now they didn't just have one candidate, they had two. For three years, they had not found even a single potential thaumaturge, and now…

"Suck on it, Mitchell," he muttered to himself.

Then another showed up, somewhere around Nevada. Another up in the Portland area. Another. Another. Another.

Up until ten seconds ago, James wouldn't have been able to think of a single thing that could bring him down. Now, however, his eyes widened as he stared at the map. All he could think was that this looked like some sort of post-apocalyptic mushroom cloud map with the steady flash of nukes.

This was good.

Right?

His voice when he called again wasn't quite so certain. "Uh, LeBlanc? Seriously, you should get in here."

CHAPTER SEVEN

"Hmm," LeBlanc said, several minutes later. Her face was studiously blank, but James could sense the slight edge of worry behind her words. "I feel foolish that I had not considered this possibility."

"Just to make sure we're in agreement..." James rubbed one temple.

"We have a surplus of potential candidates," she pronounced. Her hands were clasped in front of her sternum in the very image of any proper lady. "I believed your change in recruitment techniques was warranted due to our earlier dearth of success, but..."

James squinted. He'd been awake far too long, and LeBlanc's habitually formal speech was not helping. "Okay, so to be clear, you thought we might find no one, but you never anticipated finding too many people?"

LeBlanc hesitated. "Yes," she admitted after a moment.

"How flattering."

"I know you are somewhat sleep-deprived, but please do not be childish about this." Her tone was reproving. In the dim light, he could barely see the outlines of her face. She took a break to sweep across the room and turn the lights on. When she came back, it was to study him gravely. "After no recruits in three years, I do not think any of us anticipated such a large number of them."

"You're right." He sighed. He had let Mary Mitchell get too far under his skin, which was why he was beginning to mistrust this.

"Go take a shower," LeBlanc instructed him. "There is a plate of food for you in the kitchen. Actually, there are several, one for each meal you have missed."

"Er…"

"I will watch." She settled into one of the chairs gracefully, her multicolored skirt swirling around her and her brown eyes fixed on the map. "Nothing is availed by you being exhausted and unbathed, James."

"Right."

James headed upstairs to the bedroom suite he had used for several years now. The master bedroom was for the head of the council, and the next two nicest rooms went to James and LeBlanc, who lived here the most often.

His room had deep red wallpaper above dark wood wainscoting and a thick rug over wooden floors made from massive slabs of wood from the old trees that had been common in North America three centuries ago. The windows had glass panes that had become wavy with age and were bordered by heavy velvet drapes.

It was a little old-fashioned for James's taste, but the house had been the property of the council for centuries, and he did not have the will to make over a piece of history.

It was strange to see the old closet filled not with heavy gowns and suits but instead with t-shirts and jeans. He pulled out clean clothes and laid them on the bed before stripping off his days-old shirt and pants, wrinkling his nose at the smell.

Maybe that was why he hadn't seen LeBlanc lately.

As in many older houses, the larger rooms had windows on two sides to maximize the sunlight, with one of the remaining walls butting up against a central chimney. Unlike many similar houses, however, this one had magical seals to stop drafts and mold, which James quite appreciated.

He also appreciated the magical boost to both the water heater and the water pressure. Slumped against the wall while the hot water beat down on him, he scrubbed his hair and decided to shave.

It was the right decision. Clean, with a fresh shave and new clothes, he felt like a new man. He headed downstairs and devoured most of the plate of food while standing over the sink, something LeBlanc would not have approved of. Then he went to rejoin her, bringing two mugs of tea.

She gave him an appraising look as he sat down. "You look as if you feel better."

"There's a crash coming on," James admitted as he sipped his tea.

"It is long overdue, I believe." She smiled. "Now, while you were gone, I did one test and also came up with an idea, though it will take some experimentation to get right."

He gave her a curious look.

"First, due to your…pessimism, I tested to make sure that the results coming through on this are accurate and are tied to human users of magic, not anything such as ley-line flares."

James nodded. LeBlanc spoke calmly, but as usual, there was a weight of experience behind her word. James remembered that she had been instrumental in mapping the distribution of magic across North and Central America, including the ways in which human use of magic affected the distribution.

"Thank you," he told her quietly.

"Imagine how little we would like to find out we'd panicked for no reason," she said with a small smile.

"Agreed. And the other idea?"

"Well, it occurred to me that this…" she gestured gracefully at the scrying map, "while useful, lacks both precision and historical data."

James frowned at her. He was refreshed, but he still wasn't tracking. Then it dawned on him. "Oh, so you want something that will keep track of where there has been magic so we don't miss anything by being out of the room?"

"Exactly. And some way to get more exact readings. I think we should be able to modify the spell tomorrow to allow for historical readings, as well as setting up smaller scrying bowls to get more exact readings inside states where we see magic use."

"You're a genius," James said fondly.

She smiled. "Perhaps. Regardless, I think you should sleep."

"Mmf." James sighed. "I just don't want to miss—"

"If you miss the flares because these people only tried magic once, there will hardly be a problem," LeBlanc said practically. "We have always known there were those who had enough talent only to do one spell. Perhaps we were simply unaware of how many there were."

"How comforting."

"Rest," she said severely. "All else can wait. Once we have the other spell up and running, we can begin journeying to meet our prospective candidates. I for one am looking forward to some milder weather."

James nodded and found himself ushered firmly toward his bed.

***

"Ted. Ted." Christian poked the side of his friend's head. "*Ted.*"

Ted's answer was a groan.

"Time to go up to the bar, Ted."

Ted picked his head up quickly and tipped sideways. "Whoa. Holy…what, wait?"

"Time to…you know what, one second." Chris took out his

wallet, counted out the price of their drinks and a generous tip for their waitress, and pondered the engineering puzzle of how to move an exceedingly drunk HR manager across a bar without doing anything that could be construed as an "HR incident."

Eventually, he managed to coax Ted to the end of the booth's bench.

"Ted. Come on, Ted. Ted, please."

"Got your back," Ted said woozily. "You line 'em up, and I'll… knock 'em down. Something."

"Uh-huh." Christian looped his friend's arm over his shoulder and stumbled to the bar. It was good that he had Ted to manage, he reflected, because if he didn't, he'd be thinking about what was waiting for him.

But they'd been sitting in the corner for three hours now, and he was finally getting reckless enough to talk to Kera.

It was strange. He'd brought Ted along to give him confidence, but somehow, Ted's lack of confidence had been the push Christian needed.

Once they got to the bar, Ted leaned awkwardly against the counter while Christian pulled out a barstool and strategized how to get his companion propped on it. After a brief struggle during which Ted more than once resembled a newborn flamingo, Ted was seated and Christian, panting slightly, got himself onto his own stool.

Ted tipped his head up. "Hi," he said genially. "I'm a lightweight."

"Are you?"

The voice made Christian's head jerk up. There, staring amusedly at Ted, was Kera. Like a scene from a horror movie that he could not stop from happening, he watched as her eyes tracked to him. There was a mix of curiosity and…recognition?

"Yer pretty," Ted said. He sounded sleepy.

"I am not," Christian said before he could stop himself.

"Oh, I don't know," Kera disagreed. "You have a nice face."

Christian stared at her and realized he had forgotten every word he had ever known.

She smiled slightly before nodding at Ted. "I hope he's not driving. I'm pretty sure there's a law about that sort of thing."

"'M not driving," Ted said sagely. "I never drive. Who wants a car in Los Angeles?"

"I see." Kera was cleaning a glass. She looked as if she didn't want to make fun of Ted but was amused by his antics.

"I'm just here because he needs me," Ted confided to her in a stage whisper. He pointed vaguely in Christian's direction.

Christian froze, but Kera didn't seem to realize that Ted had inadvertently told her the truth.

"I see," she said again, definitely hiding a smile now. She went to put the glasses back down and winced as she nicked the back of one hand on something behind the bar. Unfazed, she grabbed a cloth to clamp over the line of bright blood. "So, you guys from around here, or are you visiting?"

Christian considered her question. He wasn't sure if that had been a joke. Did she recognize him? Was he supposed to say something witty?

God, I hate not having social skills. It was why he'd gone into IT, dammit. He wasn't supposed to need them.

While he was still trying to figure out what to say, Kera set a beer in front of him—and not just any beer, either. A Killian's Irish Red, his favorite.

He frowned slightly as he lifted it in thanks. "I, uh, thanks. This is my favorite."

"I know," Kera threw over her shoulder.

"You...do?"

She put down another glass, checked her hand, and came over to lean on the bar. "You mentioned it at the study group one night. How Killian's was your first underage illegal beer, and you'd had a soft spot ever since. I always told myself I'd buy you one sometime, but we never got the chance."

Christian went still with the bottle halfway to his mouth. His heart seemed to have gone off-rhythm and paused to reset itself.

"Hey!" The call came from someone down the bar. "Can I get a refill over here?"

"You sure can," Kera called back. "It's your right as an American." She winked at Christian. "I'll be back, but flag me down if you need me. Oh, and…" she pointed, "he's about to fall off his stool."

She headed off to fetch the other patron a beer, leaving Christian to unceremoniously haul Ted back to stability on the stool.

"She remembers me," he hissed at Ted.

"Heyyyy," Ted said, nearly falling off the other side. He waited until he was upright again. "That's good. Right? Wait. Did she seem to like you?"

"I don't…not sure." Christian was fairly sure she'd said something about buying him a drink, but now that she wasn't standing there anymore, it seemed less like that would actually have happened. "What do I do next?"

"Oh." Ted swayed and then focused intently, looking like an owl. "Just, uh, you know. Talk to her and stuff. See how it goes. You can ask her out later, as long as she doesn't do that thing that women do where they suddenly turn to ice because you randomly said something wrong that pissed them off." He coughed and readjusted his position on the stool. "But don't worry." He patted the bar comfortingly, perhaps under the impression that it was Chris's hand. "That, uh, probably won't happen. Shouldn't have mentioned it."

Christian would have been worried except that he'd had an idea, and it was one that might just work. He scribbled something on a napkin as he waited for Kera to come back, and when she came over, he showed it to her.

"You remember that test we had on parallel algorithms?"

"Sure."

"Well, I'm having a problem with this one fucking line of

code, and I keep feeling like it's something to do with that." He flipped the napkin around to show her.

Kera leaned on the bar as he explained the framework around the line, using multiple napkins to sketch out the process flow. He remembered her as having a good head for troubleshooting, and he was pleased to see that he had been correct. Neither of them had the answer by the time she straightened up to take a look around, but her questions had guided him closer to the answer, and she was actually listening to what he was saying.

He felt like he was walking on air. Plus, he might now have a shot at finishing this project, which had been stalled on the back burner for three weeks.

"You're very smart," Ted said sagely to her. "Very smart. Blonde bar lady…knows code." He nodded again owlishly.

Christian flushed bright red. "I am so sorry about that. He does know better, or he will by the time tomorrow is over."

To his surprise, Kera looked more amused than anything. "I'm a blonde bartender. That was far from the most insulting comment I've gotten this week alone."

"Ah. Right." Christian looked around. "I'm sure you have a better appreciation than most for what alcohol does to the human brain."

"Precisely."

"Why not dye your hair?" Christian asked her. Then he frowned. "I shouldn't have asked that, should I?"

"Eh," Kera commented, "almost makes me feel like I'm back in college. Typical coder problem-solving, right to the point. Total detachment and the problem would be solved, admittedly. Now, since there are no extra parameters to provide nuanced information, the subroutine will be shit for reuse, but it's valid given the input." With a sigh and a pat on the bar, she disappeared to help another customer.

As Chris stared into the space she'd vacated, Ted leaned in by his ear.

"Chris," he said, tugging the man's sleeve. "Did I not understand that because I'm drunk, or because it was…you guys… computer stuff?"

"Computer stuff," Christian replied, staring after her. "Isn't she just…"

"Perfect," Ted agreed, nodding sagely. "Chris?"

"Yes?"

"I don't feel so good."

"I guess I should have seen that coming. Let me pay, and we can go." Christian pulled out money as Kera came back. "Hey, sorry. Have to get this one to someplace with water and aspirin." He spent a moment agonizing about how much of a tip to leave so as not to look ostentatious, then handed the bills over. "Here you go."

"Sounds good." She took the money when he handed it to her, not looking at the bills. "It was nice to see a familiar face."

"Same," Christian said, smiling for a moment before he started to worry he looked dorky. He flushed and gave an awkward wave before heading for the door with Ted stumbling along beside him.

Kera slid a tab across the bar to one of the other drinkers with a professional smile. Unfortunately, he seemed to be the type who got crabby when he drank, and he had been looking for a fight to pick all evening.

He gave her a surly look, apparently having chosen a topic. "What's up with those two geeks? Why you treating them like they're…" He waved a hand. "Can't even hold their liquor."

Kera tried to keep her tone pleasant, but she knew there was an edge to it. "One of those geeks was a classmate in college. He helped me during one of my courses, and I had the opportunity to return the favor just now. Pretty sure he at least deserved a beer and a nice chat. He was patient, kind, intelligent, and funny. And did you see how he helped his friend?"

The man blinked.

"Do you do that for your friends?" Kera asked him. "Or the ladies in your life?" She paused and used one of the smiles her mother had taught her; the woman did have good skills. In this case, she had skills that made her look both totally pleasant and like the person on the receiving end of the look might not make it through the night. "I might not like your answer, so think before you speak."

There was a moment where she worried she had pushed too hard. Cevin always had her back—he knew his female employees would get harassed and was fully willing to give those patrons the boot—but as Stephanie said, it was always better to defuse a fight than win one.

In a pleasant surprise, however, the man leaned back and seemed to contemplate her words, his eyes going distant as she went to check on someone else. When she returned, the grouchy man was standing up and leaving a couple of bills on the counter. "Something extra," he said, "for your Oprah moment." He nodded and walked out.

Kera accepted and processed the money, wondering bemusedly if she ought to consider giving "tough-love" advice to more of her customers. It might be profitable. On the other hand, she suspected the line between profitable advice and advice that made people angry might be harder to find than she'd like.

She did another quick scan of the place, then checked the time. Turning to address the whole bar, she yelled, "Last call!"

CHAPTER EIGHT

Johnny waited in the lot behind the Mermaid.

It hadn't taken much research to find out that the place was run by a guy named Cevin. Johnny could look these things up online, but he preferred to find them out the old-fashioned way, by speaking to waitresses and bartenders. The way employees spoke about their employer was a good barometer for judging how to put pressure on them.

In this case, the waitresses seemed to like their boss. That probably meant he did all the gentlemanly things like walking them out the front before leaving alone.

He also apparently had a motorcycle. Johnny didn't know much about bikes, but this one looked well-maintained. With how parking could be in LA, maybe Cevin just stored the bike here.

Johnny remained where he was, draped in shadows, as patrons straggled across the pavement at the end of the alley. Some called drunken goodbyes to one another. Directions were shouted to taxi drivers.

It wasn't too long before the back door opened. Johnny stayed where he was for a moment, and his caution was justified when he saw that there were two people in the alley with him now. One was the thin, almost sickly-looking man Johnny had tagged as "probably Cevin," and the other…

Was the blonde who had shot him down earlier. Johnny's hackles rose, but he forced himself to stay still.

"What a night," the blonde said to Cevin.

"Bad night?"

"Nope. Definitely *some* sort of night, but not that."

Cevin shrugged. "I was gonna say. Looks like you made some decent tips. Don't take this the wrong way, but I think you're good for business. Let's just say the bar tends to be busier when you're there, and my sales have gone up."

She shrugged. It seemed she didn't care much, which didn't do anything to endear her to Johnny. "Maybe. Anyway, g'night, Cevin."

"Take care." He waved to her.

It was only when she went over to the bike that Johnny realized she was wearing leathers over her bar uniform, and his eyebrows shot up. The bike was *hers*? Seriously?

She fastened her helmet and adjusted it, flexed her hands inside her gloves, and then swung one long leg over the bike. A brief readjustment of the bike and a wave to Cevin, and she revved it smoothly into motion. After a brief pause at the street, she banked into a gap in the traffic.

Showtime, Johnny mouthed silently to himself. As Cevin turned toward his truck, the other man pulled out a cigarette and a pocket lighter, allowing the flame and the cherry glow to draw attention to him.

Cevin stopped where he was.

"So," Johnny began, his tone low and casually conversational, "Cevin, right? We need to talk."

Cevin squinted into the darkness. "You were in the bar today. Back corner."

Johnny ignored that. "I'll be straight with you so we can get done with this ASAP. There's the easy way to have this discussion, and there's a more difficult way."

Cevin said nothing, but his eyes strayed to his security camera, which was aimed at the space right beyond the rear door where the truck was parked. He frowned when he saw the shattered lens and turned his head slowly back to Johnny.

Johnny smiled. "So, let's get down to it."

Kera was three streets away before she remembered her little clutch—specifically, the one into which she had stowed her tips after the shift. She had put it down to flip chairs up onto the tables, and she hadn't picked it back up.

She groaned. She was just beginning to wind down. Hearing Zee purr beneath her had a nice, relaxing effect after a shift, and the air felt cool and heavy. It was about to start raining, something she had anticipated fondly when she thought she was close to home.

But if she went back now, she'd probably have time to catch Cevin. She knew from experience that he liked to chill out in his truck, smoke a cigarette and listen to a song or two before heading home. Everyone had their own rituals.

"Sorry, Cevin," she muttered. "Setting your relaxation time back a couple minutes. Oh, and rain? I'd appreciate a few minutes' grace from you."

She banked right and headed back toward the Mermaid.

Cevin crossed his arms over his chest and let out a deep breath. He wasn't naïve; he'd heard all sorts of stories from other bar owners over the years, and he made sure to take action when he needed to. The result was that he hadn't ever clashed with any of these gangs because he got rid of the problem before it came to a head.

This time, he had failed.

He supposed it had to happen sometime, but part of his brain was still spinning in the background. He hadn't heard of any new gangs in the area or extortion attempts. These guys had come out of nowhere.

The other man was taking an excessively long time to take a drag on his cigarette, which had Cevin itching to go for one of his.

He didn't want to take his eye off the ball even for a second, though. He knew the other man was waiting for him to make an offer first, so he was going to draw a line in the sand. "The answer is no," he said bluntly. "Whatever the hell it is you're proposing, there's never a good reason to get involved if the sales pitch starts off with someone waiting in an alley to make threats."

The other man chuckled. "Careful, friend. You need to not jump to conclusions. See, this right here is one of those moments that could take you down the difficult path." He strolled forward at a relaxed pace. The red tip of the cigarette floated through the darkness in time with a gesture.

Cevin said nothing. Of all the things he despised, this was one of the worst: veiled threats and then artfully hurt feelings when someone called them on it.

"Don't worry," the man explained, "I'm not looking to take any of your income if that's what you think. This isn't a protection racket."

Cevin raised an eyebrow. That did not put his mind at ease.

"All we want is an agreement that we'll be left alone to do our thing," the man said smoothly. He took a drag on his cigarette. "We leave you alone, and you leave us alone."

"Oh?" Cevin's eyes narrowed. "And who are the people I'm supposed to turn a blind eye to? I'd like to know who'll be preying on my customers."

"That hurts," the man said, his voice heavy with fake emotion. Cevin could see the faint outline of an exaggerated, theatrical expression of shock. "To make a reasonable proposal, and for you to assume that I'm going to be harming someone. No, sir. All we do is provide–"

He was cut off by the growl of an engine as Kera pulled back around the corner atop her motorcycle. Both men looked over, equally ill at ease with this new element to the conversation.

The shadowed man snapped his face back toward the bar manager. "You call her back?" There was no hint of congeniality in his voice now.

"You see my hands move?" Cevin was cursing inwardly. The last thing he wanted was for someone else to get involved in this. "No, for the record. I didn't."

"Well, you might want to get rid of her." Johnny's voice had taken on an edge of annoyance. "Pronto."

Kera stopped the bike near the corner of the bar and climbed off before taking off her helmet. "Hey, Cevin. I was a dipshit and left some stuff in the breakroom. Can I get back in?"

Cevin knew he had to be the one to put her at ease and get her out of here. He saw her do a once-over of the other man. She couldn't be seeing much, save for the glowing cigarette in his hand, and Cevin told himself that she would cue off his mood. He dug into his pocket, produced a ring of keys, and tossed it to her. "Here you go. Make it quick though, okay?"

"Sure." She caught the keys, walked straight to the door, unlocked it, and stepped in.

When the door closed behind her, Kera took a moment to think. The tension outside—the sense of wrongness—was obvious, but she knew it would be better if she didn't try to intrude or do anything stupid until she had a better idea about what the hell was going on.

Who the fuck was that? There wasn't another car, which meant the person had come up the alley on foot, and it hadn't been very long for them to have done that since she left: arrive, *and* start a fight of some sort.

Which meant he had probably been there when she and Cevin left the bar. She felt a prickle on the back of her neck, and instead of going to the bar to grab her clutch, she went directly to the security camera monitors and checked the one viewing the back lot.

Her eyes narrowed when she saw that the screen was black. Cevin was methodical. All of the staff got paid precisely on time, the bar was scrupulously clean, the cash register always balanced…and the security cameras were always on. One lapse she could have overlooked, but on the same night that someone showed up to confront him?

"Aw, hell," she muttered.

When she went into the main room, she hardly remembered to grab her clutch. She shoved it into her backpack absentmindedly and detoured behind the bar, scanning the shadowed shelves.

Beneath the register was a cigar box. As Cevin had told her when she'd first been hired, the box contained a Glock 19. She'd fired guns like it before, and while the grip was a little bulky for her hands, she could manage it fine. In this state, they were restricted to ten-round magazines, but she didn't expect that Mysterious Cigarette Guy had any backup. Ten should be fine.

Anyway, she wasn't going to pull it unless she was reasonably sure it would de-escalate things instead of the reverse.

She closed the box and carried it in front of her, her pack hanging from her left shoulder as she walked back to the rear door. She waited by it, pressing her face against its surface and listening to try to determine what was happening outside.

Cevin and the stranger were speaking quietly. She couldn't make out their words, but it was clear things hadn't escalated yet. Her heart was hammering in her chest. Breathing in, she opened the door, stepped outside, and let it fall closed and lock itself behind her.

The two men continued to converse in low voices. Kera pretended to ignore them and headed toward Zee, intending to drop off her pack and then assess the situation to see if Cevin needed help.

The man in the shadows had other ideas. "Perhaps," he said, loud and clear, "you need a little more convincing."

Kera stopped about five steps from Zee.

The man's voice changed direction, as though he were turning toward her. "I know you won't care if we make an example out of your piece-of-shit truck, but the girl seems to really like that bike of hers."

Kera swung her head around sharply. "What *about* my bike?" she asked before she could stop herself.

Cevin started to say something, but she never got to hear what because her answer from the man in the shadows came in the form of three sharp, cracking gunshots that echoed off the pavement.

Kera jerked back in shock, throwing herself against the wall and covering her face and stomach with her hands. With the sound dying and her ears ringing, she couldn't tell at first if any time had passed—or if she felt any pain.

When she realized she didn't, she whipped around to look for Cevin. He was on the ground, his hands over his torso, but as her mouth opened in a scream, she heard liquid trickling.

Looking over, she saw what the real target had been: Zee's gas tank.

Relief, fear, adrenaline—all of them hit fast. The anger came in a slow stream, just like the gas dribbling out of the tank. Kera stared at it, her breath coming short.

"Well," said the man, "looks like you're going to need a ride home tonight, sugar."

I know that voice, Kera realized and gritted her teeth. It was the jerk who wouldn't take no for an answer earlier.

She said nothing. Anything she'd say right now would only make things worse, and she also knew she wasn't going to draw an unfamiliar gun, aim it, and shoot before this guy got the drop on her.

He's making a point, she told herself. *He wants to scare you and feel superior, and then he'll go away.*

That didn't make it any easier to keep her mouth shut, though, especially when the stranger snickered in an unpleasant, self-satisfied way.

"Think it over," he said. "Both of you. No one needs to get hurt, right? As a sign of goodwill, I'll let you two leave first."

Kera watched as Cevin picked himself up off the ground and came over to her, swinging wide around the man in the shadows. Her boss kept his body between her and whoever their attacker was, and she saw him do a quick double-take at the box.

"Keep that for tonight," he murmured under his breath. "I'll pick it up from you later."

Neither of them spoke as they climbed into the truck, though Kera's shoulders hunched. She didn't like knowing that the man was behind them, his gun still out, ready and able to shoot as soon as their backs were turned.

Cevin's hands shook slightly as he put the key in the ignition, but he pulled out of the space and toward the road without hesitation. He always took the time to turn the truck around when he came in so he could leave easily, and Kera appreciated that now.

She didn't look back, not even after the truck had turned into traffic, and her hands didn't relax where they were clamped on the edges of the box.

Johnny remained behind, watching them leave. It was possible that some residents of the nearby housing complexes might have heard the gunshots.

No sirens yet, though.

He turned to leave before another memory surfaced. What was it that blonde had said? *No, thanks? Not interested?*

He raised his pistol, a Beretta 92FS that had once belonged to the LAPD, and fired two more rounds, one into each tire.

"Aww," he commented. "Now you're going to have to spend all the tip money you made tonight getting new tires, honey. Too bad."

He smiled as he slipped into the shadows and was gone.

CHAPTER NINE

Kera managed to keep quiet for about a block, at which point she became aware that her fingers were going white from how hard she was gripping the box. She tried to unlock her jaw to speak and only succeeded in making a growling noise.

Cevin shot her a look. "You okay?"

"Of course, I'm not okay!" Kera burst out. She stared at him. "Are you *kidding* me? That son of a bitch *shot my bike!*" With each word, her voice rose until she was shouting, and she banged one fist uselessly against the door. She wanted to scream.

It could have been one of them. She'd thought it *had* been one of them, which made her angry about caring about Zee, but she still *did* care about Zee, and—

"I'm so sorry, Kera."

She shook her head and looked out the window so she wouldn't have to make eye contact. "It's not—"

"I wish there'd been a way to warn you," Cevin continued.

She looked at him sharply. *I'm so sorry.* It hadn't been a platitude; he blamed himself for her getting caught up in it. She took three deep breaths, counting them. She was fairly sure from what she'd seen and heard that he wasn't responsible for any of it, and anyway, it wasn't like he could go back in time and save Zee.

She tipped her head back against the seat.

"Hey," Cevin said.

Kera looked over.

"I'll help pay to have someone fix it up," he told her.

"Cevin…" She couldn't afford to fix it right now—damn her mother for being right again—but this seemed like too much.

"Shouldn't cost too much," he said. "Besides, property damage is part of the deal when you own a business. I'd rather be a boss who treats people right. Besides, I was afraid it would blow up, so I guess we were lucky."

"You know that doesn't actually happen, right?"

He shot her a grin. "Joking, joking. Anyway, I'm sure the pros can handle it."

"Look, I appreciate the offer," Kera told him, "but that's a hell of a big favor, and it really shouldn't be necessary. I *am* a pro. Well, sorta. Just need to fix the holes in the tank and repaint it. I can do most of that with what I have. I even picked the paint job specifically because it doesn't show every scratch like the shiny ones do."

"That's thinking ahead," Cevin replied with a grin. "You know how I never wear white shirts? Same idea." He cleared his throat. "Just, you know, not as badass. Also, I don't remember your address from the background check, so you're going to have to give me directions."

Giving him the directions proved to be a good distraction, and both of them relaxed as the drive went on.

"Where should I put this, by the way?" Kera asked at a stoplight, holding up the cigar box.

"Under your seat is fine." Cevin's expression was halfway between embarrassed and guilty. "It's good that you didn't try to use it. It's, uh, not loaded, truth be told."

"Okay, but he also had the drop on me," Kera told him. "Not a lot of good is going to happen when one person has their gun out and the other person's is in a box."

Her employer chortled. "I suppose not. Even less good would have come if you'd pulled the trigger on him and gotten nothing but a click, but I'm impressed that you brought it out. You're a little feistier than I expected. If someone had asked me to guess who on my staff had shot a firearm before, I wouldn't have guessed you. No offense."

Kera shrugged off the comment. "My mom wanted a genteel princess, but my dad let me try whatever I wanted—martial arts, woodworking, motorcycles, guns. I stopped shooting regularly when my ears kept ringing too bad." She saw Cevin open his mouth and cut him off. "*Yes*, I was wearing earplugs. Still got tinnitus, though."

Cevin nodded and followed her silent indication to pull onto her street.

"So, who *was* that guy?" Kera asked. "Maybe I shouldn't be asking about it, but let's say I'm curious."

"I'm not sure," Cevin confessed. "He wanted to make some kind of arrangement where I let him 'do his thing.' I figured he was there to shake me down for protection money at first, but he claimed that wasn't his game, so he probably wants to be able to push drugs."

"Ugh," Kera groaned. "The joys of operating a small business in a large city. Are you sure it was only one guy?"

Cevin thought it over. "One guy alone in the parking lot as far as I could tell, but I'm sure he's got other people he works for. Or working for him. Who knows? Might be three assholes in a bargain-basement gang, might be the whole fucking mob."

"Could be," Kera acceded. "You can bet they'll be back to try to force the issue sooner or later, though, especially if he got like this after a single discussion. I don't have any bright ideas on how to deal with it, but if I think of any, I'll let you know."

"Same." He grunted. "But don't go thinking this is your problem to solve, okay?"

Kera didn't comment.

"Kera…"

"Fine." She shrugged. She knew Cevin wanted to keep his employees safe, and she wasn't going to worry him.

She also wasn't going to stop thinking about it. It was the only thing that kept the feeling of powerlessness from swamping her.

When they arrived at the warehouse, Cevin insisted on waiting outside to make sure she got in safely. He stayed until she had opened the door and waved, and it was only when she was inside with the door locked that she heard him pull away.

Once he'd left, she dropped her backpack on the floor and stood staring at her room. When she'd left this morning, she'd been annoyed at her mother, sure she was doing the right thing with her life.

Right now, she wasn't sure what she thought about anything. The crash was coming after the adrenaline rush of their confrontation in the alley, and she wasn't sure what to do to keep going.

She rubbed her face. "Shit," she muttered into her hands, then she took a deep breath. "Food. Change. Come on, MacDonagh, keep moving."

She brought her backpack over to the table and went to the fridge, where there were the remains of some pad thai she had ordered two nights ago. She set it to heat in the microwave, then changed out of her work clothes into pajamas.

When the pad thai was gone, along with two full glasses of water, she allowed herself to consider going off autopilot. She looked around. She could hang up the gym equipment, except she would certainly need another shower, and probably some tools she'd have to go to a store to get…

Which she couldn't do without Zee.

She could do some martial arts forms, she supposed, but her stomach was too full for that.

She rubbed her face again and went over to the bed to check her phone. Since she hadn't used it for most of her shift, it still had an almost-full battery. When it opened, it was still on the reading app she had used.

"Ugh." She was not up for staid business reading tonight.

Then she remembered what the book was. Grinning, she sat up and scooched over to the wall so she could sit and read.

To her surprise, there wasn't much in the way of an introduction. She would have liked to have read the history behind this book, like where it had been found and who was thought to have written it. The title seemed modern, but the wording in some of the spells was archaic, which led her to believe that it had been written in some sort of old English.

"Ye olde spelle booke," she mused to herself as she flipped to the end. No appendices or 'About the Author' pages there, either. "Curiouser and curiouser. What d'you think, Zee? Someone dug up an old grimoire, scanned it, and gave it a fancy modern title?"

She looked up as she finished speaking and her smile faded. Zee wasn't there, of course. In fact, Zee wasn't even in an auto shop, warm and toasty while waiting for repairs. No, her bike was out in the rain with a punctured gas tank.

The craziness of the night threatened to overwhelm her for a moment, and her chin trembled.

There was one thing the jerk hadn't counted on, though: anyone who tried to scare her or browbeat her into doing things their way was in for a *big* surprise. It hadn't worked in grade school when Eva Lucas had tried to get everyone to stop talking to Amanda Maynor. It hadn't worked in high school when her mother tried to keep her from learning how to shoot guns. It hadn't worked in college when several professors *and* her cheerleading coach had tried to keep her from majoring in Computer Science.

And she sure as *hell* wasn't going to let some jerk who didn't understand the word "no" shoot up the bar. Cevin might be blaming himself, but Kera knew where the shooter had first started disliking the Mermaid—and she knew that people like him wouldn't just take one concession. They'd walk all over you if you gave them the first chance.

When he came back, she was going to be ready for him. She had no idea how, of course, but she'd come up with something.

Maybe there was a spell somewhere in the book.

That was the dose of humor she needed to get back on an even keel. With a grin, Kera tapped over to the table of contents and scanned through the spells.

"Forgetting something… Oh, shit, is that *really* brain bleach? Maybe even the ancient druids had stuff they wanted to forget." She snickered as she tapped to turn the page. "Purifying water, probably useful. Finding water, also useful. Ah, here we go: fire spells."

Once she was in the relevant section, she scanned it. There were spells for extinguishing fire, spells for lighting candles or creating a spark in kindling, and *several* warnings about starting a fire you couldn't put out without magical means.

If this weren't a book of magic spells, Kera would say those warnings came from experience. As it was, maybe they just had good sense.

One section in particular caught her attention: Fire. Kera didn't have to think for more than a second.

"Yeah, fire sounds good, and I know just where I want that asshole to feel it. So, ancient book, how do I do this? Is there a potion, or…"

There was no potion. Instead, one was supposed to move one's fingers much in the same way as snapping them, the idea being to conjure the mental image of a spark striking from flint. At the same time, one must seek to connect one's inner power to the ambient power that covered the world. The book noted that what had primarily been thought of as 'ley lines' were not lines and tended to shift over time.

"Whatever," Kera muttered. "I don't care where they are. I just want to light this guy's crotch on fire. All right. One, two..."

The flare of light caught her by surprise. She yelped and scrambled back on the bed, running into the wall immediately. Her fingers were smarting. She looked at them, then at the empty air where she *knew* she had seen a flare of magic.

"No *way,*" she breathed.

CHAPTER TEN

When James awoke, it was not to the pale sky of an early winter morning, but instead to the strong, direct rays of midday sunshine.

For the first time in weeks, he felt well-rested. He sat up and stared out at the blue sky with a smile on his face before pushing the covers back and standing up to stretch. He pulled the spread up his bed. He used magic for things such as drafts, not for smaller things like making a bed.

Besides, it was always better to start a day with attention to form and detail.

He came downstairs in a chipper mood and was nearly done with breakfast when Mother LeBlanc arrived in the kitchen. She poured herself a small cup of coffee, laced it liberally with sugar, and came to sit with him.

"You look restored," she told him.

James, his mouth full of eggs and toast, nodded.

"You will be pleased to know that the activity on the map continues." She sipped her coffee. "And though my eyes could be deceiving me, I believe I see some recurring locations."

"Did *you* sleep?" James asked her. He had never been sure she did things like that. Mother LeBlanc, in his mind, existed without the constraints of other mortals.

"Yes," she said in a way that made him wonder further.

He finished his food while pondering the possibility of immortals masquerading as humans. After all, sometimes folktales got things right. Perhaps they were right about vampires, too.

Had he ever seen her teeth? He grinned around a mouthful of food.

"I assume there's a reason for your mirth," she commented.

"I was considering the idea that you might be immortal," he explained cheerfully.

"Ah. Well, in that case, I would have wasted a great deal of time on unnecessary caution." She sipped at her coffee. "Though, given the aforementioned immortality, perhaps the wasted time should not concern me too much."

"That's the spirit. Shall we start working on the changes to our map?"

She nodded and stood, bringing her cup to the sink. She thanked him in a low voice when he took it from her and led the way through the darkened hallways.

In the council chamber, the map lay deceptively still. There were presently no blooms of light on its surface, which disappointed and heartened James in equal measure. He wanted to learn where their new recruits might be.

"We *should* be able to modify it so that lights don't show up only when the magic is actually being practiced," James said. Since he had developed the original spell, he was taking the lead role in modifications. "What I would like to do is add a time component, with the color changing to show how long it has been since the magic was used."

"That is very clever." Mother LeBlanc sounded impressed. "I had not thought of that, but of course it will help us determine who is most in need of immediate intervention." She tapped the corner of her mouth with one finger. "But how exact is it?"

"That's the question," James said. "I've thought about it two ways. First, should we allow enough variance that someone practicing magic on one side of their living room doesn't show up as a different event from them practicing it on the *other* side of their living room? One assumes yes."

She nodded.

"But what about apartment buildings?" James pointed out. "Multiple people on different stories of the same building, or people who share a wall?"

"I wouldn't think there would be many of those."

"Neither would I," James pointed out, "except that we initially got far more potential recruits than either of us imagined."

LeBlanc nodded, her eyes distant as she thought.

"How *would* one make it more or less exact?" she said finally. "You mentioned the mechanics of it in abstract at the meeting, but nothing in-depth."

James explained, pulling out the notebook he had used to create diagrams of the spell. Not for the first time, he wished there had been more advances in the field of thaumaturgy.

Magic was a force humans could summon, and it could be exhausted, just as human energy could be exhausted. The mechanics of that were not well-known, however. While there had been two notable thaumaturges who'd worked to codify the differences in spell-working techniques, as well as some, like LeBlanc, who had studied the magical fields around the earth, the number of thaumaturges was vanishingly small compared to the number of humans.

Therefore, where science had several hundred luminaries who had changed the course of a field, thaumaturgy could not boast the same thing.

Nor, of course, was it safe to expose the existence of magic in order to gain more insight.

While James explained, LeBlanc produced a notebook and fountain pen from the folds of her dress and took notes. What language they were in, he did not know, but he did not recognize the alphabet. Perhaps it was her own shorthand.

The two of them had rarely worked together, and he was pleased by the questions she brought to the topic. It did not take long for them to settle on a method of determining individual magic users and less than the usual number of tries to get the spell up and running.

"What we really need," James said at the end, "is someone to… what do they call it in software?"

"I am not the correct person to ask, James."

"Fair enough." James spun his hand to indicate that he was thinking. "That thing where you test something a *lot* to make sure it doesn't run into problems? Quality! QA, that was it. I don't think anyone has ever done that with thaumaturgy before."

"You have a good point," she conceded. "Perhaps one of our new recruits will help us with that. In the meantime, we both need rest."

James nodded. He had only woken up two hours ago, but he was exhausted from the magical workings. Over time, one grew better at using magic without drawing on one's own energy, but complex workings were always exhausting.

"The one problem with living in the middle of nowhere," James muttered, "is that you can't just order a pizza. I could really go for…oh, eight pizzas or so right now. You?"

"Barbecue," Mother LeBlanc said with a smile. "Slow-roasted meat, freshly-made cornbread, some greens, black-eyed peas… oh, and sorrel."

"I don't think I've ever had it."

"Then you should hope some of our new candidates are in Jamaica," Mother LeBlanc said lightly. "Even the chefs in New Orleans don't make it the same way."

Sven watched as Pauline marked locations on a map. So far, the group had found success in Little Tokyo and Chinatown, but Sven had struck out at the club he and Johnny had gone to the night before.

Anxious about his tally, he'd gone to two more bars as well to bump his numbers up.

Unfortunately, he couldn't tell from Pauline's demeanor if she was angry. Her face hadn't so much as flickered when he gave her his stats.

She finished making a note and looked up. "Where is Mr. Torrez?"

"Uh." Sven scrambled mentally. Was he supposed to be covering for Johnny? That was the general rule, but Johnny hadn't mentioned anything in particular.

"Mr. Jensen, it is not a difficult question. Do you know where Mr. Torrez is or not?"

"I...no." Sven shook his head. "We met up after the first set of bars to debrief, then we got your text and headed out again."

She watched him for a second longer, using her silence to make him speak.

It worked.

"He'd mostly had success," Sven said. "Just one place seemed like a miss. The Mermaid." Under her steely gaze, he felt much smaller than his six-foot-plus stature. "I don't know where he went and in what order, though."

Pauline went back to her notes without comment, but she shot a pointed glance at Lia.

The other woman pulled her phone out and began texting furiously. Sven assumed it was a business-speak version of "Where the fuck are you?"

"With these locations *plus* the party..." Pauline considered. "Yes. Mr. Jensen, you will move on to Stage 3. I believe you were the one who initially identified the gangs working in this district?"

"Yes." Sven decided not to comment on the hint of a Russian accent that had emerged.

"Good. You will do your best to stoke violence between them."

"You want me to start a gang war?" Sven wasn't sure what was going on.

"Were the instructions unclear?"

Sven tried to decide how far he was willing to push this.

To his surprise, Lia spoke up for him. "Ma'am, part of why he's here is your vision of a peaceful city. While you, of course, are not obligated to tell us your reasons, I think he wants to understand how short-term violence will lead to long-term peace."

Sven shot her a grateful look.

Pauline nodded. "Very well, although I prefer my employees speak for themselves. Ask yourself this, Mr. Jensen: if all of us are here to create a better world, why did we not join the police?"

Because I'm not a fucking narc, and I'm in it for the money? "I… don't trust the police, ma'am."

"Nor should you," Pauline said, nodding approvingly. "They are powerless. The methods they have at their disposal are useless. They are hamstrung by their own incompetence and by the weakness of politicians, and that is what we are about to show them." She paused for a moment. "*You* will stoke violence between the gangs. News reports will come out. People will be afraid. The police will be able to do nothing to help them, and then…*we* will help them. *We* will restore peace."

Sven knew better than to look at Lia. He only nodded as if he understood.

As if this wasn't completely ass-backward.

"The police cannot stop them," Pauline said, "so they will know they cannot stop *us*. They will also know that to take us out is to return to the chaos and violence that made them look so bad. They will let us be."

Oh. When she put it that way, it wasn't the worst idea.

Sven was about to speak when the door was thrust open and Johnny strode in. The other man was grinning, his clothes rumpled and the smell of perfume clinging faintly to his shirt. It was obvious what he'd been doing to be late.

"Good night," he announced.

Sven sensed that Johnny was about to make a spectacular ass of himself. He should stop that from happening. After all, Lia had saved *his* ass. He might as well save Johnny's.

"It sounds like we both had good results last night," he said, trying to convey with his expression how urgent it was for Johnny to bring things back on track. "We will be starting Phase 3 soon."

"Oh, we had good results, all right." Johnny took a seat and propped his feet on the table. Sven could still smell the alcohol on his breath. "After that little bitch at the Mermaid tried to play tough with me, I needed a little something, you know? Went and got wasted with a bunch of models."

Pauline's face had gone icy.

"Did I say that blonde was hot?" Johnny continued. "She might be hot, but if you can't see the tits, they might as well not be there, huh? Three models are better than one snooty rich girl."

Pauline was done waiting for him to speak. "Mr. Torrez, did you do *anything* productive last night?"

"Oh, sure. Got you the four bars I mentioned. Not the Mermaid, but I'm going back there tonight. That guy's not gonna hold out much longer, an' the models aren't too far from wantin' in. That's a whole market we haven't tapped."

Johnny had saved himself by the skin of his teeth. Pauline's expression changed to something more contemplative. "It's hardly an untried market," she said, "but yes. We might. Their drugs are usually supplied by their handlers, but for those coming to LA domestically, we might have an in."

Lia was taking notes.

"Mr. Jensen, explain Stage 3 to Mr. Torrez. And Mr. Torrez?"

"Yeah?" Johnny ran his fingers through his hair.

"I expect you to be on time to meetings and appropriately attired." Pauline's voice was perfectly pleasant, but it gave Sven chills. She left without another word, and Lia trailed after her with a pointed glance at Johnny.

When they were gone, Sven dropped into a chair. "Do you know how close you were to getting your balls cut off?"

"Woman like that could do better things with my balls." Johnny gave him a grin and made a crude gesture. "Might loosen her up."

"Johnny, I'm serious. She is *not* in the mood to play around. We have work to do."

"Damn straight. I'm gonna show blondie—"

"*No*," Sven interrupted. "Seriously, Johnny, *leave* it. We have a lot to do."

"Like what?"

"We have a gang war to start." Sven stood up and held out his hand to pull the other man up. "After you shower."

CHAPTER ELEVEN

For a moment, when Kera woke up, she felt as if she had finally slept enough.

Then she cracked an eye open to check the time and was struck by one of the worst headaches she'd ever had.

"Owwww." She pressed her hands over her eyes, only to have the distinct feeling that she'd been hit by a truck. Her muscles hurt. Her hands hurt. Her eyes hurt.

What had she *done* last night? Gotten ragingly drunk and then found a horse to get kicked by? She squinted at her arms and saw nothing in the way of bruises, though it was difficult to tell, given the unholy brightness of the sunlight. She sat up and looked around the room.

"Seriously, what the *hell?*"

Her first thought was that she had been robbed. The walls, the table, the fridge…all of the surfaces were covered with sticky notes. She distinctly remembered when her mother had sent her a care package with supplies for "the office I just know you'll have soon, honey," and Kera had said that she wouldn't ever use that many sticky notes, especially ones with flowers on them.

At a glance, it looked like she had used them all. Last night.

"Is there a new drug I don't know about?" Her eyes were getting used to the light, though the headache was still there. She could just hear the news headlines now: *Police confused by the emergence of OrganizeX, the drug that makes people compulsively take notes. OfficeMax reports unprecedented first-quarter sales.*

She didn't realize she was hearing a trilling noise until it stopped. Kera sat up a little straighter, wincing as muscles ached and spasmed, and looked around. Not the clock, which said 2:14PM. That meant it was probably her phone, which she did not see anywhere.

She looked at the post-it notes for another moment, then her eyes settled on the empty space on the other side of the room.

Where the hell was Zee?

"*What?*" She threw the covers up and bounded out of bed. The pain in her head and her muscles was *nothing* compared to the rage rising in her chest. Someone had come into *her* house, taken her baby, and—

Put up several hundred sticky notes?

Kera hobbled to the door as fast as she could and wrenched it open to make sure she hadn't left Zee outside. The fragile hope collapsed as soon as she saw the empty patch of concrete that served as a driveway and ramp.

"Fuck." She slumped against the doorframe, only to nearly leap out of her skin when there was a beep from somewhere around her feet. "What the—oh, hey."

Her phone was between her shoes.

Why had she put it *there*?

She bent down to get it, wincing. The screen showed a missed call and a voicemail from Cevin, which made her frown. She couldn't remember if she was supposed to work today—she also couldn't remember which day it was—but she couldn't be late since it was only 2:15 in the afternoon. The Mermaid wasn't even open yet.

Cevin. She had a vague memory of being here in this door, and—

His truck. She blinked at the empty street. Why would Cevin have been here? She sorted through several possibilities in her head, each stranger than the last.

Then it came back to her in a rush, like she had stumbled all the way through a patch of dense fog and could see the shapes of memories ahead. She had been at the Mermaid when someone had confronted Cevin. There had been a gun. Zee…

That was why Zee wasn't there. The thought came with barely any relief. No use knowing where Zee was when he had bullet holes in his gas tank.

"Fuck," Kera said, and she took only a hollow pleasure in what her mother would say if she could hear her swear like that.

She closed the door behind her, went back into the big open space, and looked around.

"Okay. Some asshole shot Zee, Cevin drove me home, and I went crazy. But, like, in an organized way." She hobbled over to the table and began looking at the post-it notes. They all had her writing on them—unsurprising, now that she knew what had happened to Zee—and seemed to be arranged like some sort of quality assurance checklist.

Her stomach interrupted her thought process with a growl, and she realized how hungry she was. She was at the fridge in a second, yanking it open to stare at the food inside with a groan of frustration. Eggs that were past their expiration date, a bag of shredded cheese, and a green pepper that didn't quite look to be in its prime anymore.

She didn't have the willpower to order food in. Kera grabbed the bag of cheese and the pepper and began shoveling cheese into her mouth with one hand while washing the pepper with the other. She chowed down on the pepper like an apple, spitting seeds into the sink occasionally, then stared at the empty cheese bag and the pepper innards confusedly.

This wasn't like her. She tried to eat healthy. She had never gotten out of sorts when she was angry or motivated by an empty stomach.

And she was getting increasingly worried because she couldn't remember much of last night.

She considered, then took her phone over to the bed to listen to the message from Cevin, which she put on speakerphone.

"Hi, Kera," her boss began, sounding less than cheerful. "Listen, don't bother coming in today. After we left, that guy apparently shot out your tires, too."

"That asshole!" Her eyes widened, and her hands balled into fists. "Those tires were brand new."

Cevin's voice went on, his words echoing hers. "Real asshole move. It looked like the tires were brand new. Anyway, I took your bike to a shop this morning since I figured the tires would at least be an easy fix."

Kera groaned and pinched the bridge of her nose. "They were special orders."

"But," Cevin continued, "it turned out they were special orders. I should have known you'd have primo stuff since you love your bike so much. Regardless, I had them match the size and place the order in the meantime. One set and a spare. Anyway, it will be three days before it's ready. Maybe more, but they're hoping three."

Kera groaned again and propped her arms on her knees. How was she going to get to work? The Mermaid wasn't *that* far, but it was farther than she could realistically walk.

"So, I thought I'd give you some PTO. Take a couple of days paid. I'll cover you for the time being. Since that prick shot up *your* vehicle to send *me* a message, I guess I feel responsible." He sighed.

Kera grimaced and looked at the phone, guilt worming through her chest. The asshole with the gun had been hoping to teach *her* a lesson, too.

"All I can say is that I'm sorry about last night," Cevin concluded. "I've got more cameras coming in and extra lights for the back. We won't be caught with our pants down like that again, I promise. If you, uh…" He paused. "If you don't want to come back at all, I'll understand. Just let me know. Take care of yourself."

He hung up, and the phone beeped as the message ended.

Kera sat staring at the phone and feeling a peculiar sensation in her stomach, one that had nothing to do with the cheese and the pepper. Though Cevin's message had been predictable, touching on all the topics she would expect, she couldn't help but feel that she had anticipated all of it, down to the exact words he had used.

"This isn't still a dream, is it?" she asked aloud. She gave herself a light slap across the face and determined that she was indeed awake. "Huh. And *ow*."

She got up and went into the bathroom, where another surprise awaited. She stopped and stared at the note stuck to the mirror before approaching it suspiciously and pulling it off to read it.

Check the back of your hand. You had a cut there last night. And the witch stuff is <u>real</u>!

She noted that the word "real" was double-underlined. There was more on another series of notes.

Also, be REALLY careful with the memory spell. Maybe just stay away from that one.

Bet you can't remember the talk with Mom, either. Because I can't right now, and I wrote myself a note to make sure I remembered it if the brain bleach spell worked. If we could make a product out of this, we would be rich!

Kera felt like something was fluttering around in her stomach. She rubbed her eyes again. "I am too hungover for this," she said to no one in particular. "Or…whatever. Headache." She looked at the note again. "Who is *we*?"

Of all the things she needed today, her past self writing notes to her future self was not on the list.

Her stomach was doing weird flip-flops. The witch stuff was real!

That was ridiculous.

So why are you so afraid of it? a snide part of her mind wondered.

She ignored the little voice determinedly, opened the cabinet behind the mirror, and pulled out a bottle of ibuprofen, downing two capsules with a swig of water. When she was done, she still wasn't ready to think about the book, so she decided to wash her face. And moisturize it.

Her stomach hadn't stopped doing weird things yet, and it struck her that this was an excellent time to floss. She did so with extreme care, made sure to brush her teeth for the full two minutes, then rinsed her mouth with Scope.

After that, she couldn't think of anything further to do in terms of stalling.

She returned to the bed and looked at the phone as if it were a venomous snake that was about to strike. Gingerly and almost without looking at it, she brought up the reader app and the witchcraft book.

She remembered having opened it. She even remembered joking about lighting that asshole on fire.

What she *didn't* remember was highlighting a bunch of sentences and paragraphs, adding a series of notes to each suggested posture and image, and then adding the note, *"This would be easier if I didn't remember the wrong attempts and forget the right ones."*

The notes had been taken over a span of hours. How much sleep had she gotten?

She went back to the table and began tracing her way through the notes, referencing them against headings in the book's table of contents. There had been method to her madness.

"Did I seriously stay up late doing quality control testing on how to perform *spells?*"

If that was the case, it presented a lot of possibilities—ones she was too tired to explore at present but too curious to leave alone.

Her screen dimmed, the battery indicator switching to red. Kera sighed as she went to get her charger from her backpack. There was part of her bag of trail mix left, which she poured into her mouth and chewed like a chipmunk, cheeks bulging out.

God, she was hungry. Apparently, that was what magic did to you.

"This is ridiculous," she told herself firmly. "Magic is not real, Kera. The fact is, you've developed a drug problem."

It was a little bit worrisome that a drug problem was her best-case scenario, but she couldn't think of anything else it could be. Because if the magic was real, that meant…

She didn't even want to think about what it meant.

On the other hand… She looked down and flexed her fingers. She *had* gotten a scratch.

CHAPTER TWELVE

In general, the company Christian and Ted worked for was a mess of bureaucratic nonsense, needlessly specific dress codes, and corporate-speak that only the top-level executives could deliver with a straight face.

However, there were occasionally good perks, such as the full hour the salaried employees got for lunch. A half-hour didn't give people nearly enough time to drive out, buy food and eat it, and return to work, *especially* in Los Angeles traffic.

Even if one wasn't hungover, which Ted definitely was today.

Christian had driven them both to his favorite burger place nearby—independent, every bit as good as In-N-Out, and far less likely to be packed at lunchtime—and was now eating with gusto while Ted stared into the middle distance and looked queasy.

"How you feeling, buddy?" Christian asked around a mouthful of food.

Ted gave a low moan and dropped his head onto his crossed arms.

Christian tried not to snicker. "The burger will help, you know."

"Strongly disagree," Ted said, his voice muffled.

"Come on. Carbs, protein, some grease."

Ted made a gagging sound. "Why would nature make it so you're supposed to eat when you feel like you're about to throw up?"

"A glitch in the programming?" Christian tried to keep it from being *too* obvious that he was laughing at his friend. "No one ever said nature was an expert coder, and it probably didn't account for vodka when it was writing the operating system. Try drinking some soda first. Carbonation's supposed to be good for an upset stomach." He took another bite of his burger and savored the medley of greasy beef, fresh vegetables, and sauce.

Ted nodded in resignation, though he didn't pick his head up. "In…a minute."

"You're at least doing better today than you were last night," Christian pointed out.

"Not true. Last night, it didn't feel like there was a railroad spike being driven into my brain."

"Yes, but right now, you're managing to sit in a chair without falling over."

"Irre…something. Non. *Not.* Not relevant." Ted twitched his fingers weakly.

"Irrelevant."

"That's the one."

Christian shook his head and took another bite. He chewed and swallowed before saying, "Nope, *very* relevant. I kept having to prop you up on the bar to keep you from falling off the stool… which probably made me look caring and heroic in front of Kera, though. So, in a way, our expedition was a success."

"Yeah," Ted mumbled, picking his head up and staring at the burger with undisguised wariness. "You're welcome."

"Anyway," Christian went on, enjoying the free entertainment, "you weren't the one paying. It cost me over fifty bucks to make that happen. Free booze does something to a man, doesn't it?"

"Yup," Ted agreed. "It does a thing. I'm not sure what, but I *do* know that I hate myself." He picked up a fry and examined it carefully before taking a cautious bite. He ate the rest of it and picked up a handful. "So, Kera."

"Yes?"

"The supermodel who can code. Sounds like you guys talked in college. Does she, uh, have a sister?"

Christian laughed. "Not sure," he admitted. "Her family's all back east somewhere."

"Good," Ted acknowledged. "The best kind of family. Far away." He ate another fry with an expression of grim determination.

Chris finished eating and crumpled up his wrappers before stuffing them in the bag. "So, I want to go back, but not too soon. Don't think I'm ready. Not to mention, coming in two nights in a row will make me look needy and stalker-y. We don't want that."

"Correct," agreed Ted. "Plus, there's no way you can possibly do it without me, and I'm fairly certain I'm going to need another day to recuperate. Or three." He looked at his sandwich, shook his head, and continued with the fries. "Any sooner, and I think my liver will cut itself out of my body."

Christian nodded. "Deal."

They'd snagged a place near one of the trash cans, and Christian tossed his wrappers in while Ted tried to keep eating.

A few bites later, Ted said contemplatively, "Stephanie."

"Hmm?"

"The other waitress. Black girl."

"Ah, yeah. What about her?"

"Can't let you start dating a goddess and just leave me behind," Ted explained.

"Oh. Well, we'll work on you next time." Chris grinned and downed the last of his soda. "Seriously, though, thanks. I would have stayed in the booth all night if you hadn't been there. Instead, I got to talk to Kera, and it…went *well*."

He still couldn't believe that part. She had known who he was. She had remembered his favorite beer.

She had said she'd always wanted to buy him one.

That couldn't be real, right?

Ted, meanwhile, seemed to have more prosaic concerns. He moaned and shuddered. "I'm glad my sacrifice was not in vain." It seemed that a second spell of nausea was hitting him, but with Ted, it was tough to be sure when things were real versus when an act.

"Yes, yes, your sacrifice." Christian rolled his eyes. "Come on, buddy, let's stop at a drugstore on the way back and get you some Tums."

When Sven was done explaining Pauline's plan for a gang war and police non-intervention, Johnny, now showered, stared at the map on Sven's phone and frowned. He took out a cigarette, lit it, and took a few puffs before responding.

"You think she's all there?" He looked at Sven speculatively.

Sven sighed. "I'm…not sure. Scares the hell out of me, though." He rubbed at his head. "But that's the way it is with anyone who runs a group, right? They all see the world a bit different."

Johnny nodded. "Just wanna make sure I'm not signing up for some cult shit. I'll kiss ass and show respect, but you want me to do crazy shit with rituals? I'm out."

"Nothing like that yet." Sven pulled out a wad of cash Lia had come to drop off. "Just some good old-fashioned shit-talking and bribery."

"That, I can do." Johnny grabbed about half the bills. "You want Chinatown or Little Tokyo?"

"I'll take Little Tokyo." Sven didn't want Johnny to start any more shit at the Mermaid.

When the two parted ways, Sven took the time to watch Johnny drive off. Sometimes he worried about his friend. Johnny claimed he was willing to kiss some ass, but the truth was that he had too big an ego to do that without a damned good reason.

Sven was sure of two things: first, that Pauline could provide a reason, and second, that he didn't want to be there when she did.

It was a short drive from the rental office to Little Tokyo, where he parked out of the way and strolled around to get a feel for the place. Three gangs operated here, mostly minor players who had aspirations of greatness with nothing to back it up—the kind of people who talked a big game but always chickened out.

It was up to Sven to get them to take decisive action.

He wasn't going to start by asking them to attack each other directly, he thought. He was going to get them to pump up their confidence first by preying on the easier marks—regular civilians.

Once they were on a high from that, the tensions should spill out on their own.

He spotted his first group of candidates pretty quickly: three young men wearing their colors a little too obviously, both looking for a fight and afraid of starting one. Sven wandered closer, hands in his pockets, and made a show of watching them.

It wasn't long before they noticed him, though it was long enough that Sven didn't think much of their chances in a fight.

"You looking at something, Grandpa?" one of them asked.

Sven laughed at them. "Watching you."

The three of them looked at one another. They had expected him to back down, and now that he hadn't, they didn't know what to do. The two who hadn't spoken both motioned for their friend to keep going, clearly glad it wasn't them in the hot seat.

The one who had spoken cleared his throat before adopting a more confrontational posture. He advanced on Sven with his jaw up and a sneer on his face. "You got a problem with me?"

"Eh." Sven made a show of fixing a stray lock of hair. When he started out in this business, he'd gotten endless shit about being a ginger. He'd learned to own it over time. "Been outta town for a while and wanted to see who'd taken over here. Heard it was the Dreads."

The last comment was calculated. These young men weren't Dreads, they were Vox, and they wouldn't take kindly to him calling out their opponents.

"You heard *wrong*," the first man said right on cue. "Vox runs this place."

"Looks like no one runs this place," Sven said, raising one eyebrow. "This is what passes for running something now? Buncha kids standing around with their colors in their pockets? What you standing around for?"

They stared at him, taken aback.

Sven leaned against the outside of a bus stop and crossed his arms. "Not a hard question, boys. You on a lunch break? Gonna be badass in fifteen minutes? Or did you just get tired of jerking it while playing *Grand Theft Auto* and decided to come outside and play dress-up?"

The boys looked murderous now.

"Shut up," the first one said. "You're past your prime, old man. You don't want to start shit with us."

"Start shit? I could whip up a crew today and own this place by tomorrow." Sven held up his hands. "Not gonna, but you'd best get your shit together before someone else sees you with your pants down."

"The reason you don't see anything going down is that we *own* this place—" the first one began.

His words trailed off in a gurgle as he felt the press of Sven's pistol right below his ribs. Behind him, his friends froze, hands reaching for holsters under their coats.

"The reason I don't see anything going down here," Sven said pleasantly, "is that this neighborhood has been shit for years, and the only people here are toothless old ladies like you. But it's coming up now. You got those nice, shiny cars over there. You got the office crowd that ain't watching their wallets. You got the trust-fund babies." He gave an exaggerated sniff to indicate where all the trust fund money went. "You want to get steamrolled, just keep playing. You want to survive what's coming, you best get your shit together."

He stepped back, and his gun disappeared into its holster under the edge of his t-shirt.

The boys stared at him.

"You're lucky I saw you first," Sven said, "and not whoever that other gang is. You might get the drop on them if you take control now." He gave a mocking salute and headed out. He wasn't worried that they'd shoot. They'd just gotten their asses handed to them, and they'd take it out on someone weaker.

Like one of those office workers with an unguarded wallet.

So would the other gangs, once Sven had gotten under their skin, too. Little Tokyo was about to explode just enough to scare all the business owners.

Then everything was going to get nice and quiet when Pauline took control. Sven smiled to himself. He shared some of Johnny's concerns about their boss, but he was also glad not to be in one of the boys' club gangs he'd grown up with, all macho posturing and shit-talking.

Took forever to get anything done when everyone was trying to one-up one another. Pauline got shit done, and it was already easy to see her running circles around the other gangs out here. Soon they'd own a cool few districts of LA, and they'd be swimming in cash.

Sven detoured down an alley, heading for Dread territory.

CHAPTER THIRTEEN

Kera tucked her still-wet hair under a beanie and grabbed her backpack. She was ravenous and not looking forward to a walk, but she desperately needed food.

Besides, it was probably good to leave her apartment at some point. The bonus was that maybe by the time she came back, the world would be back to normal. She doubted it, but it was possible.

Her phone beeped as she walked, and she pulled it out to see a message from Stephanie, asking if she was okay. With Cevin tight-lipped and ordering a lot of extra security cameras, the other waitresses were on edge even before he mentioned that Kera would be out for a few days.

Not wanting to worry her, Kera wrote back as boring a reply as she could manage, making it seem as if she had just gotten a bad illness. She ended with, **The past day has been a haze, honestly.**

It was true, she reflected. The only thing was, she was fairly sure it had been a haze because she had accidentally hit herself with a memory wipe spell, and it had overshot whatever she was trying to erase.

Of course, she couldn't remember what she had been trying to erase, so she couldn't tell if it had worked as intended.

We'll just steer clear of that one for now, she told herself.

At the Kims' store, she waved at the counter, surprised when she only got a distracted wave in return. Assuming Mr. Kim was just tired, she got started on her grocery shopping. Her appetite being what it was, she had to remind herself not to load up on groceries. After all, she would have to carry them back.

She had been so incredibly hungry lately that she tried to get some calorie-dense foods, however, grabbing several packets of nuts and trail mix, some granola and peanut butter, crackers, and a block of cheese, along with vegetables that she added more out of a sense of obligation than anything else. She also added a dozen eggs and some whole milk, figuring they were somewhat healthy.

On her way up to the counter, she also grabbed three composition notebooks. She was getting tired of having everything she owned covered in Post-it notes.

Mr. Kim raised his eyebrows at the large amount of food.

"Are you having a dinner party?" he joked. "You will serve breakfast foods?"

Kera smiled as he rang it all up.

"I didn't hear Zee when you came in," Mr. Kim commented.

"Oh." She struggled with how much she should tell him, given the circumstances. "Zee is…in the shop." She tried to find a way not to mention what had happened. "There was an accident."

"Oh, no!" His eyes widened. "You do not look hurt—"

"Oh, not that kind of accident." Now she felt both flustered and guilty. "I'm so sorry for worrying you, Mr. Kim. Someone did some damage to my bike, but I'm okay."

"Well, I am glad for that, at least." His face relaxed, and she again saw the strange quiet behind his eyes.

"Mr. Kim, are *you* okay?"

"I—yes, Kera, thank you very much. It is good of you to ask."

But she noticed that his hands trembled slightly as he started to scan her groceries. His movements were even stiffer than usual, but *that* didn't seem to be what was bothering him.

She looked down, uncertain of what she should say. Even when he was in pain, Mr. Kim seemed to be in high spirits. She had never seen him look *scared* before. Scared and sad.

As she packed things into her backpack, Mr. Kim leaned over the counter to look out at the parking lot.

"Are you walking home with that?" he asked her.

"Yes. It's a nice day out." It really was, she told herself. Many LA natives would consider the day cold, but after a lifetime of New England winters, she found it pleasantly warm.

"I could have Sam drive you," he told her. "He has just gotten his permit, but I assure you, he is very good with the car. I recall you saying you lived over in that warehouse, yes?"

"Yes." Kera smiled. When she'd first moved here, the Kims had been incredibly helpful in teaching her about the neighborhood.

It was sweet of him to keep looking out for her, but she didn't want him to go to any trouble. Kera demurred with a smile and several rounds of thanks, then paused awkwardly. "If there's anything I can do to help…"

Mr. Kim gave her a smile that was both kind and heartbreakingly sad. "Your parents did well when they raised you. Go, be young, and have a good day. Enjoy your breakfast party, eh?"

Kera nodded and slipped out the door, but on her walk back to her house, she couldn't stop thinking about Mr. Kim's expression. Apparently Sam wasn't in trouble of any sort, and Mr. Kim's arthritis didn't seem to be the source of his problems.

Was the shop in trouble? Kera's parents had started multiple businesses over the years, and they had taught her that all businesses had runs of bad luck. Perhaps sales hadn't been what they should be. Maybe there were repairs needed.

She told herself it wasn't her problem to solve, but the truth was that the Kims were some of the nicest people she had met in

LA. She didn't stay in contact with any of her former classmates, and—

She stopped dead.

Christian. Between the jerk shooting Zee, Mr. Kim's worry, and the tiny detail that apparently magic was real and she could do it, she had entirely forgotten about Christian.

It had been good to see him. She had seen him come in a couple of times, but he had never come over to say hi. Frankly, she had expected that. When you were dressed in a work uniform, you tended to become invisible, even to people you had known well.

But it seemed he *had* remembered her, given that he'd asked her to take a crack solving his work problem. She smiled as she started walking again, hooking her thumbs into the straps of her backpack. It had felt good to be troubleshooting code again. It was always equal parts infuriating and satisfying, but the rush you felt when you fixed something just couldn't be beaten.

When she got home, she decided to eat before doing anything else. After consideration, she decided to make her omelet with three eggs.

Then she added two more eggs.

Then another one, just to make it an even half-dozen. She fried some peppers and onions to go in it and poured in the mixture, shaking her head.

"You're not going to be able to finish this, Kera," she told herself, only to wolf it down so quickly she burned her tongue multiple times.

"Who needth fire thpellth?" she muttered to herself. "If that athhole cometh back, I'll jutht throw an omelet at him."

With her hunger temporarily assuaged, she set herself to collecting the notes she had taken on Post-its. She had given it some thought on her walk, and she batched the work into three stages: gather all the notes in one area, sort them into topics, and then take down the information.

By the time she was done, she not only had a good idea of where her limitations lay in terms of various spells, but she *also* had a large pile of notes about things she had been trying to forget.

Given that she couldn't remember an eighth-grade play costume mishap, a conversation with her mother, or what her notes called "a clusterfuck of a date with a Silicon Valley dude-bro," she could only assume she was doing fairly well with the brain bleach.

The only problem was that it seemed to "bleed" a little bit, the memory wipe spreading to other related memories or times, and the effect became more pronounced when it was cast more often. On a second read-through of her notes, she could see that this effect *had* escalated slowly.

And apparently, it had managed to erase most of her memories of the night.

Presumably, that wouldn't affect people who were only trying to forget one thing, but she had no idea how she could sell it. It wasn't like *everyone* could do magic, right? Maybe she'd wind up as one of those people who dressed in billowy dresses and wore a lot of crystals and just help very rich, eccentric celebrities.

That really didn't appeal. She'd make a boatload of money, of course, but something about deceiving them didn't sit right with her, even if most of them probably deserved it.

She had this skill, and she wanted to do something *useful* with it.

Given that the memory spell was problematic at best, she decided to return to her work on the fire spell. In her opinion, it was better to master a few techniques than to learn many that she could not use very well.

All of her practice thus far had hinged on what she could make the fire *do*, but right now, she wanted to work on the gestures that made the fire appear. Could she make the gesture from her side and not with her hand out in front of her? Could she do the magic without making a gesture?

She didn't know, but she wanted to find out.

Practicing magic, it turned out, was a lot like coding. Once you started, it was difficult to remember to come up for air. Kera practiced while the sun sank in the sky, pausing to jot down notes and occasionally look up the healing spell for fingertips that had caught a stray spark.

By the time she stopped, she had developed a fairly good idea of where her boundaries were. The important part of determining what caught fire was to focus on where the fire should be and how it should ignite the material it would be using as fuel. The *gesture* could be made anywhere, but she couldn't seem to make the spell work without one.

This is when it would be very useful to have a teacher, she thought. She couldn't shake the idea that the visualization was far more important than the gesture, but she had nothing to base that on.

When her stomach let loose with a growl, she realized she was ravenous again. Not only that, her pants genuinely seemed a little bit looser.

Just my imagination, she told herself, but she also made a mental note to buy a scale so she could keep track of her weight. Maybe using magic was even more efficient than interval training for burning calories.

Forget the brain bleach. That's where the money was.

She cooked the other six eggs with as many vegetables as she could fit in the pan and grated cheese over the top of it. She was beginning to get sick of eggs after eating so many in one day, but that didn't stop her from shoveling food into her mouth with grim efficiency.

She really wanted spinach for some reason, though she knew it wasn't nearly caloric enough.

Had she gotten anemic? She usually ate pretty well, so she would be surprised to wind up with some sort of nutritional deficiency, but anything was possible, especially when it turned out that she was some kind of witch.

Was there a message board she could go to? An FAQ for her to look through? "Commonly-noticed side effects from starting to practice magic?"

She shook her head and organized her notes on the fire spell while eating nearly an entire bag of trail mix.

When she was done, she was abruptly so tired that it was all she could do to get into bed. She fell asleep without even changing into pajamas and slept the dreamless sleep of pure exhaustion.

CHAPTER FOURTEEN

With the scrying spells enhanced, the only thing that remained was to find a way to check in on the spell from afar. That was why the next day, Mother LeBlanc found James perched on a rusty ladder, trying to install a wireless webcam with a minimum of fuss.

She did not interrupt. In fact, she was so quiet that when James finished his work and she asked what he was doing, he nearly fell off the ladder in surprise.

"I beg your pardon," she said gravely. "I thought you were aware of my presence."

James waited for the hammering in his heart to subside before he climbed down the ladder. Once on solid ground, he stretched his arms and hands.

"Oof, that one was difficult."

"I did not realize the installation of these contraptions was so difficult," LeBlanc observed.

"It's not supposed to be." James rotated his neck, which had developed a persistent crick. "The thing is, you're supposed to use adhesives or nails, and I wasn't going to do that in this house."

"Ah. Very wise." She sat gracefully. "Though I would have liked to see Mary's face if she thought you had."

James snickered. "We could tell her I did."

"Indeed, we could." She gave a conspiratorial smile. "So, what did you use to put it up, then?"

"Magic." Seeing her disapproving look, James shrugged. "I needed to make sure the connection was never going to go out, so I had to work with it anyway. This was a very small piece of power, considering."

"I know that, but we are soon going to need all of our powers," she told him. "We do not have any idea who we might meet. It is best to be prepared for anything."

"I know." James sighed. "We'll just have to pack a bunch of energy drinks and hope for the best."

"Why you people persist in choosing the least civilized ways to take in nourishment, I will never know." She slid her hand into a pocket, and when it emerged, it was holding a fresh beignet, complete with powdered sugar. She smiled beatifically. "I've missed these things," she told him before biting into it. The powdered sugar sifted down and disappeared before touching the fabric of her dress.

James stared in wonder. He considered asking her if her dress could reproduce brand-named foods like Cadbury Creme Eggs or Kentucky Fried Chicken's mythical and closely-guarded eleven herbs and spices but decided against it.

"I don't suppose you have more of those?" he asked finally.

"I do indeed." She produced a pretty china plate covered in a layer of donuts and then two cups of coffee that, if the smell was to be believed, were about as strong as jet fuel.

James took a bite and briefly believed he heard angels singing. The beignet was heavenly: perfectly cooked, just a touch too hot, and crisp without being greasy. The powdered sugar melted in his mouth and he chewed slowly, trying to savor the experience.

"That was incredible," he said when he was done.

"Thank you." She smiled. "Though mine are nowhere near as good as those at Café Du Monde. Perhaps if we stop in New Orleans, we will have time to go there."

James nodded in agreement, his mouth too full for him to speak. When he was done, he pointed out, "As you've probably noticed, we've been seeing a steady stream of flashing lights in the New Orleans area."

LeBlanc smiled back. "Of course. I would expect nothing less."

"And," James added, "one that keeps coming on and off in Arizona. Possibly a California escapee? Or it might be the sort of person who lives in Sedona. They'll believe anything."

"You're overlooking a possibility," LeBlanc reminded him. "A Navajo shaman, perhaps?"

"True, but unlikely to be related to our book, surely."

"Perhaps, but we wouldn't have known of them before, and we might do well to begin reaching out to other associations across the country."

"Mmm." James nodded quietly, thinking. His eyes were locked on the map, and eventually, he said, "You remember the *Men in Black* movie?"

"Mm, no." LeBlanc's nose wrinkled. "I'm not a fan of Will Smith."

"What?" James adjusted his glasses. He would have expected LeBlanc not to have heard of the movie but was not prepared for her to have an opinion on the star of the film. "Why don't you like him? I thought *everyone* liked him."

She lifted her shoulders elegantly. "He strikes me as arrogant. He's been in Hollywood too long, ever since that Bel-Air show, whatever it was."

"You saw that?"

"James, I *do* try to keep up with popular culture."

"News to me," James said. "Anyway, one man's arrogance is another man's swagger. Will Smith has *swagger*, dammit."

"You are entitled to your opinion," the woman observed. "But he doesn't appeal to *me*. In any event, I believe you were trying to make a point?"

"Oh. Right. Well, there's a scene in the first one where they use the *National Enquirer* as a way of staying abreast of weird events. No one takes it seriously, so it's an easy source of useful information for those in the know. I say we go online and do something similar. Find websites devoted to reporting strange or paranormal events or kooky conspiracy theories. Could be a goldmine of information while we're traveling."

After mulling it over, LeBlanc gave an appreciative nod. "That works. We know which states our candidates are located in and the general area. It would be nice if we could improve the scrying process, but it would not be a good use of our time to remain here and do so." She took a sip of her coffee and let her breath out slowly. "Yes. I do believe it is time for us to set out."

"I think it is." James looked around and felt an unexpected pang of something like nostalgia. He was still here, of course, but he rarely left anymore. This trip would take him far away from the place he called home.

Of course, when they returned, there might be someone with them who would be seeing the house with new eyes.

Would they appreciate it? Would they understand the history of the place, or would they be used to more modern ways of life?

"What happens," he asked her, "if we find someone and they are not compatible? If the world has moved on too far for us to train new recruits?"

LeBlanc smiled, a curve of her lips that transformed her. "You are very young, James."

"You don't look nearly old enough to say something like that," he pointed out.

"I know, but it is true. Ours has never been a profession with thousands of adherents, and the world has changed immeasurably many times before now. Through it all, we have persisted."

James considered her words. "And if this time, we do not?"

She pulled out her pipe, and a puff of smoke curled through the air, the smell sweet and pleasant. As with the powdered sugar from her beignets, this smoke would stain nothing.

"When I was young," LeBlanc said finally, "I believed the world needed to be remade. Then I got older, and I believed just as fervently that the generations before us had faced trials as great or greater, and their wisdom would guide society better than our desire for something new and different."

James nodded.

"Now I think perhaps that society functions as…oh, what is it called? The way things tend to equalize over time. Matter fills the empty space. A dye mixes with water. We think of ourselves as upholding a great tradition, James, but we are different from those who came before us, just as the world is different."

James waited, uncertain of where she was going with this.

"If our line dies out, perhaps it will be because we have served our purpose," LeBlanc said finally.

"No." He refused to accept that.

She smiled. "I do not think we will, but it is good to ask these questions."

"The world needs us," James said. "We have sat back for far too long, and now we see chaos spreading. The world is unstable. It needs the balance we can bring, or as you said weeks ago, we may come to a time when there is a crisis only we can solve, and *only* if we are at full power."

"I agree," she said readily. "And yet, I think there is much in the fact that you have chosen a new way to find recruits. Those we find next *will* change us, just as you and I and every member of the council has changed us."

James nodded.

"And since I see I have not set your mind at ease, if nothing else, we will erase their memories." She smiled.

Lovecraft cringed. "I always hated that spell. When I first learned the damn thing, I didn't know how to control it while experimenting on myself, and it kept re-casting itself. Ended up having to leave messages all over my damn apartment."

His companion laughed. "I think we all did. I wrote them in charcoal on the baseboards."

Refocusing on the task at hand, James grinned and turned back to his laptop. "Okay, let's start on Reddit and see what we can find for conspiracy sites."

LeBlanc eyed him. "Just when I think you have nothing left to surprise me with, you pull something out of your own little version of my skirt. However, don't you think you had best begin packing?"

"Packing." James shuddered. "I hate packing. Plus, we won't have much room in the Phantom."

"I beg your pardon?" She frowned at him.

"Oh, didn't I tell you? I thought that instead of getting rental cars, we could just take my Rolls." James had done very well for himself in his career and had been born to money. One of his most prized possessions was a Rolls Royce Phantom VI, which he had painstakingly upgraded to include climate control.

"I see," LeBlanc said. "Well, in that case, I shall pack accordingly. Come along, James. James. *James.*"

"Clicky buttons," James said, but he allowed himself to be ushered out of the room. "How should I pack for the south in winter, by the way?"

"As if you *won't* be assaulted by ice and snow at every opportunity." LeBlanc shuddered as she looked out the window. "By the way, be prepared to have a *very* good argument as to why someone from a lovely part of the country should come *here* to learn magic."

"It's pretty here," James protested.

She did not dignify that with a response.

CHAPTER FIFTEEN

Johnny and Sven sat at opposite ends of the bar. Sven's hair was distinctive on its own. Put the two of them together, and they were a noteworthy pair.

And they were only here to observe. They didn't want to be linked.

Their efforts the day before had inspired immediate results. Johnny's tap into a police scanner had caught several hysterical calls from yuppies who didn't know what to do when a mean kid took their lunch money.

The police, of course, couldn't do much. They showed up to take down details and then they left, the yuppies left, and the gang members came out of their alleys and apartments again. There was a new energy in them, a hunger for confrontation.

Johnny knew all about that. He'd been eleven when he'd first mugged someone, and he'd been on a high for days afterward. Once you realized you could just take what you wanted, the world was a different place. You learned the smell of weakness. You even learned to savor a look of hatred. After all, taking what you wanted felt good, but it felt even better when the person hated you and they still let you do it. That was a bigger win.

You'd be chasing that high for the rest of your life.

It was why Johnny still didn't trust Pauline. In his opinion, you could judge people by two things: what they wanted and what they were willing to do to get it. He couldn't get a handle on what she wanted.

A peaceful world? That was bullshit; she wanted something more. Power wasn't what people wanted, either. They wanted power so they could *do* something with it—usually, be rich.

But everything about Pauline was bland. She didn't buy diamonds or drugs. He'd never seen her enjoy a meal. She seemed to go out of her way to make herself not stand out. He was left with a boss who didn't seem to want anything in particular but would stop at nothing to make sure she got…whatever it was.

That was dangerous. She'd probably need to be taken out at some point.

Johnny's attention was drawn as two young men bumped into each other, crossing the room. Both had seen the collision coming, and neither had backed down. They stepped back to glare at one another, and Johnny's eyes flicked over to meet Sven's for a moment.

It was so, so easy to tip the balance.

Words were exchanged. Johnny couldn't hear what they were, but the specifics weren't important. The important part was that it escalated. Expressions grew colder. The two got up in each other's faces. Hands went to hidden weapons.

It only took one friend standing up for the battle lines to be drawn.

Johnny stayed where he was. They wouldn't take notice of him unless he got in the way, and he didn't intend to. He wanted to see who tried to de-escalate things.

Those were the voices that needed to be silenced.

Sure enough, they came out of the woodwork, two or three guys on each side who tried to hold people back. They spoke to their friends quietly and urgently.

They weren't successful. The first shove came, then the next. The friends trying to de-escalate were looking even more worried now. One of the braver ones put himself in the middle to try to calm both sides down, only for someone on the other side to take him down with a punch.

After that, it was chaos. Johnny sat back and sipped at his drink, not bothering to hide his smile. The bartender was yelling, the gang members were yelling, and people had gone running for backup, but all of that was too little, too late.

The battle lines had been drawn. The gang members had gotten their first taste of inspiring fear and compliance, and they weren't going to stand for anyone denying them. Before too long, this district was going to be in total chaos.

A brawl was one thing, but flying bullets didn't care what colors you were wearing, so when the weapons came out, Johnny put down his drink and a few bills and slipped out with Sven. The two of them stood on the sidewalk.

"Going well," Johnny said.

Sven nodded.

"I have to say, I've been on their side of it a few times." Johnny jerked his head toward the distant shouts and crashes. "Never started one from the outside. More fun than I expected."

"I told you you'd like this job," Sven pointed out.

"I'm beginning to think you knew what you were talking about after all."

"Yeah, and speaking of that, there's a meeting tonight after the party. Don't skip it, don't be late, and *don't* show up drunk."

Johnny gave an ironic salute and headed to his car.

It was time to see how Chinatown was doing. He wanted to go back to the Mermaid, but he knew that the longer he waited, the more satisfying it would be.

Best learn some manners while I wait, blondie.

If he weren't a thaumaturge, James would not drive vintage cars. There was a stately elegance to them that could not be matched, but they were finicky and prone to breaking down.

Since he *was* a thaumaturge, however, he had all of the skills necessary to keep rust from accumulating and parts from breaking. As with most thaumaturgical skills, it took less magic the more you knew about the subject. A luck spell on an entire engine would quickly drain power; very targeted spells regarding certain chemical reactions and heat distribution points achieved a smoother result with less of a draw.

All of which meant James could take a road trip of any length in his Phantom in unsurpassed comfort without worry that any pieces of the car would break.

He was going to squeeze as much enjoyment out of this trip as possible.

Mother LeBlanc had her own worries. "Don't you think it will attract a great deal of attention to travel in such a luxurious vehicle?" she inquired when she first saw it.

"Probably," James said cheerfully.

"All of a sudden, reports of strange occurrences begin," she said. "Then a vintage car with northern plates appears, and someone from the town disappears."

"You make us sound like serial killers."

"More importantly, like people who end up on the radar of intelligence agencies," she said severely as he loaded their suitcases into the trunk.

"You're no fun, you know." James went to hold her door open.

She did not immediately move to get into the car. "James, surely I do not need to explain my reasoning?"

"Of course not." James nodded. "At the first sign of undue interest, we will find a place to store the car and continue on in something unremarkable. A station wagon, perhaps." He shuddered.

She smiled as she got into the Rolls. "I don't think we need to go quite *that* far."

They set out as the sun was near its peak, and James took a few moments to study the house in the rearview mirror as it curved out of sight amongst the hills and trees. Like many old houses, it lay at the end of a long driveway, far from the road... and difficult to navigate in the snow or rain.

When it came to avoiding attention, every little bit helped.

Their first stop would be Charleston. While James was surprised not to see any lights in New York City—the sheer number of people suggested that *someone* qualified would be there—he was looking forward to a leisurely drive down the coast. He intended to cut over south of Philadelphia and go through Delaware, rather than taking the more utilitarian drive down Route 95.

"I don't suppose you'd like to do a proper stop in New Orleans?" he asked Mother LeBlanc.

"If the candidates remain, we certainly should." She nodded at him.

"No, I mean a *proper* stop. Not business." He gave her a smile. "I've never been."

"And?"

He looked at her. "And what?"

"There's something more behind your question." She was smiling at him.

"And I'd like to know more about you," he told her honestly.

"I do not think you will learn as much as you hope," she told him with a smile. "The city hides many more secrets than even I know. That is one of its charms."

He accelerated onto the highway and gave a contented smile. This car drove like a dream.

He spent a moment enjoying it before returning to the subject at hand. "Why *did* you come north?"

She did not respond at once. Then she asked, "Why did you leave the city?"

"To be honest, I appreciated the solitude." He occasionally missed things about New York City, but its frenetic pace exhausted him. "I'm much more suited to being a hermit than a businessman, and I appreciated the slower scale of the workings we do."

She absorbed that with interest. "Interesting. I wouldn't have guessed that."

"Strange, how many years you can live in close proximity to someone and not learn the details of their life."

"Strange, indeed. And to answer your question, I left because magic in the bayou is a solitary thing. One is not shown the way or even the path. I came to magic on my own, making sense of a question in my soul, but I was not content to practice it alone."

James, who had always thought of her as very solitary, began to wonder if he had misunderstood her all these years.

"In a sense, I suppose I always expected to leave," she said after a moment. "Just not to go *quite* so far."

"And now you want to help others find their way instead of making them go it alone," James said quietly.

"Yes." The word was simple.

"And if the ones we find aren't good candidates?" James had been turning the possibility over in his head.

"Then nothing is lost, and the world is a bit safer."

Magical explosions were rare and often explained away by earthquakes or gas leaks or strange malfunctions in equipment, a symptom of aether destabilizing around an individual. It was not uncommon that stronger thaumaturges would begin to destabilize as they delved too far into their power, necessitating a memory wipe and a power block.

Such measures were both essential and painful for those who carried them out.

"Do not borrow trouble, James," he murmured to himself.

"Hmm?" LeBlanc glanced at him.

"Something my grandmother used to say: don't borrow trouble."

"A wise woman." She settled back in her seat. "Let us enjoy the drive."

While Sven and Johnny worked the streets and bars, Pauline was working the networks that held the up-and-comers, the most successful in the city. She smiled, laughed, shook hands, hugged people, and kissed them on the cheek as needed. In all things, she was pleasant and unremarkable. Everyone might know her face, but it was her goal that once this city was hers, people would not know she ran it. She would still be one of them, mingling and hearing their opinions.

They would know she supplied them with the things they wanted, but they would never realize that she used that to guide them.

The party—or networking event, as the hosts preferred to call it—was mostly confined to the first floor of the house. A few people had drifted out into the gardens, though the night was chilly enough that they came back in before long. The upper floors were off-limits aside from a carefully marked stairway path leading to a spare bathroom.

Pauline had noted this with approval when she'd first arrived; keeping everyone together would make it easier to work the crowd. The hosts knew she was involved in something less than legal, and her invitation meant she had their approval to cultivate relationships with those here.

And she did, shaking hands and introducing herself as well as letting others introduce her to their friends, or letting those friends find her on their own. Many were reckless, but some were nervous, afraid of their own curiosity.

Pauline had streamlined her process. They had already made their decision before they came to her, and all that remained was to remove the obstacles in their way. She listened to them, and she steadied them when they were nervous. In some cases, she slipped small packets into their grip while shaking their hands, and in other cases, she dropped merchandise into their pockets during hugs. She savored their grateful glances. They wanted her. They needed what she could do for them.

Once she'd made the rounds and relieved herself of the supply she'd brought, Pauline slipped away from the main crowd into a pleasantly cozy little alcove where a couple of faux-Greek busts looked down from a banister draped with ivy. She pulled out her phone.

The banking app she used was exceedingly good at updating its information within a single minute of any changes to her account. Reviewing the details of her balance, she nodded with approval. Everyone had paid her.

Save one.

She was patient. She took the moment to clear her mind and relax while she counted to sixty in her head and refreshed the app.

Nothing.

The delinquent individual's name was Darius Landham, and Pauline found him after a short scan of the main crowd. He was loitering in one of the corners, chatting up a curvy, naïve-looking girl.

Likely, he was distracted instead of intending to default, so there was no need for unpleasantness, just a reminder. Pauline carried that certainty with her as she moved toward him. She walked with a steady, deliberate stride, different from her movements during other parts of this party.

She knew the angle of approach that tended to catch someone's eye, and it wasn't long before his gaze flicked up to assess what he was seeing.

The look on his face said it all. From the sudden wary shift in the eyes to the way his breathing paused, it was clear that he realized the mistake he had made.

He coughed, cleared his throat, and nodded to the girl. "Excuse me a sec." Then he turned away from her and pulled out his phone, busily tapping the keys. When he pivoted back around, it was to give an almost imperceptible nod in Pauline's direction. He resumed his potential conquest, but the tension remained in his shoulders.

Pauline slid into the shadows and checked her phone again. The final payment had come in, and her balance was what it should be. She smiled.

Her business concluded, she excused herself from the rest of the party. She had business at the office, after all. She would let the rest of the ones here enjoy their night, well-supplied with her goods.

They would be back for more.

CHAPTER SIXTEEN

Kera lay face-down in her bed. She was not asleep, but it would be ridiculous to say that she was fully conscious or functional.

"Oh, man," she moaned, rubbing the side of her face and the back of her neck. "I should have taken up running marathons. I swear, that would be a less-painful day-after than this is." She sat up and rubbed her forehead, where she could feel either the beginning or the end of a massive headache.

She could only hope it was the end.

She stumbled to the coffee maker and prepared a pot of extremely strong coffee, and returned to bed as it brewed.

The floor beside the bed was strewn with notebooks. She had ordered a batch of them rush-shipped, and it looked as if she had filled over half of them already. She flipped through the pages, some spotted with water or vaguely singed, her writing growing neater or more of a scrawl by turns. Some of the notes were to remind her of things that had happened recently or could not be ignored, mundane things.

Others had to do with the plethora of spells she'd tried out—specifically, which effects she needed to be most aware of. It was good information, just impossible to search through quickly.

Even now that she was clear of the worst effects of the brain bleach spell, her practice was simply generating too much data for her to hold in her head at once.

She had thought this would be better than the sticky notes, but she was going to need *another* filing method. Something on her phone, perhaps, that she could search by keyword.

She definitely didn't have the energy for that right now. At the moment, she had what felt like a bad sunburn on her shoulders and lower back. She had cast the strongest healing spell she could manage on herself before she fell asleep last night, but it hadn't been enough. She'd just been so exhausted that she fell asleep anyway.

She sighed as she came to the relevant note, the final one from last night.

Do not perform the Firefly spell. It sets your ass on fire. Not fun.

The other fire spells had been relatively straightforward, more a matter of changing the type and intensity of fire than anything else.

Firefly was different.

"God, seriously?" she muttered. "What kind of sadistic prick puts spells in a book that noobs can use to make themselves burst into flames?"

Having achieved precisely that last night, she'd fallen to the floor and rolled around until the flames were extinguished.

After that, she'd been done for the night.

She went to get a cup of coffee and returned to bed to read more carefully through the night's notes.

Once she'd achieved basic competence, she'd branched out into new types of spells. The one that created a dazzling cascade of colored lights was interesting, though probably not useful as anything except a parlor trick. Maybe a diversion if she ever needed to sneak around. Still, on the plus side, it had been one of the few spells that hadn't come with any adverse side effects or potential hazards.

Another spell created a miniature cacophony of animal sounds that always seemed to be just around the corner, stomping and scratching and snorting as anyone nearby struggled to figure out where they were but never found them. When Kera had tried it, it had lasted for about five minutes and spooked the hell out of her, despite the fact that she knew it was fake. She could only imagine the effect it would have on someone who was unprepared.

Perhaps the most useful one, though, was a minor enchantment whose effects could be best described as bolstering one's luck.

After reciting the incantation and performing the necessary hand gestures and so forth, Kera had found herself swelling with manic confidence, under which lay a sense that things would work well. To test it, she'd flipped a coin, picking heads each time.

She'd ended up getting heads on seventeen out of twenty tosses. Technically, that was possible according to normal odds, but it was not very likely.

She'd then conducted a further test by throwing a glass filled with water into the air and trying to catch it at an awkward angle. Somehow, her hand had grasped it perfectly before it could slip away and strike the floor, though part of the water had sloshed out.

She wondered, though, if the spell might have nasty side effects like most of the others. Perhaps it would make her overconfident in situations where the odds were already so terrible that the spell only boosted her up to having a one in five chance or something like that.

Approximately a third of them didn't produce any effects, something she suspected was a personal failure. She seemed to have a knack for magic, or *thaumaturgy*, as the book sometimes referred to it, but she was still a novice. They might be worth a try again later.

Of course, given that she kept expecting to wake up from this dream in which magic was real, maybe she wouldn't get the chance. Her eyes strayed to the phone on her bedside table. She hadn't told anyone what was going on, though it was a constant struggle not to call someone—anyone—and spill the whole story.

If a bartender does magic alone in her apartment and no one sees it…

By this point, it was very clear that this was real and not a delusion, but she didn't know how to process that. How could it be that magic existed and no one knew about it? How had she stumbled across the book on Amazon?

Could anyone else see it?

Or was that the "special genetics" her mother had always talked about? Kera laughed and shook her head. There was no way in hell her mother, she of the white-collar job recommendations, would ever believe magic was real.

The pain in her shoulders brought her back to the present. A deep breath escaped her lungs, and she willed away the burning sting. It wasn't as bad as it had been earlier.

Once her brain had caught up to where she was now and she'd admitted that she was feeling marginally better, she concluded that the apartment needed to be cleaned the hell up and that she needed some food.

Apparently, magic did not help with chores.

Grumbling to no one in particular that it was probably better than getting hit on at work, Kera plunged straight into the tedium of picking up the piles of clothes and minor trash lying around, cleaning up the burnt detritus and smashed object shards left over from her magical experiments, wiping down the major surfaces, and sweeping the floor.

It only took about forty minutes to get things back to an acceptable level of order and decency, by which time the skin on her back was noticeably better. "There," she muttered, wiping her hands against one another.

She looked for her tablet, which she'd tossed on her bed. Annoyingly, a red light indicated that it was almost out of juice.

Sighing, she plugged it into the wall outlet and sat within charging-cable range while pulling up the web page for *How to Be a Badass Witch*. A couple of quick taps and swipes, and the paperback copy was on its way to her doorstep.

"Eat that, you POS," she told the tablet. "As of tomorrow, I won't have to deal with your high-maintenance crap anymore."

It would probably be easier to annotate, too. As Kera stretched, a vague rumble in her stomach reminded her that she planned to eat now that she was done cleaning. There was a good Chinese place only about ten minutes away on foot, and she could use the exercise and fresh air.

To the extent that LA's air could be considered fresh, of course.

Her stomach wanted her to go immediately, but a quick look in the mirror told her that wasn't a wise idea. She hopped in the shower, not bothering to wash her hair or do anything else that might take too much time, then put on fresh clothes and fished out her phone. One brief call later, the restaurant's proprietors were preparing her Mongolian beef and vegetables, as well as two egg rolls and an order of crab rangoon. She glanced out the window to check the weather. Slightly gray out, but no sign of rain.

"Good."

The girl tucked her hair into a black baseball cap. It would provide her with some protection if it did start to rain, and, of course, blondes were very much a minority in the City of Angels these days, so she preferred not to draw undue attention while she was on run-of-the-mill errands. The fact that the Firefly spell had burnt the ends into an irregular mess didn't help, either.

She also made sure to wear a shirt with full shoulders that would cover the lingering burns from her little foray into incendiary magic.

Outside, the air was pleasantly mild. Winters in Southern California did not always have the sunlight that people associated with the region, but the middling temperatures were, in Kera's opinion, pretty nice—a welcome contrast to the hundred-degree heat waves in the summer.

She strode down sidewalks and across streets at a brisk, modulated pace. There was no need to hurry, but she wanted to get proper exercise out of it. Besides, the slower she walked, the easier it was for random dudes to try to strike up a conversation because they wanted to "just talk."

Strange, how often "just talking" turned to the subject of phone numbers.

Nine minutes of trotting past mural-adorned buildings and through busy intersections later, Kera arrived at J's Peking Kitchen. The place was popular enough to do a steady business, but fortunately, the trend-chasing hipster types hadn't latched onto it.

Yet.

Within, she stood in line behind two couples before reaching the counter and giving her information to the young woman, who promptly fetched her order. Kera admired the understated traditional Chinese decor while she fished in her pockets for her card. The aesthetics of the place matched its food: not gimmicky, but pretty damned good regardless.

Smelling it once she'd paid and received her bag, her stomach positively thundered with need, and she resolved to walk faster on the return trip than she had on the way there.

It *almost* worked.

Halfway home, she had to stop at a crosswalk to wait for the electronic signal to hold up traffic on her behalf, and a small cluster of people formed around her.

Including two young men, whose eyes locked onto her immediately and stayed there.

Well, shit, she thought.

One of the guys, the shorter and thinner of the two, led the way, with his friend following. He stopped right at the edge of her personal bubble and put himself in front of her face.

"Hey, girl," he opened. "What you doing carrying all that heavy-ass food by yourself? You want someone to walk you home? Or maybe you need a drink..."

Kera turned to stone. "No, thank you," she stated. "I'm busy and *really* not in the mood."

Her shoulders and back were starting to sting again.

"Oh!" The lead guy grinned, not fazed or deterred by her standoffishness. "So, you sayin' you free *tomorrow* night? 'Cuz I got some time off myself, and I know this new place out on Alvarado Street that you'd love. Have a *real* good time, meet some of my friends."

Kera sighed. "No, that *isn't* what I'm saying. I'm not interested at all. Leave me alone and find someone else, please and thanks."

The larger dude frowned, but in a way that suggested he got the point. He put a hand on his friend's shoulder and tried to turn him away. "She ain't going out with you, man. Come on."

The lead guy shrugged his buddy's hand off with a sharp motion and glared at Kera.

"See," he began, "now you pissing me off, 'cuz you *assuming* things I ain't never said. All I wanted to do was talk to you, see, and maybe get a drink. You jumping to all kinds of conclusions..."

The signal changed, and Kera was the first person in the group to begin moving over the crosswalk to the other side of the street. Much to her chagrin, the stubborn young man followed close behind her, rambling a stream of aggravated nonsense while his friend occasionally tried to dissuade him.

They tailed her for almost a full block before she finally spun around and confronted him.

"Leave me alone *now*. I won't ask you again." Though her stomach had tightened and her skin prickled with tension, she wasn't afraid of the guy, and her lack of fear gave him pause.

He stopped in his tracks, recognizing that the situation had escalated but refusing to back down. Instead, he took a step forward and stuck his face in hers.

"Bullshit." He scoffed. "You ain't got *no* reason to give me that kind of attitude. I think you owe me and my friend here an apology. We ain't leaving until you say you're sorry for wasting our time. And when you said 'leave me alone,' you forgot something. You didn't answer what I'm about to ask, which is, 'Or else what?'"

Kera stood her ground and stared back at him. She'd been carrying her brown paper bag of food with both hands, but for the moment, she supported it with one, leaving the other free to act but hidden from the guy's sight.

"You don't want to mess with a witch," she told him. It might have sounded ridiculous under other circumstances, she realized, but she said it with full conviction.

So much for not telling anyone else that magic was real, and this guy wouldn't have been her first choice if she'd been thinking about it.

The young man burst out laughing, but she thought she could detect an undercurrent of anxiety in him. Possibly he thought she was crazy.

It didn't matter what he thought, though.

"Oh," he jeered, "so you one of those little Wiccan bitches with the purple stars on their profiles and shit, and you gonna use that to try and get out of apologizing. Well, you *ain't* scaring me and my boy here. We staying until you—"

While he blathered, eyes focused on her face, Kera's free hand performed a rapid sequence of gestures. A second later, a tiny, barely perceptible flash of light appeared at waist level, then a curl of smoke rose from the crotch of the young man's pants.

His eyes shot downwards abruptly, and as his bigger friend moved around from the back to see what had happened, the guy screamed. Flames were starting to curl from the juncture of his legs.

Kera nodded. "I suggest you slap that out right away. It doesn't go out easily. Trust me, I know."

Both the lead guy's hands and those of his big friend were furiously smacking and swatting at his groin, but the flames refused to die. Kera turned away as the dude fell to the ground in a panic, then pulled his pants off and kicked them away while a crowd formed around the pair to watch. Many pulled out their cell phones to record the incident.

Kera crossed the next street, hoping the delay wouldn't mean her food was cold by the time she got home. She found herself smirking as she walked, and the ache in her shoulders didn't bother her as much as it had a few minutes ago.

"I warned him," she murmured.

CHAPTER SEVENTEEN

Kera jerked awake to the sound of her phone going off. A bleary look at the clock showed that it was 11:02AM, early enough that it probably wasn't Cevin. He knew she was a night owl; her job required it, after all.

She picked up the phone and sighed when she saw who it was. She had no desire for another motherly lecture at this hour, *especially* when she was bone-tired from doing magic.

Which, of course, she couldn't explain to her parent.

"What did I ever do to deserve this?" she asked no one in particular. Then she swiped a finger to answer the call. "Hello, Mom."

"Hello, Kera, dear."

Kera flopped back on the bed and closed her eyes. "Uh-huh."

"I just wanted to say hello and check how you were doing," her mother continued. "Since we live so far away, we can't see you every week."

Yeah, that's terrible. "Uh-huh. Um, I was asleep, so…give me a moment to get my bearings here, okay?"

Her mother sighed loudly. "It's after eleven in California. Is it really necessary for you to sleep in so late? Kera, if you're hoping to get a job in an office, how are you going to answer calls about interviews? How are you going to present a professional image?"

Kera stared blankly at the ceiling. "I...don't..." *I want to go back to sleep.*

"For example, have you made *any* progress toward what we talked about last week?" her mother asked.

Kera wracked her brain, trying not to succumb to her rising confused low-level panic.

The magical forces of thaumaturgic memory bleach seemed to have struck again. She had no recollection of having spoken to her mom on the phone last week. She could not say with any certainty what they'd discussed.

"Dear?"

The answer came with a shaft of sunlight and a choir of angels. Her mom was more or less a broken record, which meant...

A boyfriend—a boring boyfriend—or job things.

"I'm making progress, Mom. I'm just doing it at my own pace. There's plenty of time."

"Kera, you don't understand how quickly time can go by." Her mother sighed. "At this rate, you'll still be working at the bar when you're thirty and the tips won't have gotten any better, and all of the people from your class will have gone far beyond you. It doesn't need to be that way. Someone of your intelligence and potential can go on to much bigger things."

"Yes, I know." Kera stifled a groan.

"I was heartened when you said you were trying to develop a product," her mother told her.

What product? Crap. "Uh..."

"I can't imagine how you'd make 'mind bleach' work, but I'd certainly like to try it if you invent it."

Her mother was clearly joking, but Kera started to smile.

"Actually, I've made some good progress on that."

"Oh." Her mother didn't seem to know what to say. "Well, why didn't you say so, dear?"

"I just woke up and was getting my bearings," Kera reminded her.

"I see." Her mother didn't sound convinced. "Now, what about a boyfriend, hmm?"

The woman was relentless. "If you *must* know," Kera said, "I spoke to a guy who was in one of my college study groups, and we might see each other again, so who knows. It's something, right?"

As soon as the words left her mouth, she knew she'd made a terrible mistake.

"Kera! How wonderful. Tell me all about him." Her mother's voice was climbing steadily in both volume and tone.

Kera held the phone away from her ear with a grimace. "Um…"

It was useless. There was no going back now. She sent a mental apology to the universe at large for whatever she had done to deserve this and described Christian to her mother. Between her description and her mother's questions, the whole thing took close to ten minutes. Kera had never been asked to describe so many things about a person before.

"Okay," she said finally, "it's been nice talking to you, but I need to run some errands."

Her mom let out another sigh. "I understand, dear, but take everything I said seriously. I know I sound like a nag, but remember, it's *your* life and happiness on the line, and that's all I care about. Goodbye."

"Bye, Mom." Kera hung up and stared at the phone, annoyed. "How does she *always* get the last word in?"

She downed the glass of water on her nightstand and wandered into the bathroom. She was up now, so she might as well shower and get on with her day. The only problem was…

"Son of a *bitch!*" She stared into the mirror, jaw hanging open.

Her hair now resembled a mostly-mature wheat field on the fifth of July after a crew of dumbasses had launched a battery of illegal commercial-grade fireworks.

Kera strode to the table and began flipping through notebooks and looking at post-its. It took her time to piece together what had happened, but it looked as if she had started the night with a memory spell to check how bad the "bleed" effect would be over time.

The answer appeared to have gone past "bad enough not to do it again" and fully into the realm of "really fucking bad."

"Goddammit." Not only could she not remember which it was, but she also couldn't remember which fire spell had made her hair look like this.

She sighed and opened the table of contents on her phone, scrolling through spells for one that might repair the damage. Unfortunately, nothing stood out. There were a lot of spells one could use to keep things from breaking, but none that she could see for fixing them after they had broken. The only thing she could see that might work was a healing spell, but given that hair was not live tissue, she wasn't sure it would work.

Five minutes later, she could say two things with certainty: first, that the healing spell did *not* work on hair, and second, that she was ravenously hungry.

She downed a handful of trail mix before getting dressed and stuffing her ruined hair under a baseball cap. She didn't consider herself overly vain, but she couldn't quite bring herself to go out with that train wreck showing.

She wished she could pay someone to fix this mess for her, but she didn't have the spare money right now for something so expensive. She knew she was lucky that Cevin had the decency to give her paid time off, but her hourly rate was a pittance compared to the tips she would have made.

Of course, if she were working, she also wouldn't have done this to her hair. She shook her head and slipped out the door, heading for a salon nearby that also sold do-it-yourself products.

When she got home, she unloaded the contents onto the table and opened the instructions, which turned out to be an insanely thick packet of information with more steps than she would have imagined. Grousing, she turned on the TV for some background noise and began working her way through the mixing and prepping necessary to put the mix on her head.

Kera's eyes wandered to the screen as the talking heads got past the opening pleasantries and began to focus on the main story of the day.

Namely, that the world was fucked.

"Throughout Los Angeles and its suburbs and satellite cities in Southern California," the anchor on the left opened, "tensions have been on the rise due to a perceived increase in violent crime, particularly muggings and armed robbery. According to the LAPD, the uptick in robberies represents only a marginal increase compared to last year's statistics. Nonetheless, Chief Alvarez has outlined a plan, working in tandem with community organizations and other city agencies, to put a stop to the worst of the crime wave and bring the numbers back down."

Kera nodded, frowned, and looked back at her instructions sheet. She tried to clamp her mind down to keep from thinking of the incident in the Mermaid's parking lot, but it was impossible. The prick's voice and the cracking report of his gunshots rose again in her brain, momentarily blocking out the anchors' spiel and the obligatory random commentary from eyewitnesses on the street.

She allowed herself to fantasize about what would have happened if the prick who'd shot up her bike had dropped his gun that fateful night and she'd had the opportunity to kick the living shit out of him. A girl could dream, couldn't she?

Virtutis gloria merces, she thought and gave a chuckle. It was the MacDonagh family motto and meant, *"Glory is the reward of valor.*" She had seen it nearly every day of her life since it was printed on the banner at the top of the MacDonagh crest, and her parents kept a copy of that hanging in the living room.

Kera had always thought the idea of a family motto was insanely pretentious. This was America in the twenty-first-century; having aristocratic roots in Ireland or any other "old country" was of little relevance. In truth, nobody talked or cared about such things.

But right now, it made her wonder if she should have done something bolder in the parking lot. She knew the general self-defense advice was not to escalate situations, but that meant people like the man who'd shot Zee got away with things a lot of the time.

Him and all of the other people who were apparently part of this new crime wave.

The news had moved on from the story about the crime wave, but their other stories weren't any happier. An insurance firm had been overcharging their customers, corrupt local officials were implicated in the unfolding scandal, and another drought was expected come summer. Unexplained phenomena had erupted here and there throughout the United States, with conspiracy theories rapidly popping up on the Internet to try to explain them. There was also the usual political claptrap in reference to the upcoming midterm elections.

Kera sighed. "Only news is bad news, it seems. Then again, I can't be bothered to stick around for the heartwarming human-interest piece at the end. I've got bigger fish to fry."

She looked down at the bottle in her hand and at the weirdly purplish goop within it, hoping she'd made the right choice and that her new hair wouldn't look too fake, or that she wouldn't accidentally stain her ears black or anything similarly stupid.

A few days ago, she wouldn't have worried about that, but a few days ago, she hadn't lit various parts of her body on fire and then wiped her memories of how she'd done it.

"Here goes," she remarked, stepping into the bathroom and pulling on the plastic gloves.

An hour later, she was pleased to say that her hair had turned out well, or as well as it could. To her surprise, the shade of black she had picked—with brown undertones instead of blue, per the receptionist's advice—didn't seem jarring to her, nor did it make her look overly pale.

That was the good news. The bad news was that she was almost out of groceries. She downed the last of the trail mix and considered what to do. She couldn't keep ordering food in, not without a proper paycheck.

She wouldn't mind seeing Mr. Kim again, especially to check if he was all right.

She changed out of her stained work shirt, now with hair dye stains to match the grease stains, and pulled on an unassuming shirt, slacks, and jacket and admired her new hair in the mirror. Dyeing it really had been a pain in the ass, but she'd pulled it off. No obvious blonde patches remained, and the roots weren't noticeably lighter than the ends. There was some slight staining on the back of her neck, but it wasn't really noticeable.

She savored the fresh air on the walk to the store—for one thing, the hair dye had stunk up her apartment—and was pleased to see the proprietor behind the counter. "Hello, Mr. Kim," she called.

He gave her a smile, less distracted than he had been the day before. "Hi, Kera, how are you? Did you change your hair?"

"Yeah." She shot him a smile. "I figured I could stand to look better."

He chuckled as she gathered supplies: more eggs, a couple of salads, and cans of tea from the fridge, a package of toaster pastries, and more trail mix. She also threw in a couple of bars of dark chocolate. Normally, she didn't have much of a sweet tooth, but she was so hungry and tired that junk food of all sorts was appealing right now.

She finished selecting her stuff and laid her groceries on the counter, spreading them out slightly so that Kim could get a clear look at each as he rang them up. He nodded and peered at the items with a rapid scan, then raised a hand to punch them into the register.

His face contorted momentarily in pain as he flexed his fingers. "Arthritis again," the old man grumbled. "For the last two days, I thought it was flaring *down* again—like you said, eh? Usually it leaves me alone for a week between times when it gets bad, but this time, not so lucky. Makes me worry that it's getting worse. I suppose I should expect that. I'm not getting any younger."

Kera frowned in concern as Mr. Kim punched keys and rang up her total. He didn't seem as strained today, but he *was* suffering.

She paid and pulled the food items back together to start bagging them so as to spare Mr. Kim the pain of having to grasp them. He reached out with his right hand while waving cantankerously with his left, indicating that he didn't feel it was necessary for her to do that. As his hand brushed hers, she thought of something.

"Hey," she said lightly. "Could I, uh, try something?" She pointed at his hand.

He turned his hand over as if looking for dirt, then chuckled wryly. "If you are thinking of cutting off my hand, I have already considered it."

She smiled at him. "No, not that. Uh, *reiki*." Yeah, that was a good cover. "You've heard of that, right? I've been learning it in my spare time. It might help your arthritis."

"Reiki? I work in Little Tokyo." He gave her a wry smile. "Many people have been trying to sell me their services. I think it is mostly up here." He tapped at the side of his head. "But if you think it will help, I will let you try."

"I do," Kera said. "The worst thing that can happen is nothing, right? No charge, by the way."

"Hah!" Kim laughed. "If it does work, I might have to start giving you a discount."

She inhaled, cleared her mind, and mumbled the incantation for the healing spell under her breath, cupping her right hand over Mr. Kim's knuckles while holding his palm gently with her left. As she'd done with herself over the last couple of days, she channeled the beneficent forces at work in the universe—what the book called "miraculous forces"— into a person afflicted with pain, seeking to counteract it.

As she had before, she perceived a faint, warm light. Not anywhere she could really *see* it, but somewhere nearby, hiding and yet all around them.

This time the rest of the effects were different. She didn't feel the pleasant, comforting tingle because she was not the recipient. Instead, she felt as though someone had tapped a vein in her arm and was draining something out of her.

Her vision clouded and her head swam. Kera released Mr. Kim's hand and stumbled against the counter, grasping fiercely at the surface to keep from falling to the floor. Dazed weakness nearly overwhelmed her.

"Kera! What's the matter?" Kim leaned across the counter urgently to grasp her hand.

"Urgh." She pushed herself upright, blinking and shaking her head. "I-I'm not sure...what happened." The dizziness was starting to clear, but she still felt badly enervated. Her hands and feet trembled.

Mr. Kim continued to watch her closely as she gathered up the two plastic bags' worth of supplies, and the bell rang as a young couple came in.

Kera waved a hand, trying to come up with a fib on the spot. "I guess I should have eaten lunch. I think I'm okay now, though."

Mr. Kim sat back, looking at her worriedly, and with a great deal more assessment than she wanted to see.

"I'm all right," she told him. "Sorry to worry you. I hope you feel better." She left the counter, working hard not to let herself tremble. Her hands felt weak, making it difficult to carry the bags.

As she pushed out through the doors, though, in the reflection of the glass, she saw him look at his hands, flexing them and staring in wonder.

Outside, she allowed herself to process what had happened. Healing others was clearly more difficult than healing oneself, something she would have to keep in mind. Further, she guessed that Mr. Kim's arthritis had been very bad; much worse than she'd thought and worse than the relatively minor burns she'd dealt with previously.

Healing him had required her to donate a large amount of her vital essence and channel more power than she'd realized. She hadn't thought to place a limit on how much the spell could take from her and give to him, so it had simply taken as much as the job required.

Could she limit the amount of power a spell took? She'd have to find out.

Let this be a lesson, Kera, she told herself and winced since she imagined the admonition in her mother's voice. *Read all the fine print of a spell before you use it, especially on someone else.*

Walking home was a struggle. The two grocery bags felt like they weighed forty pounds each, and the half-mile or so that separated her home from Kim's store might as well have been a marathon.

Still, if she weren't so tired, Kera would have laughed out loud, and if she weren't carrying grocery bags and completely exhausted, she would have punched the sky in victory. Some good had come of what she'd done. She had used her power not just to set things on fire or wipe her memory but to *help* someone.

On the other hand, she was shaking so hard that it took her three tries to get her key into the lock. When she blundered through the door, she dropped one of the bags and had to pick up some of the food. Now that her body and mind knew she was safe, she was edging toward collapse.

Kera set the bags on the floor beside her refrigerator and hastily stuffed the cold or spoilable items in. She barely got the milk into its usual place on the fridge's door shelf before she half-collapsed to her knees.

"Screw this," she muttered. The dry stuff could wait until tomorrow.

She pulled herself back to her feet and stepped toward her bed, intending to undress normally, but once she reached the edge, she collapsed onto the mattress and passed out in her clothes, no longer caring.

CHAPTER EIGHTEEN

Kera was almost positive she'd been having a dream that her phone was ringing. It might have been that once her *actual* phone went off, the dream added it in as an extra touch.

Whatever the case, she woke up to beeping.

"Shit!" she blurted, and she jerked herself awake, feeling groggy, confused, and incredibly hungry. She snapped her head toward her bed table. The phone's screen was lit and the ringtone seemed to echo in her brain, suggesting she'd barely missed being able to answer it. She rubbed the sleep crusts from her eyes, pushed her hair back from her face, and waited to see if the caller would leave a message.

A minute or two later, the phone beeped again. An icon appeared over her voicemail, and she recognized the number—Cevin's.

"Well," Kera murmured, "this is either the good news I was hoping for or *really* bad news. Eh, Zee?" She glanced at Zee's empty spot and winced. She couldn't get used to not having Zee around, and given that this call might be to tell her that Zee was beyond repair, the reminder of his absence was particularly unwelcome.

She contemplated having some breakfast and a shower before listening to the message but decided she wouldn't be able to enjoy either with the possibility of bad news hanging over her. She tapped the screen and chewed her lip as the message queued up.

Cevin's tone was surprisingly chipper. "Hey, Kera. Cevin here. I've got good news."

"Oh, thank God," Kera muttered.

"You can come on in whenever you're ready to get your bike picked up. Everything is fixed, and as I mentioned, the cost was covered. You won't have to pay a dime. The one catch is that I can't pick you up anytime today. I need to be at the Mermaid, so you'll have to catch a bus or something. Or wait till tomorrow. Let me know when you make up your mind. Or just show up, in which case I guess I'll see you when I see you."

The phone beeped and returned to the automated voice that informed Kera she had zero unread messages remaining.

She leaned back, closed her eyes, and smiled. "*Finally.*" She sighed. The haze of sleep was clearing from her head, and aside from the gnawing hunger, she was surprised by how good she felt. Sixteen or so hours of sleep could do that to a person.

The girl rolled off the bed and onto her feet, resolving to get active as quickly as possible. The gnawing hunger seemed to be a constant now, but she didn't want to take the time for a big meal. The sooner she had Zee back, the better, and she could always grab something to eat once she had transportation again.

She got dressed quickly, ducked into the bathroom to comb her hair, and then on a whim, added some dark eyeshadow. Something about the way her new hair framed her face suggested that it would look good.

When she was done, she blinked at herself in the mirror. It *did* look good. Really good, in fact.

Not to mention, the look was appropriate for a witch.

There was a bus stop a block away, and from what she

recalled of the schedules, one of the shuttles ought to come by within the next fifteen or twenty minutes. She grabbed her backpack, put her motorcycle helmet in it, and headed out.

The day was sunny again and warmer. As usual, she turned heads, but nobody accosted her. There was only one other person —an elderly Latino gentleman, not likely to try his hand at flirting—at the bus stop. Kera let him have the bench while she leaned against a signpost.

As she waited, she pulled out her tablet and opened *How to Be a Badass Witch*. She wanted not only to review the details of the healing spell but also to check for any notes she might have added at an earlier time and forgotten about.

The memory spell was proving to be a real liability.

Sure enough, the chapter entitled "How to Heal Minor Injuries and Ease Chronic Conditions" included a disclaimer about overdoing it.

Kera bit her lip and narrowed her eyes as she read. She was irritated with herself for having overlooked the book's warnings. Granted, when she'd read it earlier, she had been in a hurry to get relief from her burns, so the fine print and provisos had eluded her attention.

The book's authors clearly mentioned that the spell was only to be used for relatively low-level and non-life-threatening wounds. For long-term diseases or chronic pain, it was important to employ it within certain cautious limits.

Here, past-Kera had added a note. It read, *See last page of the Intro. AND DON'T TRY TO CURE CANCER!*

She snorted. *I should have written, "Don't try to cure arthritis." If curing that is dangerous, cancer pretty much goes without saying.*

Scrolling back to the end of the book's introductory chapter, Kera soon found the passage her note referred to. Here, the authors included a disclaimer under the word IMPORTANT, bolded and in caps.

A higher-level spell, it explained, or in some cases, a low-level spell stretched too thin or made to do too much, could severely overtax the thaumaturgist, and in extreme cases, lead to injury, mental health problems, and death. Such miraculous works required tremendous expenditures of energy, and the caster would be responsible for all of it.

This, they elaborated, was why the book did not go into detail on highly powerful spells and why open-ended ones like the spell of healing came with admonitions to self-impose careful and sensible limits on how much would be used *before* beginning the incantations.

Kera nodded, rankled at the idea that the unpleasantness in Mr. Kim's shop could have been avoided. "I'll keep that in mind for the future," she murmured to herself, quietly enough that the man on the bench would not hear her.

The bus pulled up. The girl slipped her tablet into her pack, stood up, and boarded. She was relieved to see that the vehicle was only running at about two-thirds capacity for the time being. Crowded buses were never fun.

Once settled in and confident that no other passengers were going to try to bother her or strike up a conversation, Kera slipped her tablet back out. She'd only read perhaps a third of the spellbook thus far and was curious what other mischief the volume might contain.

A few stops later, when they were halfway to the Mermaid's corner of Little Tokyo, the bus had rapidly filled nearly to capacity. It nonetheless paused in its route to pick up an old lady, who slowly hobbled in.

Kera, seated near the front and on the left, saw that the most likely candidate for getting up and standing was a young man in a seat one row ahead of her and across the aisle to the right. The elderly woman hesitated in front of him, giving him a moment to consider donating his place while she adjusted her glasses and feigned confusion.

To her annoyance, Kera saw that the guy was clearly

pretending to ignore the woman and waiting for her to pass, assuming that her plight couldn't possibly be his problem.

The driver was looking over his shoulder in irritation at the delay. The other passengers exuded restlessness.

She could get up and give the woman *her* seat, of course, but Kera had a better idea, one that wouldn't let the young man think he could get away with this stuff.

She leaned slightly to the side and pantomimed a stretch of her right arm while her hand wove in and out of the motions for a minor spell. One designed as a "poke" or minor stunning blow to be used against a hostile person, it caused a slight but painful muscular convulsion in a tight, concentrated part of the body.

Of course, it included a stern warning not to use it on someone's throat, eyeball, diaphragm, testicles, or anything else delicate, but Kera had another target in mind.

She felt the gluteal muscle was more appropriate anyway.

She gave the final flick of her index finger, and the young man reflexively jumped to his feet, hand going back to massage his ass.

"Oh," the old woman said, "thank you, sir." She put a hand on his shoulder to steady herself and also to push him away as she sank into his seat.

A round of applause rose from the other passengers in the front half of the bus for the guy's goodwill and decency, and the driver moved them onward.

The young man looked around in confusion. "Uh, yeah," he stated, "no problem. It's the right thing to do." He nodded at some of his newfound admirers.

Kera, meanwhile, turned her eyes back to her book.

She got off at the stop at Alameda and 3rd Street, which was barely a block from work. Though she was feeling spry enough that she could have walked farther, she'd been separated from Zee for long enough. Quicker was best.

Since she was not scheduled to work today, Kera pushed through the front door rather than bother with the rear entrance.

"Careful" wasn't her usual *modus operandi,* but she would go with it for now since she didn't know what variety of new security measures Cevin might have implemented. She'd have to ask him about that after she got Zee back.

Within, the place was nearly dead. They'd opened less than an hour ago, and there was still sunlight to spare.

One of the male waiters, a guy named TJ, noticed Kera at once but did not appear to recognize her.

"Hello," he said over his shoulder. "Please seat yourself, and I'll be right with you. Or there's space at the bar."

Kera grinned. "Thanks."

TJ was busy clearing a table of glasses and plates, so she strode past him to the bar proper, where Cevin was getting things ready for the evening. He shot a quick glance at the new arrival.

"Good afternoon, ma'am," he greeted her. "Have a seat. What'll you have?"

Kera decided she could delay the reunion with her baby by an extra minute for the sake of playing along. "Hmm. How about a motorcycle?"

Cevin squinted and looked up again, now staring her full into the face, his mouth slack with befuddlement. She tried not to burst out laughing as the gears in his mind turned. He was apparently struggling to discern if she meant a Blue Motorcycle cocktail as he attempted to figure out if he knew the person in front of him.

"Kera?" he asked finally.

She cracked up. "Yes, it's me. I didn't think I looked *that* different."

He shook his head, blushing. "I suppose you do. You could have warned me. You've...changed. Not in a bad way, but not what I was expecting." His eyes moved over her, and she considered the possibility that black hair somehow drew more attention to her figure.

"Meh," Kera responded. "It's only the hair and a little makeup."

Cevin came out from behind the bar. "Well, your hair looks a *lot* different. Did you also cut it? And I'm guessing more than a 'little' makeup. Don't get me wrong, you look great. Just… different from your normal look."

She shrugged. "Thanks."

He gestured at the side hall, and they walked toward his office. "Is this because of that jackass? Are you, like, trying to make sure he won't recognize you if he shows up again?"

"Nah," the girl replied. "If I bump into him in a dark alley or empty parking lot again, he's going to be the one who ought to worry. I burned some of my hair off while cooking, so I figured I might as well blacken all of it. That was why I applied for the bar instead of the kitchen."

Cevin chortled. He didn't laugh often, and she had to admit it was nice to hear him in a better mood for once. "It happens to the best of us, I suppose."

"Anyway," Kera continued, "who knows? I might keep it dark so I don't get the constant dumb-blonde jokes. Those got old somewhere around, say, ninth grade."

Her boss opened the office door, and she immediately fixated on a full set of black leathers laid out on the spare chair. Protective biking gear.

She gestured. "Are those for me?"

"Well," Cevin observed, "they'd be a little tight on *me*."

She smiled. "You didn't have to do that, you know. Not that I'm complaining. Thanks, Cevin. For everything."

He nodded. "You're welcome, Kera. I feel responsible. You should never have been involved in that incident. Speaking of everything, let's go have a look at Zee."

Something swelled in her chest. She wanted to jump up and down like a kid but forced herself not to. Cevin had called her "ma'am," after all. It would have been unbecoming for her new image.

Cevin led her out the back door, and she noted that he'd replaced the camera and added a couple of new lights.

"Did you change the security code or anything?" she inquired.

"Yes." He waved her through while he handled closing and locking the door. "When you work next, I'll give you the new one. For now, your bike's in the bed of my truck. I picked it up earlier on my way in."

She paused at the sight of the sleek black cycle lying on its side, with its two healthy replacement tires, which were exactly the right kind. "Man." She sighed. "You don't know how much I missed this damn thing." She waved at the truck bed. "It's okay, Zee, we're going home."

Cevin chuckled as he climbed into the truck's bed and opened the gate. Kera hopped up beside him, removed the tie-downs, and stood the bike up while her supervisor propped up a metal rack to allow them to wheel it down rather than trying to lift it out.

Once Zee's tires were back on the pavement where they belonged, Kera turned on the engine and gave it a couple of revs. The growls of her ride were the best sound she'd heard in days.

"All good?" Cevin called over the engine.

"Wonderful," Kera called back. She shut the bike off and patted the handlebars, then leaned close to whisper, "I'll be back soon, Zee."

Cevin put the rack back in the bed and closed up the truck. "Let's go get your new outfit, and then I need to get back to work."

He punched in the code to let them back into the building and handed Kera the leathers, folded over his arm.

"Shit," she commented. "I didn't bring enough storage space to take these back with me separately, but if I'm riding home anyway, well, excuse me for a minute."

Cevin chuckled. "Take all the time you need. Just go out the front, if you could, so I don't have to deal with all the security stuff again."

Kera took the leathers into the bathroom. The lower half of the outfit, she determined, would fit over her pants, though it'd be tight. Her jacket, though, had to go. She took it off before slipping the top portion on, confident that that jacket by itself would fit in her pack.

As she headed back out, she grabbed her helmet and went to the nearest mirror to give herself a look-over before she put it on.

Damn, I'm not sure I recognize myself *at this point. It goes beyond the hair color. Something's truly different, but what? Did using magic age me? That's a disturbing notion. I swear I look a few years older. In a good way, though, so far.*

It also occurred to her that if she couldn't recognize her own image in the mirror, the son of a bitch who'd shot Zee wouldn't either, and being able to avoid him was a definite bonus of her makeover.

Nodding in satisfaction, she departed the restroom and strode past the bar. "Bye, Cevin. Am I in tomorrow?"

"Sure." He looked up and stared after her. "You, um, can have one more day off if you want, but I can use you tomorrow if you're up for it."

She smiled. "I probably will be. I'll let you know. So long."

As she glided across the floor, Cevin kept watching until she disappeared out the front entrance. Somehow, he hadn't fully appreciated her body until he'd seen it sheathed in tight black leather. Sure, he'd noticed that she was both slim and buxom, curvy in the proverbial right places, but he'd been trying not to be a creep since it was unprofessional.

In any case, he was much too old for her—old enough, in fact, that he would be able to enjoy the procession of guys tripping over one another to impress her instead of feeling left out.

He shook his head and went back to his work. "One day, the sight of that girl is going to launch a thousand ships."

It should be amusing when it happened.

CHAPTER NINETEEN

Originally, Kera had planned to simply drive Zee home and then experiment with more stuff from her new grimoire, but some-how, that didn't happen. She needed to ride.

She needed to *think*. She hadn't realized until the past few days just how much her daily rides had been a part of her routine and how much she had processed her day while she was riding home. Something about being on the bike cleared her mind in a way nothing else did.

She hadn't gotten the chance to process the last few days that way, and a *lot* had happened that she desperately needed to process. Vague, half-formed thoughts and ideas that had occurred to her over the last three or four days were starting to come together in her head, informing her of what she truly wanted to do.

Had to do, in fact.

There was so much swirling in her head: the sense of help-lessness that had accompanied the attack on her, Cevin, and Zee, the unshakeable conviction that she should have been able to do something about it, even though rationally, she knew that pulling a gun on someone who already had a firearm out and ready was virtual suicide…

There was the nagging suspicion that her mother was right; that Kera should have been doing more with her life, though, of course, her mom had dumbed it down by simply telling her to find a better job.

Then there was the way her family's historical motto had come unbidden into her mind a couple of mornings ago: *Glory is the reward of valor.*

It wasn't just her own memories and experiences that were sticking in her head, either. There was the news report she'd watched before dyeing her hair black about the beginning of a crime wave terrorizing the city. Other people going through what she'd experienced, or possibly far worse.

And of course, the fact that since she'd perused that fateful, silly-seeming book, she had discovered that magic was real, and that she, Kera MacDonagh, seemed to possess a natural talent for it.

She wanted to use it to help. She wanted to do *something*.

The sky was turning a deep reddish-orange as Kera buzzed down the streets of LA, the tall buildings of downtown giving way to the lower, humbler ones across the river. More of the ubiquitous palm trees hove into sight.

She realized that subconsciously, she'd been heading for some of the more "middling" neighborhoods of the city. The ones that weren't considered bad but were close enough to the bad ones that the people who lived or worked there had to be careful.

The kinds of places where criminals came to prey on people. She felt a flutter of worry in her chest and suppressed it. Her encounter outside the Mermaid had opened her eyes to a part of the world she had always stayed away from. One she had known was there but had never had to see.

If she wanted to help…

She needed to see how things really were.

Kera drove back west across the river again and around the periphery of downtown, then took a side street that formed the edge of a residential area. It abutted a semi-derelict zone of warehouses and weedy lots.

The shadows were deepening beside the buildings as the sky faded. At first she saw nothing, but as the last of the daylight started to die, she drove past something that caught her eye.

A rather nice Mercedes-Benz E-Class. White, fifth generation. Its owner had parked it on the side of the street, figuring that his choice of location was out in the open enough for it to be safe while also being clear of any parking violations that might have attracted cops who had nothing better to do.

It had also attracted three young men Kera instantly pegged as gang members. She might be wrong, but she doubted it.

She drove by, doing and saying nothing for now. The trio glanced sharply at her but then ignored her as she passed on. They were pretty obviously canvasing the vehicle, the area, and the overall situation.

No one else seemed to be around, and Kera sensed that they would make a move soon.

What I should do, she told herself, *is keep driving. Maybe call the cops and let them do a drive-by. Yeah, that would be the smart thing.*

She didn't want to do the smart thing. The "smart" thing was to let the world keep turning; it allowed things to stay the same. She was here because she didn't *want* things to stay the same.

"Fuck it," she said aloud. She pulled Zee around the corner, parked next to a tree, and climbed off. She left her helmet on, though, as she strode briskly back toward the Mercedes-Benz.

It came as no great surprise to see that the three gang members had encircled the car, with one leaning against the hood and the other lounging near the other side. They kept their eyes out while the third worked on the lock on the driver's side door.

The one at the front of the vehicle noticed her at once, though he didn't react. He was waiting to see if she posed a real threat or was turning a blind eye to them.

She intended to eliminate all doubt immediately. She stormed straight toward the trio, hands clenching into fists at her side.

"Hey!" she yelled, deepening her voice to disguise it. "Is that your car? Because if it isn't, you have no reason to be all over it like flies on a dumpster."

All three turned their heads to look at her. Two of them dropped their jaws in shock at her brazen stupidity.

The one who'd been leaning on the hood stood up straight and took a single step toward her. He was short and thin, his eyes were dull but malevolent. "Get lost, *maricon*. Before you get hurt, yeah?"

Kera's blood seemed to thrill as it pumped through her. They all knew how this was supposed to go: she would back down because they would make it painful if she didn't, which meant they would just get away with it.

She was changing the rules.

"No," she retorted. "That's not your car. It doesn't belong to you. You want a ride, get one the old-fashioned way. The sooner you get the hell out of here, the sooner you can do that."

The guy who'd been trying to pick the lock, average height and tubby, came up beside his friend out front. "Why don't you mind your own fucking business?" he suggested.

The third of the group trailed behind the other two. Though the largest and most muscular-looking, with tattoos all over his bulging arms, he seemed the least interested in confronting the newcomer.

"Hey," he said to his partners, "she might call the cops. Let's go."

The other two ignored him.

"No," the lockpicker insisted, pointing at Kera. She pegged him as the leader. "*You* are the one who leaves. Right now, or you get hurt."

Kera couldn't tell if they were armed. She might stand a chance against them if they weren't, but if a gun or knife came out, she'd have to reevaluate her strategy in a hurry. She hesitated.

The leader noticed. He glanced at the other two and snapped his fingers. "Get 'em."

They all sprang into action at once and charged her from three different directions.

Kera swung up her hands, ran through the incantation for the "pinch" spell, and directed it straight at the skinny guy's groin. It struck him when he was about four feet from her and he collapsed abruptly, squawking in pain and clutching his crotch.

The lockpicker was on top of her before he could react to his friend's sudden departure from the fight. Kera was already preparing another spell, the one that would augment her luck. She cursed herself for not casting that one before she'd even climbed off her bike, but there was no help for it now. She swung a fast snap-kick at the guy's generous stomach. He dodged it with surprising speed, but it halted his advance.

That gave her the time she needed to finish the incantation.

A feeling of confidence and optimism surged through her, and she recalled her three years of martial arts training. While she hadn't had time to become a master by any definition, she was far from helpless. With the aid of magic, she felt sure she could take these assholes on and win.

One thing about bullies was that they didn't expect anyone to challenge them. Often, there was nothing backing up their bluster.

The third guy, the one with the tattooed muscles, might have been reluctant to get involved in the fight, but he was in it now, and she sensed he *did* have skill. He flanked her and hit her with a strong shoulder-shove, trying to knock her off-balance and drive her toward the curb, which she might trip over. She anticipated the maneuver, ran into it, and jumped the curb, spinning around in time to send another kick at the chubby gangster.

This time her foot struck him in the ribs, though he was sturdy enough that it did little but stun him. His fist drove into her stomach, and though she moved backward in time to avoid the full force of the blow, it was still enough to knock most of the wind out of her.

Guess my luck isn't as great as I thought, she lamented, *though it could have been worse.*

As the two still standing moved around to attack her from each side and the skinny guy climbed to his knees seething with rage, she decided to try something different.

She flung out her hand, whispering a chant beneath her breath, and a shower of colored sparks engulfed the lock-picking leader. "*Shit!*" he exclaimed, his voice cracking with fear. How he interpreted those sparks she wasn't sure, though she saw him looking around for the telltale canister of a firework.

No such luck, friend, she thought with a grin.

The tattooed guy pounced on her the next moment and tried to punch her in the head, but his fist ricocheted off her helmet. He grunted in pain.

Kera stumbled back; the blow had had enough force behind it to momentarily disorient her, but her helmet was designed to protect her from motorcycle accidents. A mere punch wasn't going to do any damage.

She scoffed, then cast the muscular-convulsion spell again, this time aiming it at Tattoo's back thigh muscles.

He hopped straight into the air, shaking with pain and surprise, then tripped over his own feet. The sharp pain was too great for him to stand, let alone fight.

By now, Lockpick had recovered from the surprise of the colored-sparks enchantment, and he realized that he wasn't burnt or otherwise hurt.

And he looked *pissed.*

She needed to deal with that before his anger turned to action. Kera charged him, launching off the edge of the curb and sweeping her helmet off her head in the same motion. It knocked aside the man's fists and crashed into the side of his face. He toppled.

Her mind suddenly registered one of the tattoos on the muscular dude's arm: it was a symbol she'd seen spray-painted on buildings.

"I know you assholes," she hissed. "I know which gang you're with. This isn't your turf anymore. It belongs to the LA Witches, you hear that? If you think I'm bad, wait 'til the other ones show up."

At this point, the skinny guy had regained his feet, but his wrath had withered into fear. Rather than attack Kera, he helped the other two up. "Let's get out of here!"

Grunting and swearing in both English and Spanish, they hobbled off, not sparing her a second glance as they disappeared into the vacant lot across the street.

Kera stood staring after them, then looked at the car she'd saved. She had no idea who the owner was, of course, but it didn't matter. No one's ride should be stolen.

The rush of adrenaline died, and all at once, the fatigue and pain hit her. She nearly collapsed on the curb five or six feet in front of the Mercedes and gasped for breath. She ate healthy and walked a fair amount, and her cheerleading career had previously kept her from getting too far out of shape, but she wasn't used to strenuous activity anymore, especially when paired with the effort that came from doing magic.

And though luck had saved her from any serious effects from the two hits she'd taken, her stomach felt bruised, and several joints were aching.

"Crap," she wheezed. She probably ought to scram before someone came to check out the racket.

She just had to find the will to stand up.

The healing spell might be helpful here. Though it took energy to cast it, Kera had always noticed that casting it on *herself* seemed to provide a positive result, at least briefly. Unlike when she'd healed Mr. Kim's arthritis, she got the benefits as well as the energy drain. Still, she made sure to impose a clear limit on how much energy the spell could take. If it *didn't* work this time, she couldn't afford to spend much on it.

She closed her eyes and cupped her hands in front of her face and chest, preparing to speak the words. She told both herself and the spirits that she only needed enough to dull the pain and tiredness. She only needed to get to her bike.

And then a 7-11 or something for a candy bar.

As she completed the incantation, the mixture of subtle warmth and soothing coolness returned, and Kera felt reinvigorated. The spell had taken a portion of her mental fortitude, but the energy had been reasonable. Her stomach hurt a lot less.

She rose to her feet, jogged around the corner, and swung her leg over the seat of her bike, then buzzed off to the west.

It was full dark now, some street lights sputtering on, storefront signs glowing, taillights and headlights picking out the lines on the streets. She stopped at the first convenience store she found and chowed down on a candy bar, considering her options.

She *should* go home.

But riding Zee had both calmed her down and instilled a need to do more. The night was young, dammit, and she felt better already. Now that she'd had a taste of running people off, she wasn't going to stop at rescuing a single Mercedes-Benz. If she drove around enough, an opportunity would present itself.

Since she had no desire to be anywhere near the scene of the fight if the LAPD showed up, Kera merged onto the I-10 as soon as she saw an entrance and rapidly left downtown behind, revving Zee into high gear as she picked up speed and coasted toward Santa Monica.

Fun as it was, driving at higher speeds demanded more attention. Kera perked back up, her awareness rising, and took in the interplay of lights, the bends in the road, and the shifting positions of different vehicles.

She decided to exit near Culver Junction, but at the entrance ramp beforehand, a car shot up onto the freeway and began to waver erratically as though the driver was drunk.

Hoo, boy, she noted, shifting her attention to the vehicle. *Looks like the I-10 still needs me, after all.*

Rather than exit, she fell in behind the suspicious sedan at a safe distance. Should she try to cast a healing spell? A luck spell?

She didn't have time to try anything. Seconds later, the driver lost control and crashed into the sidewall. Flames erupted from under the crunched hood.

"Fuck!" Kera exclaimed. She braked as quickly as it was safe to do so, wove around the wreck and the other vehicles taking evasive maneuvers, and came to a stop ten yards in front of it while other vehicles honked madly around her. Panting with effort, she wheeled her bike around to the car's rear and put on the emergency flashers to ensure other motorists would either help or stay the hell clear.

Please, she thought as she dismounted and ran toward the crashed car. *Please, please, please don't let anyone smash into Zee. It's his first day back from the shop.*

But she had more important things to worry about right now. The people in the car were still alive but trapped and possibly wounded. The crash had knocked them away from the one door that still seemed operational while blocking the others against the ravaged concrete.

Okay. This is going to require magic, including some spells I haven't practiced much yet. Think, Kera. You can do this. Some of my extra luck should still be in effect from the tussle with those gangsters, right?

She was mildly relieved to see that all three of the car's inhabitants were adults; no children had been endangered. She had no intention of letting anything bad happen to these people regardless, but it took the edge of panic away.

First, she tried the "pinch" spell on one of the doors, but nothing happened. Then she pretended that the car was a living being and that its metal structure was bone and tendons and muscle tissue and tried again.

This time, the latch popped. The door was still bent in a way that meant it would take a lot of force to open it wide enough for a person to squeeze through, however.

Kera dashed forward. One of the men in the car was trying to push the popped door with his foot, but he wasn't having much luck. The other two were dazed or wounded and of no help.

Strength, Kera recalled. *Can't believe I forgot that one during the brawl. A spell to give one person the strength of five large men. Okay, the incantation was...*

It came to her out of nowhere, and she wondered if the luck spell influenced her ability to perform other magic. She hoped so.

After casting the enchantment, Kera seized the warped metal and heaved against the door, shouting and grunting, and ripped it up and away. It screeched in protest and bent backward, and the front seats opened before her.

But then the flames rushed back from the engine to lick around the steering column. The man who'd been trying to kick the door open jerked back to avoid them, moaning in fear and despair.

After she'd accidentally set herself on fire, Kera had looked at another spell that allowed the caster to lower the air temperature in a given area by as much as a hundred degrees Fahrenheit. It could be harmful if it hit any of the people inside, but if dropped on top of a blaze, it ought to balance things out nicely.

Kera swept her hand toward the steering column and the hood and spoke the words. Frost formed on the pleather and steel and the angry flames died, reduced to a couple of flickers near the front end.

Now she could focus on the people.

"Come on," she called to the man. She took his hand and hoisted him out with surprising ease. The strength spell lasted a good five minutes, and it had barely been a minute and a half so far.

Freeing the other two, another man and a woman, was harder since the man's shoulder was dislocated and the woman was barely conscious and bleeding from the head. Kera had to kick an entire seat out of the way to pull them free, being careful not to injure them further but wasting no time. The fire in the engine was spreading again as the cold spell wore off.

"Oh, God," the first man gasped. "Thank you. Thank you so much."

Kera guided the woman out into his arms, and the three supported each other as they leaned against the undamaged part of the sidewall. The witch, for her part, hopped out, hurried past them, and remounted her bike before they had a chance to ask her any awkward questions.

She was shaking as she settled on her seat, and there were spots floating in her vision. She didn't have a headache yet, as she'd had the first few times she tried magic, but she had the sense that one might not be too far down the line. She had gotten better at putting constraints on the amount of magic she used, but she had still consumed more than she'd anticipated.

Worried about her ability to drive, she blew out a long breath and closed her eyes for a moment.

By now, the first man had managed to pull out his cell phone to call 911, and two other cars had stopped nearby to check on the scene. Two women and one man had approached and were asking about a dozen questions at once. Sirens were approaching from afar, too.

"Hey," someone exclaimed, "where'd that guy on the bike go?"

That kicked Kera into gear. She was far from a hundred percent, but she wanted to get out of there before anyone found her and started asking questions. She gave the group an unseen salute, suddenly borderline-embarrassed by the display she'd put on, and revved up Zee, then gave a quick check for a place to merge before starting westward down the freeway.

Still shaky, she exited at the first opportunity. From here, it would be easy to disappear into the labyrinth of suburbs toward Century City.

A flip of a switch gave Zee a lower range of power and she eased off on her speed, coasting casually eastward. She was a long way from downtown and wanted to avoid the main roads, but she decided she didn't mind the ride. Simply being and breathing was helping her regain her strength.

It had been one *hell* of an evening, and she still hadn't eaten much of anything. She was very aware of the growling in her stomach, the edge of the headache behind one eye, and the feel of her heart pumping overtime. Her breath was warm inside the confines of the helmet.

She had grown accustomed to the effects of using magic, and having the forethought to limit her usage had helped immeasurably, but that only meant she had pushed herself close to the edge without going over.

Not long after, she saw a sign for a Greek drive-through place, and her stomach gave such a growl that she nearly wrenched the bike straight off the road. She was able to control herself, but she tapped her foot anxiously while waiting at the drive-through, and within thirty seconds of receiving her food, she was tearing into a giant gyro and fries.

That filled her up, but as she was starting the bike, her stomach gave another twist, and she rolled her eyes before going back through the drive-through line. This gyro she stuffed into her backpack on top of her folded jacket, and she tried to control her impatience to get home. She wasn't far.

Finally, Kera pulled into the warehouse, parked within it, closed the main door, and flung her pack onto the table. Then she pulled out the bagged gyro and left it to sit while she took off her helmet and boots. She didn't bother with the leathers yet.

As soon as the possibility for relaxation set in, her head swam and her stamina left her.

"Whoa." She steadied herself against the wall. She hadn't realized just how much the adrenaline and spare calories were keeping her going. She felt completely strung-out; she was coming down from all the enchantments and augmentations she'd placed on herself, like a druggie after a major high.

Kera sat on the edge of her bed. "Okay. Yeah. I'll just rest here a minute, then eat, then–"

She fell over on her side and passed out.

CHAPTER TWENTY

The hotel James and Mother LeBlanc stayed in the first night was not cheap. After seeing his room, James decided he should make it clear that he had paid for it out of his own money and not the council's coffers. He set off down the gently lit corridors, whistling cheerily to himself. It felt good to be out of the car after so many hours of sitting.

To his surprise, he found her suite empty when he arrived.

"Hello?" he asked the empty space.

"Is there something you need?" Her voice didn't seem to come from any direction in particular. "I'll be dressed for dinner in an hour or so."

"Sure, sure. And, uh, it can wait." He looked around. "Where *are* you?"

He thought he heard her chuckle, then the outlines of her spell became clear: a protective shield surrounding the *en suite* bathroom, which otherwise would be fully visible from where he was standing. He could not see inside, but from the tendrils of steam, he assumed she was soaking in a bath. Her illusion had made it seem that the room was empty.

"It's been a very long time since I had a proper bath," she said.

His mouth twitched. "By 'proper bath,' I assume you mean you're trying to make the entire room so hot, you remember why you left Louisiana."

Another chuckle. "You could say that," she agreed.

"Well, I wouldn't want to interrupt a good soak for anything as mundane as dinner. I'll order food to my room, and you can come along whenever you're done. Does that sound good?"

"Very good, thank you, James."

He smiled and let himself back out. Thaumaturges lived for a very long time, and most tended to settle either in a hedonistic lifestyle or an ascetic one. James much preferred the company of those who chose the hedonistic route.

Life was just better when you had perfectly cooked steaks and a good port after the meal.

When she arrived in his room sometime later, Mother LeBlanc looked relaxed and happy. She raised an eyebrow at James's notes and laptop, some shoved out of the way on the desk for his meal.

"I started doing ads, and all my bad work habits came back," James said, shaking his head. "I always did working meals back when I had a 9-to-5 job."

"Then I shall do the same." She sat and took the lid off her meal. "What does your research say?"

As she ate, he explained the various internet rabbit holes he'd gone down to find their new potential recruits. It appeared that their recruit was somewhere southwest of Charleston, and James had combed a distressingly wide array of police blotters, local social media pages, and more.

Whoever their mysterious recruit was, they were not hiding their tracks quite well enough to evade Mother LeBlanc and James. The incidents that were happening around them were described as "one in a million"—car crashes that ended with a car hanging precariously over a cliff, yet with no deaths, supercell thunderstorms, and gas line explosions.

"There are comments on each of the stories," James told her, "saying 'What are the odds?'"

She shook her head. "Higher than they should be."

"Yes." He was troubled as well. "We'll have to figure out the backstory for each of these."

Magic was rare enough to bind those who practiced it into a tight-knit group and powerful enough that they had to be careful about who could wield it. Even if one's power was stable, free of cracks or drains that would be dangerous to them or others, there was the matter of character.

It took a very specific type of person to be a thaumaturge. They must be determined and disciplined enough to master a very difficult skill, which ruled out a great many potential recruits. Far too many attempted to become powerful without mastering the techniques and attempted spells they could not control or which they did not have the power to complete.

Spells like that were dangerous. Not only did they often kill the magic wielder, but they could also hurt or kill bystanders. It was possible for such a catastrophe to produce a Chernobyl-like effect, though magic wielders worldwide had been relieved to learn that the Chernobyl disaster had *not* been due to magic.

Just good old-fashioned human error.

But magic wielders could not afford human error, not to mention the human ego. Thaumaturges must be careful. They must also be willing to put in effort without being in the spotlight—not simply on occasion, but sometimes for decades at a time. That ruled out many others, and James's choice of career had been a concern on the council when he was trained.

After all, how could someone who worked in advertising be comfortable out of the spotlight?

James had eventually proven that he was a good fit and his skills were good for controlling public perception, but it had been an uphill battle.

A good recruit must also be willing to use power sparingly.

Some became addicted to magic and wasted away. There was little room for error on that front. Magic was more exhausting than any endurance sport, and an addiction to magic would quickly result in death.

Lastly, a good recruit *must* be willing to forgo justice in the interests of the common good. Many recruits, driven by a desire to help the world, found themselves unable to forgive bad actors or allow them to prosper. Many descended into vigilantism and focused on criminal elements of society.

That was the largest sticking point, but one on which the council never wavered.

James knew Mother LeBlanc was worried about the person they were going to see now. Things like car crashes, supercell storms, and gas explosions hinted that this practitioner might be using magic to punish people.

If that was the case and the person was not willing to reform their ways, the two of them would have no choice but to shut the magic down.

"You look grim," Mother LeBlanc stated.

James let his breath out slowly. "Do you ever wonder if the council is wrong?"

"Of course. One must always make considered decisions." She took a neat bite of her food.

"Yes, but…vigilantes, for instance." He had never brought this up with her, accepting the council's logic over his occasional objections.

"James." She gave him a warning look. "When one must choose between punishing one person and lifting up others—"

"But what if that's a false choice?" he protested. "What if seeing these things go unpunished hurts society?"

"That is a human matter, not a magical one." She folded her hands in her lap. "A society cannot rely on vigilantes. It must structure itself to reward the good and discourage the bad, or it will fail."

James sighed. "It seems as if we might rob ourselves of good recruits. And..." His voice trailed off.

"And it is difficult to seal off a person's powers," she finished softly. "Yes. It is not a decision to be taken lightly. But, James, you do not remember the times when we were burned at the stake for magic, and vigilantism and revenge—those things draw us into the public eye. Now more than *ever*, it is imperative that we stay hidden."

He knew she had a good point, but as he settled back in his chair, he could not stop his mind from turning the problem over.

This was a new time in the world. Surely new solutions might be possible.

Or necessary.

"Where are we going next?" she asked.

"Right." He sighed. "Uh, we'll be hanging out here until we can locate this person, then fixing on our next target. I've narrowed it down to a couple of towns, and we'll go from there. Tonight, we rest."

Sven was just finishing his lunch when he heard the sirens.

He looked at Johnny, who had eaten more quickly, and the two of them smiled. Their car was one of many parked in the wide lot nearby, so the odds of anyone noticing them sitting there were slim. If they *did* notice, all they would see was two men eating lunch.

It was the perfect vantage point from which to see if the police could do anything about the escalating fights that had begun to spread.

Sven took the last bite of his sandwich and stuffed the wrappers in the takeout bag, which he put in the back seat. He'd insisted that they take his car because they'd be here for a while, and Johnny never let anyone eat in *his* car.

"How many do you think there'll be?" he asked Johnny lazily.

"One or two cars," Johnny said after taking a second to decide. He grinned. "And a couple more when they figure out this isn't Beverly Hills."

Sven laughed. He sat back and listened to the sirens coming closer. By now, even the youths who had been fighting across the street were taking notice. He could see some of them looking over their shoulders and telling the others to run.

Everyone knew how this was going to go down, except maybe the cops. If they were new, they probably thought they were going to show up and heroically insert themselves into the middle of a fight. Possibly they pictured themselves saving babies or puppies from the influx of gang violence while apprehending all of the criminals and scaring any potential wrongdoers onto the straight and narrow.

What was *actually* going to happen was that the people currently fighting were going to scatter. One or two might get caught, and the rest would wait for the police to go away and either resume their fight or return to mugging people.

Just as Johnny had predicted, two cop cars came screaming up the street, only to find the various gang members scattering in all directions. One or two hurdled the fence around the parking lot, though neither were paying enough attention to see Johnny and Sven.

"The kids are getting sloppy," Sven remarked.

Johnny nodded.

Some of the usual chases were now taking place. One of the cops was young and spry but not energetic enough to keep up with teenagers who'd been running from cops their whole lives. The other three cops didn't even try, just jogged after their friend just quickly enough to make it seem like they were expending effort.

It looked like they weren't going to catch anyone, but also like no one was going to make them sorry for coming out here.

Sven sighed and grabbed his knife. "I'll be back," he told Johnny.

He hopped the fence and crossed the street at a brisk walk. With the police cars in place, lights blazing, cars up and down the street were turning onto alternate routes.

He briefly considered stealing one of the cars, but they all had GPS in them now. Not worth it. Instead, he approached the two cars from a careful angle and made a few discreet cuts in the tires. Then he pocketed the knife and jogged back.

Johnny took a big sip of his soda and started to laugh as the police headed back. "I love this part."

Sven settled back in his seat to watch. This sort of thing wasn't what he normally did these days. It made him feel like a teenager again, someone who had just gotten into the game. He didn't realize how much he'd missed those days.

Both of their phones buzzed, and Sven motioned for Johnny to check the message.

Johnny made an annoyed noise. "That bitch."

"One of your models?" Sven asked him.

"Jealous?" Johnny sounded insufferably smug.

He was a little bit jealous. It bothered Sven how someone as unremarkable-looking as Johnny managed to have the luck he did with women. Of course, he supposed he only had Johnny's word for it that any of the events described actually happened.

Sven shrugged. "So, who was it?"

"Any time I say 'that bitch,' I'm talking about our boss."

"What is your problem with her?" Sven asked him.

"What *isn't* yours? She's crazy." Johnny watched as the policemen came back to their cars and had a shouted conversation over the roofs, gesturing about which road to drive down.

They hadn't noticed the tires yet.

"Okay," Sven said, "so...what did the crazy bitch say?"

"Now you're getting it." Johnny shrugged. "She wants a status update. Hey, look, they're figuring out the tires."

Sure enough, both sets of policemen had gotten back out of their cars and were gesturing at the tires. Both Johnny and Sven sank down in their seats as the policemen looked around.

They seemed to hope that the criminal would be waiting there with a knife, ready to be apprehended.

"She's been right so far," Sven said, gesturing at the police. "Took them fifteen minutes to get here. Then they only nabbed the guy who'd gotten knocked out at the start of the fight, and the rest of them are already off mugging tourists again. Game, set, and match."

"So, how are *we* going to calm it down?" Johnny asked. "Now that we've given them a taste of the good life."

On this point, Sven wasn't quite as certain. He shook his head. "I hope she's got a plan for that."

He pulled out his phone and sent a status update for the two of them since Johnny hadn't. It wasn't long before their phones buzzed again.

"She wants all of our original sites locked down and in distribution tonight," Sven said. "She moves fast, I'll give her that." Normally, courting business owners was a multi-week process.

"When she starts bringing in cash, we'd better get a cut," Johnny growled.

"Uh-huh. As soon as this mess is cleared up, I'll get you back to your car."

Johnny was staring into the middle distance.

Sven snapped his fingers in front of the other guy's face. "Hey. What's up?"

"Thinking about how to lock down the Mermaid."

Sven groaned. "You struck out. It happens. Anything more than half is good; you and I both know that." He looked at his friend. "Johnny. Don't go back there."

Johnny smiled, and Sven knew this was going to be a mess.

He just hoped it wasn't a mess Pauline would pin on *him*.

CHAPTER TWENTY-ONE

Kera awoke feeling terrible again, probably because it was morning. She always felt like shit when she got up during the morning hours.

In this case, 10:22.

"Ugh." She sat up and rubbed her eyes, then waved a hand in front of her mouth. "Morning breath. Wait, did I eat last night?" The rumble from her stomach suggested she hadn't, but the past few days had made her wary of trusting it.

Shaking her head to clear it, she glanced toward her table. The bag with her food was still sitting there, cold and possibly inedible now. She had a memory of downing the other gyro in record time, but she might as well not have eaten anything, given how ravenous she was.

"Oh. Well, then."

Standing up with a creak of leather, she realized that she'd slept the whole night in her new outfit. It had gotten filthy in a hurry and would need to be cleaned, despite having been in service for less than twenty-four hours. She stripped the leathers off, an elegant process that involved hopping, overbalancing, and flopping onto the bed, and draped them over her dresser, then wobbled over to the table.

Her body was desperate for calories by this point. She picked up the gyro and slung it into the microwave, giving it two minutes to kill any bacteria that might have shown up while it sat out overnight. There was still a possibility that her digestive tract would get angry at her, but she didn't care. She was famished.

While the food heated, she made herself a quick pot of coffee. She'd need it to come back to the proverbial land of the living.

This was like the worst hangover ever. She pillowed her head on her arms. Well, minus the nausea.

Small blessings.

Speaking of which… She threw a glance over to where her motorcycle stood and smiled. "Good morning, Zee. Nice to have you back. The place wasn't the same without you."

Once the food was ready, Kera didn't even bring it to the table. She ate standing at the counter, downing bites of pita, gyro meat, and tzatziki with ravenous speed and washing it down with scalding black coffee. Even wincing at the hot food couldn't slow her down. Everything tasted fantastic to her despite the less-than-optimal conditions. Deprivation made the body more appreciative.

When she was done, she stared forlornly at the empty plate for a moment before washing it. She'd get herself more food after a shower, she decided.

But first, she was going to let the food and the coffee do their job. She crumpled her wrappers and returned to her bed with a second cup of coffee, then located her tablet and fired it up. Out of dull curiosity, she opened an Internet browser and perused the morning news.

Her eyes grew wide.

"Ohhhh, *shit!*"

Good Samaritan saves desperate family from burning car on Interstate, the headline announced.

Kera gawked at the screen while she read it. Her stomach roiled with faint nausea, but mostly she just found it bizarre—nearly surreal—to be reading about her own exploits on the news.

Which, in all truth, *hadn't* been what she'd wanted. It seemed ridiculous to her that she had expected to do that without the press getting wind of it, but she really had.

"For God's sake!" She groaned. "I decide to do anonymous vigilante stuff and fail to be anonymous about it."

At least they hadn't identified her yet as far as she could tell. She scanned the article three times, afraid she was missing an identifying detail, but all anyone seemed to know was that *someone* in a black motorcycle helmet was riding around and saving people from problems. The article also stated that the bike was black, but there weren't any more details.

Kera was generally annoyed when people couldn't distinguish between different types of motorcycles, but right now, it was pretty convenient.

"So, Kera," she told herself, "I guess your idiot ass shouldn't have made the grand announcement that downtown is now the LA Witches' hood. Not sure if the article mentions *that* part, but still."

She skimmed the rest of the story. It contained, mercifully enough, no mention of her excursion into gang warfare. She doubted that reporters, cops, or regular citizens had made the connection yet if they'd even heard about it.

After all, who were the gang members going to go to? The police? What would they say, that some chick had been mean to them while they were trying to steal a car? She snickered.

Her smile died. They would have paid attention to her little ass-kicking, though. They wouldn't forget.

Her mind drifted away from the brawl, however, as she read the Good Samaritan article in more detail, no longer focusing solely on descriptions of herself. Since the journalists had known nothing about the mysterious "hero," aside from their assumption that it had been a man, they'd filled out the story with details about the family who'd crashed.

Kera was drawn in. While she'd been happy to help, there hadn't been time to think about who the three individuals in the wreck were.

It turned out that they were siblings. The two who'd been injured in the crash, she discovered, had gone to the hospital to pick up the other man, the one who'd been in comparatively good condition. He, their brother, had been admitted for extensive testing for a cancerous tumor, and the doctors had not yet decided if it was benign or malignant.

"We went there," the woman was quoted as having said, "totally fixated on him and whether or not *he'd* live. Mel and me were too upset to drive while we were bringing him back. I couldn't handle it, and the crash was my fault."

Her brother Mel, who'd dislocated his shoulder, had added, "And us two were the ones who got injured in the crash. Ironic, right? If that guy in the black helmet hadn't come by, it might have been us who died, while Jerry lived with his cancer, completely alone, without us."

Kera's gut clenched. She wasn't the overly sentimental type, but there was no way to read about the family's plight without being affected. A lump formed in her throat and her eyes began to water. This put a different spin on things.

The article's authors went on to describe in an updated section how the car had been deemed unsalvageable. More importantly, they'd received word right after publishing the story that the doctors had determined that Jerry's tumor was benign.

Mel and the woman, Daniela, might have perished for nothing, Kera concluded. Their brother was going to make it, yet without her intervention, the two might have ended up trading their lives for their brother's in a way.

Instead, all three would live.

Kera leaned back and allowed the facts and implications to sink in, trying to be stoic and mature about it. Then she burst into tears. She didn't cry easily, but with the aftereffects of adrenaline and exhaustion, she wasn't as balanced as usual.

They weren't bad tears, at least, since the family's story had a happy ending.

"Oh, hell." She sniffled and wiped her hand over her nose. "I wasn't," she swallowed, "expecting *this*."

For once, *just once*, she had done something purely right. That something wasn't a mere by-product of being a stupid, pretty, privileged rich girl, either. It had nothing to do with the fact that her parents were wealthy or that she got good grades and high test scores in school. Or that most people thought she was attractive. Nothing like that. In fact, they'd assumed she was a dude.

She'd helped someone she didn't know and would likely never meet again. It was as though a need inside her had been fulfilled, but she hadn't grasped until this moment that it had been a need. She had felt good when she fixed Mr. Kim's arthritis, but this was even better. Something about the anonymity of it felt purer.

Trying to calm herself, she looked at the description of herself in the article. It made her chuckle. "I guess the ta-tas aren't that obvious in the leathers? Sure, we'll go with that. Feels kinda nice."

She sniffled for another minute or two, then got herself under control. Rational thought returned, and she sighed. Chances were the confusion was worse because it was dark, there was fire and smoke everywhere, and everyone was panicked and confused, not to mention she was hauling around huge pieces of metal like the Hulk. In their position, she'd probably have assumed the mysterious motorcycle person was a guy, too.

So much for anonymity.

She wiped her eyes, washed her face in the bathroom sink, and came back into the main room to look at her leathers again. They *definitely* needed cleaning, being covered with debris and grime and soot from the ravaged car as well as condensed exhaust fumes, random road spray from wet patches on the asphalt and concrete, grass stains from the fight over the Mercedes-Benz, and of course, sweat.

This was another thing she could do herself, though, and she knew from experience that doing something would help steady her. She started off by wiping the surface down with paper towels, spraying it, and rubbing carefully to remove the filth without compromising the integrity of the leather. Cevin had provided the outfit as a gift one measly day ago, and she didn't like the thought of it being reduced to hand-me-down levels that quickly.

But the process of cleaning it all was tedious as fuck.

"Wait," she said with a sudden swell of excitement. "There might be a spell for this. I could've sworn…"

Kera left the leathers where they were and checked her spell-book. Sure enough, buried near the end of the contents was a formula for "cleaning organic material."

She grinned. "Hah! They thought of everything. This is going to work. I know it."

She hesitated for a moment, then left the tablet where it was and rummaged around in the cabinets. She didn't have much that was very caloric, but she found a bag of Halloween candy that she had intended to pass out.

Beggars couldn't be choosers, and she knew her body was going to rebel if she tried to do more magic without adequate energy. She was pretty sure she hadn't recovered from last night's expenditures yet. She wolfed down a few fun-size bars and several tiny bags of M&Ms.

"The things I do for magic," she murmured. "And might do again, just because they're tasty."

After a few days of trying spells, she decided to go back to the introduction and the "Philosophy of Thaumaturgy" chapter, both of which she had only skimmed. After all, they had seemed like wishful thinking at the time, the sort of thing people talked about before trying to sell you crystals.

Except that Kera now knew *this* book was for real.

Perhaps she hadn't given it a fair shake the first time because on this read, she found that it had a simple, straightforward template for its spell descriptions. The authors always began with a quick summary of what the magic was intended to do, then they detoured into the underlying theory and philosophy behind the spell—the arcane significance of it, though they didn't spend too much time on that. In Kera's opinion, that was wise. One didn't want to bore the reader, after all.

She pored over the pages in which they described the casting time, the hand gestures involved, the materials the thaumaturgist would need—in this case, none—and finally, the incantations to be spoken. Following this, they included final comments, including safety recommendations.

Kera made sure to read the short chapter in detail, then re-read it for good measure. The essence of the miracle-work involved had to do with calling upon the ancient spirits who were traditionally associated with whatever material needed cleaning and employing their help in "purifying" the structure of the substance. That made sense to Kera, though she hoped the ancient spirits didn't object to being used for something this mundane.

She read the closing commentary before she started the hand gestures.

The authors admonished the reader that this spell, like the healing formula and many others, involved a "pull" of magical energy from outside sources, which in turn pulled energy from the caster. Thus, it was wise to know one's limits.

Kera recalled the earlier portion about contacting the spirits.

So, is it really simply a case of me grabbing their power and stuffing it into the spell, or is it more that I'm politely asking for their help?

Maybe thinking of it that way is the key to getting the amounts right. Worth a try.

Rather than risk ruining the beautiful new leathers, she opted to test her hypothesis using one of the fire spells. She was very familiar with the gestures and the energy expenditure, but she had spent her time perfecting the gestures, the words, and her control, and she hadn't thought to examine her *motives*.

"Knowing what you want to achieve," Kera said aloud, "while trusting the powers you're invoking. Maybe that's it."

She reviewed the chapter on the ignition spell, then took a deep breath and mounted a candle on her small dining table.

"Here goes nothing."

While forming the gestures with her hands and intoning the words, she imagined a tiny puff of flame and heat. She put her confidence in the elemental spirits of fire to understand her intention.

A fireball the size of a modest ice cream cone erupted in the air directly over the candle. Though it was bigger than Kera would have preferred, it nonetheless ignited the wick without harming any of her other stuff.

She smiled. "All right, then. Let's move on to Phase Two."

The girl turned to the bare brick wall at the far end of the warehouse, equidistant from both Zee and her stash of workout gear, and started the spell again. This time, she envisioned a blast that, while specifically not powerful enough to destroy a structure, would suffice to kill a large animal.

The air in front of her blazed and shimmered and a roaring cloud of fire erupted over half the wall, the flames filling her apartment with heat and light, only to die a second later as they found nothing flammable to feed upon. The bricks were scorched, but otherwise, there was no damage.

She sighed. This time, though she had summoned the spell with finesse and efficiency, she still found herself trembling. She made her way over to the candy shakily and ate a few more mini candy bars, resisting the urge to write a sticky note that read, *Magic as a way of losing weight?*

Once the energy had gotten into her bloodstream, she practiced her magic further with a handful of other cantrips and parlor tricks. She used a telekinetic spell to gather the random ashes, summoned a light breeze to then blow them out the window, and tried to combat the smell by conjuring a nice lemony aroma.

The last one failed at first due to a lack of material components as a frame of reference, but then she remembered she had a lemon-scented candle. Using that and trying again, the witch quickly had the space smelling as though she'd recently made a batch of lemon meringue pies.

"Nice," she congratulated herself. "Next up, organic materials cleaning as originally planned."

She turned to her leathers, shaking her head as a stray thought popped into her mind.

A thought she really should have had sooner. She sat staring at the back wall, jaw agape.

It was weird. These spells worked. It was real magic, not merely a gimmick. The people who put this book together must have been aware of that, which made it seem strange that they'd put it on the Internet for the general public to—

A thunderclap went off in her brain.

"Holy fucking *shit*." She ran to her tablet, nearly crashing into the wall by her bed as she snatched it up and opened the ebook reader.

The publisher was listed as Thaumaturgy Publishing, LLC.

"Okay," she remarked. "That makes a certain amount of sense, though it doesn't tell me much."

The book had no credited authors to speak of either, just two pairs of initials: JL and MLB. That was all.

Brow furrowing in determination, Kera looked up HideMy-Ass, her favorite VPN, and used it to conduct an anonymous search on the mysterious and redundantly-named Thaumaturgy Publishing.

As far as the Internet was concerned, the company did not exist. The sole evidence that any such limited-liability corporation *did* exist was the book and the places where it was listed for sale. They had formed for the sole purpose of releasing their grimoire, then faded back into the mists of time.

Kera let her head drop into her hands.

"I don't get it," she mumbled. "Why would a publishing company not want to be found? And if they don't want the usual degree of attention, what does that say about *me* being found by *them?* Or by God-knows-who?"

Clamping down on the rising tide of dread and anxiety, Kera looked at her widely dispersed possessions, particularly the stuff associated with her strange new hobby. Someone had published this grimoire—someone who didn't want to be found. Someone who knew the spells worked.

She wasn't sure if they wanted to find her, but she needed to consider that, as well as the possibility that they weren't friendly.

First up: plausible deniability.

"I need a lockbox," she concluded. "Or at least a regular box. I know I have one of those."

She spent the next hour cleaning, reorganizing, and gathering every last one of her numerous notes and accouterments, then piling them into a large plastic tub with a sealable lid. It wasn't much but far better than nothing, and she might be able to magically guard it against prying eyes.

She was just deciding whether to go out and find a metal lockbox when there was a knock on the door.

CHAPTER TWENTY-TWO

What the heck?" Kera muttered. She tiptoed over to the door, where she could see the top of a short man's silver-haired head, which looked familiar. She undid the lock and pulled on the knob to open the door.

"Mr. Kim," said Kera. "I wasn't expecting you. Is…everything okay?"

The old man's face was tight and drawn with concern, and there was a deep sadness in his red-rimmed eyes. The entire vibe surrounding him was negative. Asking if he needed help felt like the natural thing to do.

"I…" Kim began, "I do not know yet if you can, but I would like to ask anyway."

Furrowing her brow, Kera opened the door farther and motioned for him to come in. He nodded his thanks and shuffled over the threshold but remained standing near the edge of her living area. He didn't seem to know how to start speaking.

"What's the matter?" Kera prompted gently.

The elderly grocer winced at a sudden inner pain, and he had to breathe in and out twice before he could finally speak.

"My wife, Mrs. Kim, is very sick. The doctors cannot do anything for her until four months from now."

Kera nodded. "What does she have?" Her hopes sank as soon as the words left her mouth; if it was something that required her to wait a third of a year for treatment, it couldn't be anything good.

Kim's frown deepened. "Cancer."

Oh, no, the girl thought, trying not to let her fear and anguish show on her face. She wanted the old man to know she cared, but breaking down in tears, as much as she suddenly wanted to, would not help. She could feel the exhaustion of the past day and night dragging at her.

Kim went on, "I have no idea if your reiki treatment might help, but I must ask."

She wasn't surprised. "It is worth a try."

"It helped my hands." He looked down at them, and his face spasmed again. "I just don't know if it would be any good for...something like that."

The warning from the book flashed in Kera's mind. *DO NOT TRY TO CURE CANCER!* The authors had been extremely clear.

But she had already made her decision. She had made it the moment she'd asked what was wrong with Mrs. Kim. She remembered the day she had come in to find Mr. Kim so worried. Probably, that had been the day of the tests, and he had been trying to put the matter out of his mind since then.

Little did either of them know that she had been studying the very thing that could help.

Kera cleared her throat. "How long does she have?"

"Probably?" Mr. Kim sighed. "Less than four months. Not much longer than that. I think they're delaying. They said it's advanced, and that the treatment centers are backed up, and the specialists are booked—" He broke off, swallowing, and finished softly, "The earliest they can promise us is July."

It was currently the beginning of March.

Kera closed her eyes for a second before she responded. "Mr. Kim, to be honest, I don't know if I can do anything, but the one thing I will say for sure is that I will try. I will do everything I can to help your wife."

The elderly businessman gave a slow, deep nod, but he did not speak. Oddly enough, he seemed to have gotten his emotions under better control than when he'd first come to speak to her. Though still concerned and melancholy, there was stoic acceptance in his demeanor.

Kera moved over and patted him on the shoulder. "Okay? Let's go."

It was Wednesday around lunchtime—1:06 pm, to be exact. Pauline was unavailable since she and Lia had other engagements, but she'd given Sven and Johnny the keys and necessary information to let themselves into their rented office.

They arrived in Sven's car this time but had a nice official slip of paper to display on the dashboard to validate their parking.

"After all," Sven snickered, "we wouldn't want to have any problems with the law."

"Right." Johnny unbuckled his seatbelt and climbed out, firmly shutting the passenger's side door behind him. "Getting busted for a fuckin' parking violation when we're this deep into the real shit would be way too embarrassing to live down."

Sven shrugged as he stepped out and locked the vehicle. "Couldn't be any worse than what happened to Al Capone."

"Eh?" Johnny looked over, then his brain caught up with him. "Right, tax stuff. Imagine getting busted by accountants."

"Not *just* tax evasion," Sven protested. "Guy was one of the greatest criminals in American history. All the legendary shit he did and the feds nailed him for *tax evasion*. There ought to be a law against that."

Johnny chuckled as they made their way to the elevator. Unlike when they were on the job in bars, they were both dressed in nice, moderately expensive suits and jackets that had been freshly pressed last night, and both wore mirrored glasses and carried briefcases. Nothing distinguished them from any other business drones going about their daily affairs in downtown LA.

At least, nothing visible to the average person. Sven had a Ruger LCR snub-nosed revolver, chambered with .327 Federal Magnum, carefully tucked into a small holster at the back of his pants and hidden by his coat.

Johnny had thought about getting another gun for concealed carry since his old Beretta 92, great pistol though it was, was too big to properly conceal during open daylight activities. At night, he could get away with stashing it in a shoulder holster under his jacket. But he was saving up to get his car's seats reupholstered.

And ammunition was more expensive than ever lately.

Their conversation turned to casual law-abiding shit as they walked across the street and into the massive building. The warming of the weather, how the Dodgers were looking so far in MLB Spring Training, and the latest news on the stock market.

Once safely inside their office, they locked the door behind them and relaxed in the reasonably-comfortable chairs, opening their briefcases to go over the material they'd gathered.

"Okay, so," Johnny began as he passed a list of bars and hotspots across the table, "the Palmary, Verduro's, the Angels' Den—that one's the strip club—the Alphonse A. Bar and Grille, Park's…"

Sven nodded his way through the litany of them, running his finger down the list. "Hey, what happened to that one fucking place…uh, the Azul?"

Johnny scowled. "They turned out to be morons. We're better off without them."

"Oh?" Sven raised an eyebrow. This was the Johnny he'd known in college: whip-smart, with an unmatched sense for people. His recent preoccupation with the Mermaid had been troubling to Sven, but the fact that Johnny had cut off the Azul made him think the man was getting back to normal.

Hopefully, Johnny would stop being so suspicious of Pauline. Sven *really* didn't want Johnny to be right on that front. Disentangling from this mess would be a bitch and a half.

Johnny was still focused on the Azul. He laughed as he leaned back, chair squeaking. "The guys running the place were a little too...*enthusiastic* about the arrangement, shall we say."

"Oh, no." Sven groaned.

"Yeah. They decided that they were gonna 'help' us, so they promised me that they'd have drugs available soon from their end. Next thing you know, boom. Arrested. Businessmen of the Year right there."

Though the room was reasonably well-soundproofed, they both stopped talking as footsteps passed by outside and waited until silence returned before resuming their discussion.

Sven shook his head. "Who the hell thinks, 'Oh, drugs! *That* should be easy to get into'?"

"Too many people watched *Breaking Bad*," Johnny said. "So many fucking trust-fund babies in business school, acting like they were Walter-fuckin'-White. They aren't, and neither is some random guy who owns a bar."

Sven nodded. As Johnny spoke, the two of them had been laying out markers on a map and would be sending a carefully itemized list to Lia for distribution later that night. Given that they were weeks ahead of schedule, everything was going great.

"We got more places than she expected," Sven said. "Pauline didn't say it, but Lia told me."

"We'll get more," Johnny promised.

Sven looked up, every sense on high alert. "Where are you thinking?"

"You know where." Johnny leaned on one elbow and moved a marker into position over the Mermaid.

The fact that they'd resisted would, under normal circumstances, make him less than enthusiastic about going back. He liked it when his job was nice and easy.

But in the case of that *particular* establishment, he had his own non-professional reasons for looking forward to seeing the place again. And the blonde who worked there.

And if necessary, her precious little motorcycle.

Sven sighed and tried to come up with the words that would dissuade Johnny from this course of action, but he knew he wasn't going to be able to. People like them didn't just give up on things. Whoever that little white girl was, and whoever owned that bar, they'd made the mistake of not just turning Johnny down but insulting him.

You never did that in a situation like this.

Sven knew that if it wasn't Johnny who went to teach them a lesson, it would be someone else. He looked over. "Just don't let the police get wind of it, huh? They've been around more since we touched off our little war."

"I won't." Johnny smiled. "Just me and them. Little chat. We're all gonna be real friendly. I'll hit 'em Friday morning."

CHAPTER TWENTY-THREE

Today was a workday, but having gotten such an early start, Kera wasn't worried about being late. There was plenty of time. Besides, trying to help the wife of one of the nicest men she'd ever met was more important than being one hundred percent certain she'd be her usual five to ten minutes early for clock-in.

She'd rather deal with this today than take the chance of the cancer doing irreversible damage. She knew the spellbook had cautions against this for good reasons, but she couldn't live with herself if she didn't try to help.

Mr. Kim had taken the family car to Kera's warehouse apartment, and he offered to give her a ride. She accepted since it was still only late morning. She had hours until she needed to get ready, so taking Zee in preparation for going straight to the Mermaid seemed pointless.

"Kera," the grocer began as they pulled out onto the street, "I appreciate this. Maybe it's too big a job for you or for anybody, but it is all we can do now. My wife thought you were a nice girl when she met you. She'll be happy to see you, but she's tired and in pain, so please understand that."

Kera nodded, clasping her hands in her lap to keep them from trembling. *Is this the stupidest thing I've ever done?* Out loud, she said, "I understand. Fortunately, performing reiki doesn't require much from the subject. All the work will be on my end, so, um, in theory, she can sleep through the whole thing." She swallowed. "Probably."

It was a short drive, but Kera didn't bother trying to make conversation. She needed to think. There had to be some way to examine Mrs. Kim using magically-augmented perception to determine how bad the cancer was. To figure out if it had gone malignant and was spreading.

Removing the disease was clearly out of the question, but if she could channel the minimum necessary to stop or slow the spread of the tumor or to empower Mrs. Kim's body to fight back more effectively on its own...

There was a chance. There *had to be* a chance.

The car pulled into a small, semi-hidden lot behind the Kim family's store. As they stepped out of the vehicle, Kera assumed that the old man would lead her in via a rear entrance, but he went around to the front and entered the shopping floor as if he were a customer.

Sam was behind the cash register, and he waved at them.

"Keep watch here," Mr. Kim told his son. "We hope this will not take too long. It's to help your mother. Remember that before you think about complaining."

The boy nodded; his face was somber, making him look more mature than his years would suggest. Kera wondered if he knew how bad the cancer diagnosis was and guessed he didn't.

Seeing him, she felt even more obligated to do the right thing.

Kera followed Kim the elder behind the counter, then they walked down a short, rather dim corridor to a staircase sequestered around a corner. The old man ascended first with steady, deliberate steps, and Kera modulated her pace to match his.

Once on the second-floor landing, Kera realized the Kims had managed to hide their home within the store building. She'd suspected as much, but it was difficult to tell from outside.

The place was nice, cozy, clean, and decorated in a tasteful style that blended American and Korean influences.

Mr. Kim turned to her and pointed at a little mat. "For your shoes," he explained.

Kera pulled her boots off and placed them on the mat while he did the same. When they were finished, he led her around another corner to a small living room furnished in warm colors, with a profusion of potted plants arranged in the corners or on shelves. A medium-sized flatscreen television rested against the far wall, currently dark and silent.

On a couch at the side of the room lay Mrs. Kim. Kera sucked in a breath at the sight of her. She looked noticeably unhealthy and looked far worse than the last time the girl had seen her about two months ago when the cancer was either latent or at least far less advanced. Before things had gone wrong enough to seek a diagnosis.

Mr. Kim padded to his wife's side. The woman looked much like he did: wiry, compact, round-faced, and with hair that was mostly gray. Kera was pretty sure the lady's hair had been half-black previously. It was hard to tell if she was asleep or simply resting in a half-conscious state of pain and exhaustion.

"Ye-Jin," the old man began, "Kera is here to see you. Say hello."

Mrs. Kim roused, her housedress rustling as she turned her head to look at Kera with dim, sleepy eyes. Her face was drawn with pain. "Hello, Kera," she said. Her accent was heavier than her husband's. "I hope you are good. Please forgive my appearance. I am not...well."

Mr. Kim took her left hand between both of his, then spoke to his wife softly in Korean. Kera was unfamiliar with the language, but she caught the word "reiki" and watched as the man flexed his hands as if to demonstrate something. Presumably, he was explaining the girl's success with his arthritis and their faint hope that her skills might be able to do something for the poor woman.

From the way she grimaced, it was obvious she didn't have much faith, but after another moment of cajoling, Mrs. Kim lay back and relaxed again while her husband beckoned Kera over.

"The cancer," he said, "is in her colon. She has much pain every day lately. She agreed to let you look her over and do what you can. Please be careful, and let me know if you need anything at all."

The girl tried to smile. "Okay. I'll do what I can. Stick around for a few minutes if you could. Again, I can't promise that this will work, but if it does, it's going to take a lot out of me, so I might need someone to help me up and get me a cappuccino, or something like that."

"Of course," Kim replied. "Anything you need or want."

While Mr. Kim waited and watched, statue-like in his calm patience, Kera examined the woman on the couch, running her hands gently over her abdomen and extending her mind out in the way she had when casting previous enchantments. Under her breath, she spoke the incantation of the first verse of the spell, describing the problem to the forces being invoked.

Or, as she had done earlier today, to *ask* for their help in figuring out what it was.

As the chant reached its end, Kera quickly imposed a sharp mental limit on how much magic was to be worked: only enough to determine the nature and extent of the illness. There would be no healing yet, not until she had a clearer idea.

The subtle tingling warmth and the vague sense that lights were glowing beneath her or in her peripheral vision came back, and a mental picture of the internal workings of the ravaged body before her took shape behind her eyes.

The tumorous growth had indeed gone malignant and was spreading. She didn't know enough about cancer to say whether it was terminal, but the picture that emerged was of a disease that was already serious and growing far worse. Mrs. Kim might have a chance, but *only* if something were done to stop the metastasis and soon.

Kera took a moment to steady herself. A plan had formed in her head, and she nodded as she committed to it.

Okay, she reflected, the book said not to try to cure cancer. What it didn't say was that it was impossible to cure cancer. In other words, it could be done; it was just a really bad idea for a novice, which she definitely was. Then again, she was not going to try to cure it per se. The goal was merely to weaken and delay it. To fortify Mrs. Kim until the treatments could do the rest of the work. She could manage that much, couldn't she?

Since Mrs. Kim had her eyes closed and might have slipped into unconsciousness again, Kera looked at Mr. Kim. "I, uh, I think I may be able to do a little something. Enough to ease her pain slightly and perhaps give her the strength she needs to fight it so it doesn't spread. I've never done anything like this, but it's worth a try. Might help her get through the next few months until she can get in for treatment."

Nothing she'd said was a lie or a distortion. Except that she intended to perform thaumaturgic witchcraft rather than reiki, it was a perfectly honest assessment.

He nodded, and his eyes went past her. "Ye-Jin?"

Kera looked back as Mrs. Kim opened her eyes again and gave a barely noticeable nod.

Kera took a deep breath. She was going to do this, but she estimated that it would take far more energy than she'd ever expended before, including the surge she'd accidentally employed in taking care of Mr. Kim's arthritis.

I need to push back the cancerous cells or kill them while beefing up the healthy ones or convincing the body's immune system to fight it. Something to that effect. Shit, I wish I'd read up on cancer, but I think I get the gist of it.

She turned to Mr. Kim. "I'm going to need a bunch of food and drink. Stuff with lots of calories and energy. Fattening, sugary stuff. Maybe some caffeine, too. It will keep me awake and alert while I do this."

"Yes," he said. "Sam and I will get you as much as you need. I will be right back."

The old man hurried out of the living room and down the stairs. As Kera listened to him leave, she placed her hands back on Mrs. Kim's stomach, inhaled, and got to work.

"Sam!" Mr. Kim barked as he hustled out of the back hallway into the space behind the counter.

His son turned around, startled. "Uh, yes, Dad? What?"

"We need to get some food for Kera. She said lots of calories and caffeine and energy. Anything that can make you fat, grab it and put it in a sack to take up to her. Are there any customers?"

The boy glanced around the floor, then checked the security cameras just to be safe. "No, not at the moment."

"Okay. Close the store for a few minutes, then help me."

Sam rushed to the door to flip the *Yes, We're Open!* sign around to the *Sorry, We're Closed* side while his father unfolded a large paper bag and began stomping through the aisles, heading first for the candy, junk food, and sodas.

Mr. Kim extended his arm and knocked multiple chocolate bars and bags of honey-roasted peanuts into the sack, then added some fattening-looking cheese and pretzel bites before going to the cooler and grabbing a couple cans of cola as well as two energy drinks.

Sam came up behind him. "Uh, want me to hold that?"

"No," Mr. Kim chided him, "get your own sack, boy, and start packing up more food. The more calories, the better."

The younger Kim shrugged and did as he was told, grabbing

the nearest bag and filling it with blocks of cheese, bottles of honey, and packaged muffins, especially the kind that were frosted or contained chocolate chips. Kera didn't look like she ate much of this stuff, but he knew better than to argue when his father used that tone.

Besides, his father looked *hopeful* for the first time since his parents had gotten back from the doctor that morning. They hadn't told Sam what was going on, but he knew it was bad.

He shook his head and tried to focus. "Hey, Dad!" he shouted. "According to this back label, this stuff has five hundred calories per serving. Is that going to be enough?"

"Well," Mr. Kim shot back, "how much is one serving?"

Sam snapped his eyes back to the packaging. "Er, one cup."

"Ha!" His father scoffed. "Eight ounces. That's less than sugar. Unacceptable!"

"Okay," Sam replied, tossing it aside and looking for something worse. "Wait, isn't she also going to need vitamins? Like, uh, B-12, I think. There's a couple of those that people need to stay alert and stuff."

Mr. Kim, who had nearly filled the bag with dry foods and beverages, was about to add a carton of ice cream when he stopped. "Ah, yes, true. We need stuff that is healthy *and* sugary."

Sam snapped his fingers. "Cereal! I'll get a couple boxes."

"Good!" shouted his dad. "I will get the milk. Whole milk! The kind with all the *fat!*"

The boy, nodding as he picked out a couple cartons of quasi-nutritious breakfast goods, was about to suggest chocolate milk instead, but he wondered if that might be overkill.

Not wanting to waste time, Kera had initiated the enchantment while her host went to collect sustenance. She had considered that it might be better to eat first, but that could also make her overconfident about how much energy she had to spend.

She hadn't ever done something like this, and she was doing her best not to kill herself doing it.

That meant she would start small. If even the earliest and most tentative healing efforts wiped her out, she would have learned an important lesson.

Namely, that the task could not be done this way without killing herself.

In which case she'd find another way, she promised silently. She was *not* going to let this family be destroyed.

Kera concentrated and repeated the healing spell's ritualistic chant over and over. Rather than try to channel all of the magical power involved at once, she repeatedly cast the same spell in the smallest quantities she could manage while making any difference.

The room hummed and buzzed and glowed around her, or so it seemed, and the universe's divine powers stayed by her side, working with her but extracting their toll. Each tiny cluster of cancer cells that she killed or immobilized, each section of healthy tissue she cleared of corruption and restored to full health, made her feel as though she'd skipped a meal and tried to run a couple of miles on an empty stomach.

Her consciousness and attention wavered. It was the way she felt at the end of a long, hard workday, and she'd been at it for mere minutes. Not eating before starting had been a mistake.

Kera wondered if this was how diabetics felt when they were about to slip into a coma.

She paused in her medical efforts, noting that Mrs. Kim was unconscious. It was impossible to tell how the older woman was feeling.

Kera realized she'd need other forms of magic to bolster herself. She recalled a simple wake-up spell that, according to the book, had a similar effect on the brain as a cup of coffee or a shot of espresso. The authors had also mentioned some other substance but refused to identify it for legal reasons.

"Okay," the girl breathed, "here goes."

She closed her eyes, twisted her fingers around her temples, and spoke the brief string of words. Instantly it was as though a bright light erupted within her mind, and she went back to her tasks feeling vastly more alert but also strung out. Her hands shook as they passed over Mrs. Kim's abdomen.

She lost track of time. It couldn't have been that long before Mr. Kim and Sam returned with provisions, but it felt as though it had been hours.

"Kera," the old man announced, "we brought you enough fattening and sweet food to send a diabetic into a coma. This should help. Would you like a bowl of cereal?"

Sam set a bag down next to her, and she glanced into it. "Oh, wow!" she exclaimed, trying not to giggle stupidly, "Red Bull! I haven't had that crap since the last time I did Jaeger Bombs. Fuck, I love those things. That was during Spring Break in 2019, which I really shouldn't have gone on instead of studying, but you know how college kids are, and my friends basically peer-pressured me into it anyway, which was really funny since I technically couldn't legally drink at the time, not like anyone gave a shit, ha-ha." She shut her mouth, realizing that she was babbling. "But yeah, this all looks great! Goddamn, I'm hungry. And thirsty!"

The words came out of her mouth so fast she was amazed she didn't misspeak. Her trembling hand shot out and snatched one of the energy drinks, cracked it open, and brought it to her lips with feverish haste.

Mr. Kim stared at her wide-eyed. "Uh, are you sure you need that? Did you eat something before we came here? You did not, um," he coughed, "go into my bathroom with a razor blade and a small mirror, did you?"

Kera gave a laugh that was tinged with hysteria. "Nope, promise. Just…a little overtired." She had to admit, the question was warranted.

Mr. Kim waved his hand and dismissed Sam, who headed back downstairs to reopen the store and man the register.

The old man waited by her side, watching with concern as Kera replicated the process of healing his wife a little bit at a time, taking short breaks after each brief session to scarf a bowl of sugary cereal, a peanut butter and honey sandwich, a couple bags of snacks laden with orange cheese-like substance, and greasy muffins.

Each time she went back, she could see progress.

I think it's working! Kera could hardly contain her excitement, her brain blazing and reeling as it rode the energy rollercoaster, its functionality plummeting with each re-casting of the spell and then blasting back upward as she devoured junk and washed it down with caffeine. *I'm cutting the tumor off. The bastard isn't going to get bigger anytime soon. Hah!*

"Okay," she gasped as the process reached its end, "believe it or not, I think I might have improved things a little for your wife." She paused to down a candy bar filled with nuts and caramel, trying not to unhinge her jaw like a snake. "Wasn't easy, but I suspect I slowed the metastasis down, and she won't have as much pain."

Mr. Kim came up beside her and gazed at his spouse, his jaw slack. "Her skin looks better. Not so unhealthy. Maybe it's just wishful thinking, but your reiki worked so good on my hands that I believe you *did* help. If that is true…" His mouth trembled, and he turned away.

To give him privacy, Kera rustled loudly through snacks and ate two more candy bars.

"Kera."

She looked up and swallowed a giant mouthful of honey-roasted peanuts.

Luckily, Mr. Kim didn't notice her disheveled chipmunk-like

appearance. He was smiling. "I can't thank you enough," he said quietly.

Kera shook her head. Her head was swimming, but she was sure she just needed a bit more candy. "Thanks."

Wait, was she supposed to say that? Or…

She was still considering it when she passed out.

CHAPTER TWENTY-FOUR

She had no idea how much time passed before she awoke to the sound of her phone beeping and Mr. Kim shaking her shoulders.

"Kera! Your boss tried to call. That man 'Seven' from the bar, he is your boss, right? That's what your phone said."

She groaned and straightened herself. "It's pronounced like 'Kevin,' but yeah. Wait, what time is it? *Shit*! Sorry for my language, Mr. Kim, it's just..."

Just that it was 3:27, and she was half an hour late for work.

The girl sprang to her feet, wobbling and holding her head, as Mr. Kim came up beside her to take her arm and steady her.

"I am so sorry," he said. "I didn't know you worked tonight, or I would have gotten you up. You slept for about an hour and a half, and I thought I should let you rest. My wife is sleeping also. She seems much more peaceful."

Kera's thoughts crashed into each other within her skull, and she tried to impose order on them and get herself thinking rationally again like a good computer science major.

"Uh, yes. Okay. Thanks. Sorry." She winced at how stupid she sounded right now. "Could I have a cup of coffee or something? And I'll need a ride back home. My place is on the way to the

Mermaid anyway, and I need to grab some things. Cevin isn't going to be happy." She did a double-take at the look on the man's face. "But it was worth it to help your wife," she assured him.

She just needed to get a handle on herself so she didn't tell Cevin to stuff it. "I'm so sorry" would probably be better.

Mr. Kim helped her downstairs and had Sam fetch her a tall, steaming cup from the coffee station, which he brought down to a drinkable temperature by adding ice from the soda machine. Kera accepted it, thanked him, and gulped down half the cup as quickly as possible.

"Come," said the old man. "I can take you home right now. I will let you know tomorrow how Ye-Jin is. Even if nothing changed inside her, I think it did her good to see you again."

As they drove back to the warehouse, Kera felt normal mental function return, partly because her brief sleep was departing, partly thanks to the extra caffeine. Still, that dogged and oppressive sense of tiredness hung over her.

Work was *not* going to be fun.

Mr. Kim waited outside the warehouse while Kera hurriedly got ready for work. As she threw on her leathers, backpack, and helmet, the old man knocked on her front door.

She opened it for him.

"Will you be okay to drive yourself?" he asked. "I can give you a ride, but you may have to get a co-worker to bring you home at the end of the night."

She waved a hand. "Yes, I'll be fine." Changing and getting ready for work had shown her that she had the balance and reflexes to handle Zee. "Thanks, though. I appreciate the offer."

He nodded and gave her a subtle yet warm smile. "You are very welcome. It's the least I can do. Take care."

Kera gave him a hug and wished him farewell. A minute after his car departed, she buzzed down the road in the opposite direction astride Zee.

Oh, man, she moaned to herself, *maybe I should have let him drive me to the bar, after all. I think I'm okay for now, but how the hell will I be at 2 am?*

While she rode down the streets, she cast another wakefulness spell on herself, followed by a luck spell, hoping it would last through the whole evening.

Of course, the good part is that I'm over an hour late, so my shift will be that much shorter. Har, har. Small comfort when Cevin is probably going to chew my ass out over this.

She didn't think he'd fire her, but there was no way to be sure.

Maybe I'll get a different job after all, Mom.

She felt better by a small margin as she parked and locked her bike and swung through the back door. Riding Zee through the breeze had refreshed her in a way nothing else could.

Cevin said nothing as she rushed to punch in. He was glowering in an unpleasant way but seemed satisfied for the moment with her being present.

Of course, with the other employees, it was another story. She still had a tremble in her hands, and while she had managed to replace some of her energy by eating all that food, neither the process nor the food had been *good* for her. Her coworkers noticed.

"So, who's Mr. Right? Or should I say, Mr. Right Now? Ha-ha."

"What'd you take, Kera? Couldn't have been legal if it was *that* good."

"You know, I thought about taking a day off once too. Then I grew up and got a job. Still, last night must have been tons of fun, am I right?"

All the sorts of comments she expected and was in no particular mood or condition to deal with. She grimaced, pretended to smile, told people to shut up in a half-serious tone, and gritted her teeth whenever no one was looking.

It's going to be a long, long night, she surmised. *And if Chris comes back, it'll be at the worst possible time. Dammit.*

Stephanie was less obnoxious than the others, though given her curious nature, she was obviously waiting for a big revelation as to what the hell had broken Kera's perfect attendance record. She took her break before Kera did, and when she returned, she brought her friend another cup of coffee from a nearby drive-through.

"Thanks, Stephanie," Kera said gratefully. "It's been a while since I've needed this much coffee."

The other woman laughed. "Oh, I noticed. Never seen you drink it before. When the time's right, of course, we all want to hear the story."

"Yeah, whatever," Kera grumbled. She didn't feel like telling the story yet. Maybe tomorrow, but not today.

A patron came up to the bar, and she set her paper cup down on the back counter to serve him his drink. He must have noticed that she looked tired and crabby since he politely stuck to ordering his beverage and didn't try to converse or flirt.

Fortunately, Chris never showed up.

The night dragged to a close, with Kera wondering how she was still standing as the bar announced last call and the final customers filtered out into the street.

Cevin approached her. "You can't drive like this," he stated, looking her over.

"What?" she protested. "Yes, I can. I'm..." She stumbled and braced herself against the bar. "*Mostly* fine."

The boss shook his head. "No, you're not, and after what happened previously, I don't think you should leave your bike here either. Come on, I'll help you load it into the back of my truck, and then I'll take you home."

They locked everything up, checked the security cams, and headed out into the back lot. It was empty and quiet.

Kera did little. She tried, but Cevin had to do most of the

work of hauling Zee into the bed of his vehicle. As they climbed into the cab, it occurred to her that she owed too many favors to the people she knew.

Her boss piloted the truck out onto the road and headed toward her home.

"Okay, Kera." Cevin sighed, "I can see that you're not in any condition to talk about things in detail. Let's just say that this shouldn't happen again, right?"

She nodded and rubbed her eyes. "I completely agree."

"Good. You've been a good employee so far. As long as this was a one-off incident, I don't see any reason to get upset over it."

Kera scowled out the window but didn't protest. He was, if anything, being lenient with her.

Once they arrived back at her place and had Zee inside, Cevin gave her a final wave from the truck. "Goodnight. And if you need help, ask for it. See you soon."

Kera waved back and locked the door. She barely made it to bed and was unconscious within seconds of striking the mattress.

"Whuhh!" Kera grunted, flinging sheets around as she thrashed up into a sitting position.

Someone was knocking on her door, and according to her alarm clock, it was 1:58 pm.

"Oh, God," she gasped. She had come awake too quickly.

The knock came again. Struggling to her feet, she threw on a light bathrobe and scampered toward the door, shouting, "I'm coming! One minute!"

When she reached the window and checked, it wasn't a delivery driver. It was Sam Kim.

Kera threw the door open. "Hi, Sam. Sorry, I just woke up. How are, uh, things?"

The boy smiled, and for a second, it looked like he might

blush at the sight of her in a bathrobe. "Things are pretty good. Mom is feeling a little better, so that's, um, great. But yeah, Dad wanted me to bring you this."

He'd carried a tray all the way to her warehouse, and she realized it was piled with prepared Korean food covered with plastic wrap. Wisps of steam rose from it, and it smelled divine.

"Oh, man!" Kera exclaimed. "I think that's exactly what I need right now. Thanks." She accepted the tray and brought it in to set it on her table while Sam waited awkwardly on the doorstep.

He cleared his throat. "There's no charge for that, of course. My dad was worried about you. He said I should stay for five minutes or however long you wanted to make sure that you could eat a decent meal before you had to go in to your job. He also said to let him know when you're feeling better."

Kera decided she needed to guzzle some water, but aside from that... "I'm feeling pretty okay for the moment, thanks to him and you. I know you helped yesterday also."

"You're welcome." Sam shrugged. "So, is there anything else you need?"

The girl glanced up and caught a glimpse of her reflection in the shiny surface of her fridge, with the mop of night-black hair standing out.

"Nah," she told the boy. "Unless you have a blonde wig I can borrow."

Sam shot her a look of puzzled concern. "A wig? No, sorry, I don't."

She got up and waved her hand. "Joke. It's a joke. We females have a thing about our hair. Like, if there was a way to flip a switch and change the color from day to day—or better yet, hour to hour—that would be way better. Anyway, thanks again. Bye."

She saw him out and nodded as he waved at her and trudged down the sidewalk toward his family's store.

Kera sat down to eat her meal, savoring every bite and half-hoping the Kims would invite her to dinner in the future. If not, she might have to start hitting up Korean restaurants. There wasn't exactly a shortage of them in Los Angeles.

Since she'd slept well, she found herself feeling mostly back to normal after a little relaxation and a hot shower. She wasn't scheduled to be at the Mermaid until six today. When the time came to get ready for work, she swelled with confidence that everything would go well. She intended to more than make up for the near-fiasco of yesterday.

If Mrs. Kim was any better, it was worth all the misery and inconvenience. Anyway, she would definitely take the leathers tonight. It was supposed to rain.

The weather had been unusually drizzly lately. L.A. still had far less precipitation than she'd been used to back east, but rain was by no means nonexistent. Of course, summer would be on its way soon, and everyone would remember that they lived near the edge of a subtropical desert.

As she mounted her bike, she wondered idly if there were spells to control the weather.

CHAPTER TWENTY-FIVE

James Lovecraft and Mother LeBlanc walked side-by-side down the paved walk. When someone else strolled by, they fell into single file, trading positions based on who was closer to being out front.

There was a school up ahead. Classes had let out a few minutes ago, and since it seemed to be a tight-knit neighborhood where many of the kids walked to and from school, many of them had lingered to make use of the recreational equipment, harass each other, or prepare for curated after-school activities of some sort.

James adjusted his glasses. "You or me?"

LeBlanc responded, "I'll do it. You'll look like a child-stalker."

He tried to argue but she waved him off, her expression and demeanor indicating that it would be pointless to waste her time. In near-perfect unison, the pair sat down on a bench across from the main building.

Their guess was that the person involved was either a teacher or a student at this school since it was one of the common threads in their research. LeBlanc stared at the edifice, her gaze steady and unblinking. Seconds turned to minutes, and her eyes grew unfocused, hazy, and vacant. She did not move, and her breathing had grown so shallow that she seemed catatonic.

James was not fazed. All he had to do was keep an eye out for anyone who might notice how strange the woman looked.

Such as the young, pudgy-cheeked black kid approaching them right now.

Shit, James thought. *It won't be the first time, though.* Children seemed to notice far more than adults.

The kid, who had to have been in whatever the youngest grade at the school was, squinted at the witch-woman, then turned to James. "She okay?" he inquired.

"LB?" James gestured at her as though he could have meant anyone else. "Oh, yeah, she's fine. Occasionally, you see," he leaned forward, put a hand beside his mouth, and spoke in a whisper that was about the same volume as his normal voice, "she just wanders off in her head. You know what I mean?"

The boy looked skeptical but nodded.

James went on. "I stay with her when she gets like this and keep an eye on her so she doesn't walk away. See, last time she did this, the poor woman almost stumbled right onto some railroad tracks at the exact moment a train was coming! I was off volunteering at the local animal shelter—I can only be in one place at a time, after all— when I noticed her, and at the last minute, took a heroic dive and knocked her out of the way of the train. 'Oh, thank you, J,' she said, and ever since then, she's trusted me to keep watch over her when she has her little 'episodes' and doesn't have her pills on hand."

By the time he finished his anecdote, the kid's attention had turned to LeBlanc. James looked at her and saw that her eyes had returned to normal.

"Oh, she's back!" Lovecraft exclaimed. "There. Everything's fine."

LeBlanc swiveled her head toward him. The look on her face was only an iota short of a legitimate Evil Eye spell. "What did you say? I need your attention to *protect* me, all of a sudden? More often, it seems to be the other way around."

James coughed. "You heard that?"

"Mmhmm." She continued to eye him with concentrated malevolence.

He leaned toward the kid, who'd continued to watch them both in fascinated confusion. "You better run along," he told the boy. "She's dangerous."

"Dangerous?" the kid repeated, glancing at the witch-woman. He was so perplexed by their behavior that James was pretty sure he'd accidentally piqued the boy's curiosity.

He clarified, flicking his eyes toward LeBlanc, "Well, dangerous to *me*. Not so much to you. Nonetheless, if I scream, find an adult and have them call 911." At this point, he couldn't suppress a grin.

Mother LeBlanc relaxed her expression a notch, then looked at the boy and smiled. "Don't worry, I won't do anything too awful to him with you around. I'll just make him cry. He likes it. Don't you?"

It was James' turn to swivel his head in consternation. "I like it?"

The kid interrupted them. "You two are best friends, ain't you? I hear stories about older people who argue all the time, but they're really best friends."

James bristled. "I'm young," he pointed out. "*She's* the older one."

"Older?" LeBlanc asked dangerously. "Well, maybe this older woman is going to beat your scrawny white–"

"*Nah-ah!*" James interjected, waving a finger at their audience. "Young ears don't need to hear such filth."

Mother LeBlanc sighed and caught the boy's attention again. "Sweetie, would you run along so I can make him cry? Like I said, he likes it. Trust me." She winked.

"Yes, ma'am," the boy said. He added, "You two are funny as hell." He scampered off.

When LeBlanc returned her attention to James, however, his eyes had gone out of focus in much the same way hers had a couple minutes earlier. "What are you doing, James?"

His vision returned to normal with a swiftness that bordered on abrupt. He smirked. "I was looking for a miracle, and I got one. Our kid is over there." He nodded in the appropriate direction.

The witch-woman looked toward the child he'd indicated, and she did a quick mental scan of her own to confirm it.

"Well," she conceded, "aren't you lucky today?" She stood up, brushing off and gathering her colorful flowing skirts, and James got to his feet beside her.

He offered his elbow. "Shall we?"

She accepted it but said, "Yes. But next time, I'll give you a sound whooping with a switch if you tell a young kid that I need your help to keep from wandering onto train tracks. Lord have mercy!"

CHAPTER TWENTY-SIX

"Zee!" The woman named Sara laughed and slapped the surface of the bar. "You named it *Zee!* Oh my God, I love it. Honey, did you hear that?"

Her boyfriend, Maurice, chortled into his whiskey and Coke. "I heard it. You said you spelled it out? That makes all the difference. Like, it's not as funny if it's just the letter."

Kera smiled. "Well, I went to college with this chick from Australia, and apparently everyone else pronounces it—the last letter of the alphabet, I mean—'zed.' I never knew that. Fucks up the rhyming scheme of the 'A, B, C' song, doesn't it? Anyway, I named the bike in honor of weird American pronunciation."

Sara laughed again and hoisted her screwdriver in the air. "I'll drink to that. Here's to doing all kinds of shit differently than the rest of the world. An American tradition!"

They raised their glasses in a brief toast and drained them. Kera wasn't supposed to drink on the job, so she did the bartenders' trick of making a fake shot. A lot of customers wanted to drink *with* the bartender, and they were usually so nice about it that she didn't want to disappoint them.

It had been a fun night, and thus far, Sara and Maurice were among her favorite new customers. Not only were they nice—and inclined to tip generously—but they were fellow motorcycle enthusiasts. Obviously they rode bikes, and they ran a shop together that created custom rides. Maurice had slipped Kera a business card about ten minutes ago.

As much as she was enjoying her job for the moment, though, she was a little down. Something within her gnawed at her heart, a faint but persistent disappointment. Stupid as it was, she could identify it. Christian still hadn't shown up. Hadn't he said he'd be back soon?

Calm down, Kera, she told herself. He's an office drone, and it's Thursday. He probably can't afford to go out drinking on weekdays most of the time. Wait and see if he shows up tomorrow or maybe Saturday, and we'll go from there.

She didn't know why she wanted to see him again so badly. Her life had been strange and hectic lately, and her time so consumed with both work and her continuing education in the arts of thaumaturgy that she hadn't had enough time alone with her thoughts to examine them in detail.

She worked her way down the bar, checking on patrons, refilling drinks, and taking orders from people who'd just sidled up.

"So, Kera," Sara called once she drifted back toward them, "as a fellow biker, what are your thoughts on you-know-who?"

Kera frowned. She felt as though she ought to grasp what the hell the other woman was talking about, but she was stumped. "Uh," she countered, "no offense, but I *don't* know who. Sorry?" Hopefully, she added, "You mean, the Harry Potter character?"

Sara laughed it off, and Maurice picked up the slack.

"The mystery rider on the I-10 the other day."

Kera made a noncommittal noise and turned back to her work, hoping they hadn't seen the look on her face.

"Didn't you hear about that?" Maurice pivoted on his stool to look at her with interest. "He pulled a family out of a burning car after they crashed, then drove off before anyone could get a name or a picture. Hell of a thing, but I have noticed that people have been looking at us a little different since then. In a good way. Guy gives us all a good name with his heroics, I'll say that much. A lot of people still think all bikers are scumbags and criminals, but maybe that's changing."

"Oh. Yeah." Kera swallowed and shot a look over her shoulder. "I did hear about that briefly. Was busy at the time, so I guess I didn't delve into the details. Nice to have a good story on the news for once, I guess." Was she talking too much? She concentrated on scrubbing a table.

"The news was all over it," Sara elaborated. "He still hasn't come forward, and the family has been asking all over social media. They want to know who it was so they can at least thank him."

Kera thought of something then. To both cover for herself and gather information while she was at it, she queried, "Did they get a description of the bike?"

"Pffft." Sara snorted. "Nah, not really. None of the witnesses were the types who'd notice. Granted, they were busy making sure the people in the car were okay."

Maurice concurred. "If it had been us, we could have IDed it out of the corners of our eyes while checking those folks over, but most people can't. All I ever heard was someone said 'it was black.'" He cracked up and pushed his glass toward the bartender.

Kera refilled it with three fingers of whiskey and topped it off with Coke. "Black, eh? Well, that's a start."

Sara snapped her fingers. "I think someone did say it was a Kawasaki, but they couldn't tell anything else beyond that. I mean, that narrows it down *slightly*."

Brushing a strand of hair away from her face, Kera added, "That means they had good taste, whoever they were."

Maurice leaned forward and squinted at her sidelong, his lips pressed together in a weird expression. "It wasn't *you*, was it?"

Kera froze in place, but the biker burst out laughing again, and she let herself relax. Artfully, she sighed and shook her head. "No, Maurice, but thanks for your assessment that I look like a man. I was off that day. And, uh, didn't that happen way out by Culver City? I live downtown." *Shut up, shut up, stop babbling!*

"Whatever." Sara scoffed. "We'll just say he was, like, the incarnate spirit of every decent, law-abiding motorcycle enthusiast who ever got ogled like they were getting ready to rob a store."

Kera had been ogled before, but she was pretty sure it wasn't because people thought she was a criminal. "Well, I think we can all agree that if any of us sees someone in trouble, we'll try to help."

Maurice raised his newly-replenished drink. "Amen."

A little later, Kera found herself serving another pair farther down the bar. She could tell they weren't an established couple, though they seemed to be hitting it off. The woman was thirtyish, petite, attractive, and nicely dressed. The man was a good fifteen years older than her but obviously a committed bodybuilder, and dressed as though he'd come to the Mermaid straight from the gym.

The man motioned to Kera. "Beers," he stated.

"Coming right up." Kera grabbed Buds for them both and set them on the bar.

There was a lull in business for a couple minutes then. Listening to the seemingly mismatched would-be couple, Kera learned that the woman had a Ph.D. in Ecological Science.

A minute later, the big guy got up and excused himself to go to the restroom, leaving his half-drained bottle behind him.

Kera had turned to check on the bar's supply of available ingredients when Ph.D. Lady said to her, "I bet you're wondering what a smart lady like me is doing talking to a guy like him, right?"

Judging from her slurred tone, the beer had sent her well into the proverbial bag. She'd had a Tequila Slammer beforehand, and she didn't look like she weighed more than a hundred and ten pounds.

Kera turned to the woman. "Should I be wondering?" she inquired. Her eyes moved toward the bathroom, where the man had temporarily vanished.

The lady flapped her hand, dismissing the half-rhetorical question.

"I get all the brainpower-intensive problems I can handle at work," she drawled, "trying to clean up the State of California's messes and keep overdevelopment from killing every goddamn species that isn't homo sapiens. But when I'm done? Hell, no. I don't need any more intellectual stimulation."

She laughed and took another gulp of beer. Kera hung nearby, curious.

"No," Ph.D. Lady continued, "off-duty, I'm ready for some nice simple conversation and a night of quality humping. And let me tell you, sister," she nodded, "muscular guys have all the energy that's required. God, I'm going to be *so* sore all weekend!" She broke off, tittering, but forced herself back to composure as her suitor returned from the men's room.

Kera laughed along, but once she was able to get away from the pair, she rolled her eyes. "Man, older people! What the heck do they do with their lives? They're acting more like kids than I do."

The night proceeded with no sign of Chris. Business was steady but by no means overwhelming, and Kera racked up a decent haul in tips by the time 2:00 rolled around. She announced last call and served the final drinks, then helped Cevin shoo off the stragglers so they could close up shop.

In addition to the manager, Kera, Stephanie, and one other bartender were still present.

"Okay, everyone," Cevin announced, "Friday is payday, and it's technically Friday, so those of you who are here can have your checks now. Unless you want to come in for them tomorrow if you're not working, I guess."

No one did, of course, so he handed them out. Kera was last in line, and Cevin motioned for her to wait and listen once she'd accepted hers.

"Yes?" she asked.

Cevin waited as the others filed out.

"You might remember that when I gave you a few days off," he said quietly, "after your bike got shot up, I said I felt bad and that I'd compensate you for the time you couldn't work. Well, I'm as good as my word, and your check for this pay period reflects that. I figure it's only fair since in this town, being more than twenty-four hours without a ride is like being on crutches or something. Consider it a settlement for all your trouble."

Kera had pretty much forgotten about that with everything else going on lately. "Oh, yeah, right. Thanks, Cevin. It'll help. And I'm sorry about yesterday. I got wrapped up trying to help a friend after I forgot to sleep, and I passed out like an idiot. It won't happen again."

Cevin locked up the cash register. "Sounds good. I saw how tired you were, and you did a pretty good job regardless. Judging by what your apartment looked like, I can tell it wasn't because you were, y'know, getting into trouble. I can tell when someone's been on a bender, and you look pretty straight-laced."

Kera mock-glared, her hands going to her hips. "Oh, really? How would you know that?" She wasn't angry, but she felt obliged to fuck with him if he was going to say something like that. "For all you know, I might have had a wild party with dozens of different drugs, three guys at once..."

He didn't look at her, just chuckled. "As long as you keep coming to work, it's none of my business. If that's what you want to do, it's your call."

Finished with his final chores, he walked past her and motioned for her to follow as he did a final scan of the security cams and double-checked a couple of things in his office.

Kera wasn't finished. "It *isn't* what I want to do, but I'm not boring."

He glanced at her with an arched eyebrow. "Never said you were."

Kera followed as he opened the rear door. "You kinda *did*, dude. 'Oh, Kera, she's so straight-laced, she never does anything exciting.'"

"Mmm," Cevin murmured. He scanned the parking lot, decided the coast was clear, and they stepped out. "Let the record show that *you* were the one who decided to read into my words. If you want to have wild orgies with multiple guys and a pile of drugs, that's fine, but don't do it because you're trying to be interesting."

She scowled, annoyed that they were seconds away from their respective vehicles since she felt like there was a good five minutes' worth of argument remaining, maybe more. She decided to flip the script on him this time.

"*Hey*," she riposted, "maybe I meant platonically. Like, having dudes come over to watch car shows or something."

Cevin stopped and turned to stare at her.

"What?" she asked.

He shook his head and smiled, looking vaguely wistful. "Never stop being so naïve. It looks cute on you."

She smacked his shoulder. "Does my paycheck include mental-health hazard pay? It should."

"No." He pulled his truck keys out of his pocket. "I'd have to take money out. Oh, just so you know, I'll be moving everyone to electronic deposit starting next week. The bank finally cleared me to do that."

Kera snorted. "After eighteen months?"

Cevin opened his driver's side door. "It's been an affair to remember," he admitted. "And perhaps I was a little lazy. A little. Goodnight."

Kera watched him climb into the truck and fire up the engine, then decided it was time to do the same with her bike. She'd been engrossed in their little discussion, but with Cevin gone, there was no reason for her to hang around a dark parking lot in the wee hours of the morning.

Especially not this one.

For the first time in a while, life seemed halfway normal. As she rode, Kera let herself relax. Every time she went into the alley to get Zee, she remembered her confrontation with the asshole.

You need to let it go, she told herself. *The memories will fade with time.*

But it bothered her. She hadn't been able to stand her ground when he attacked them, and it was only luck on her end that he'd shot Zee instead of her. *She* couldn't be repaired as easily.

As she'd found when she took on the jerks trying to steal the Mercedes, she was far from being a vigilante superhero. Even with her augmented luck, she hadn't beaten them as handily as she wanted to.

It could have gone very wrong.

Healing people is good enough, she told herself. It was safer. Most people never got the chance to do something like help someone fight cancer or pull people out of a burning wreck. If Kera played her cards right, she had a long life ahead of her, full of events like that.

She ignored the nagging sense that it wasn't enough. It had felt good to help Mrs. Kim, not to mention the people in the burning car, but something in her rebelled at the idea that she wouldn't even *try* to stop injustice.

She clenched her jaw and tried to relax. When she was home with the door locked behind her and her leathers off, she looked at herself in the bathroom mirror.

"It's enough," she told herself. "Don't get in over your head."

But something in her recognized that she wasn't going to be able to rest until she knew she wasn't helpless.

CHAPTER TWENTY-SEVEN

It had not been a good morning.

James and LeBlanc walked slowly back down the sidewalk toward James's parked Rolls Royce. James hated this particular part of his job, and he suspected his companion did as well. Magic was rare, rare enough to bind those who practiced it into a tight-knit group, and powerful enough that they had to be careful about who could wield it.

When someone had the aptitude but lacked the other qualities they needed, certain measures had to be taken.

They had found the boy and confirmed that his capabilities were not a fluke. In fact, he demonstrated a lot of power and potential.

But he'd been unable to control it and was too willful and abrasive. He'd shown a marked tendency to ignore suggestions and instructions and rebel against them out of spite. Someone like that couldn't be trusted with the abilities of a miracle-worker.

Lovecraft and LeBlanc had been left with no choice but to bind his powers, so they had collaborated on a spell that would defeat any further effusions of magic he might attempt and block him from learning more or advancing as a thaumaturgist. It was tragic and in some ways, a violation, but the danger was too great. The boy was a danger to others and himself. That didn't make it easier.

Lovecraft shook his head. "Such potential." He sighed.

"I know," LeBlanc said quietly, "but it wouldn't have worked. We both know that. That boy's power had a leak, and he was too stubborn to learn. If all that magical force were to crack on him during his training, it could kill him. Maybe other people, too."

James made a fist for a second, then released it. "I just hate that our first one out of this process had to be *dampened*. So discouraging."

His shoulders slumped another notch. Willow trees swayed in the warm spring breeze as the thaumaturgists trudged along. The afternoon was fading to evening, with the light gaining that bronzed quality James had always found oddly bittersweet.

His dejection must have been even more obvious than he'd guessed since Mother LeBlanc made a small, comforting sound in her throat and put a hand on his arm.

"There, there, James," she said, and there was no sarcasm or irony in her tone. "We were both looking forward to this. We've needed new students to continue our tradition for a long time, but it's always been an uncertain business, hasn't it? Realistically, what with so many new prospects in such a short time, we couldn't have expected to find one who'd work for us right out of the gate. This was only the first try. There will be others."

He sighed. "Yeah, I suppose you're right. I just wish you weren't. No offense."

"None taken." She gave his arm a final pat and walked around to the passenger's side of the car, their trudge down the sidewalk having reached its end. "As long as your qualms are with reality and not with me."

He smiled.

Once they both were within the car, James slumped in his seat, and his head drooped forward to rest against the steering wheel. He let out his breath in a long, slow, rattling sound of defeat.

"Where to next?" Mother LeBlanc asked briskly. "There was another candidate in South Carolina, wasn't there?

Making a faint grumbling noise, James checked his tablet, where he'd marked the locations of their prospects.

"Uh, not far. Looks like somewhere around Morris Island."

LeBlanc gave a slow nod and the hint of a smile. "Any good barbecue down there?" She closed the door beside her and folded her hands in her lap, smoothing out the wafting folds of her dress.

"Oh!" James raised an eyebrow and perked up as suddenly as if she'd stuck a hypodermic needle filled with caffeine in his arm. "I believe I heard that Melvin's Legendary BBQ is down that way. Come to think of it," he adjusted his glasses, "maybe we can get a solid lead *and* a solid dinner."

The witch-woman conceded the point but allowed her tone of voice to grow sterner and more serious. "Perhaps. Yet, what are we going to do when we find someone we *can* teach who isn't a grown adult? This isn't the nineteenth century."

James flapped a hand in annoyance as he fired up the engine. "Let's worry about that when we come to it. Besides, if our first effort was a fair indication, we might not have to worry about it for quite some time."

"Don't be negative," LeBlanc chided. "One dead end doesn't mean that *every* end will be equally dead. We might well run through a hundred opportunities in search of the right one to bring into the fold, and it will be well worth it."

As Lovecraft checked the street and piloted the Rolls into it, he could only mutter, "If they don't have their power crack, then yeah."

His partner shook her head. "I wouldn't want that for anyone." She reached into her skirt. "Would you like a croissant?"

James glanced at the flaky golden pastry resting in LeBlanc's hand and wondered as he turned right at the next intersection, "How the hell do you keep them *warm*?"

CHAPTER TWENTY-EIGHT

Ted nudged Christian with his elbow. "So, are we doing this tonight?"

Christian looked at him vaguely. He was still coming back to reality after an excessively long All Staff meeting that had included satellite offices and some executives from New York.

Their weekly department meetings were a horror show, but *this* had been a two-hour snooze-fest, punctuated with corporate speak and exhortations comparing their work to war.

Christian had never been deployed, but he was fairly sure his work in a cubicle in no way compared to charging into battle.

"Dude." Ted plucked Christian's mug out of his fingers and filled it from the machine. "Wake up. Did you go into standby or something? Is that an IT trick? Can you teach me?"

"God, I wish." Christian held up the mug. "Thanks. Cheers." He sipped. "And, sorry, what? Are we doing what tonight?"

"Going back to the Mermaid," Ted said, enunciating each word carefully as if explaining a concept to a toddler.

"Oh." Christian put the cup on the table nearby. "I don't...meh."

"Dude." Ted pointed at one of the chairs, indicating that

Christian should sit down, then sat in another. "You want to see her again, right?"

"I mean, yeah, but—"

"And you realize the odds of that are low if you, I don't know, don't go back."

"Yes." Christian had to admit his friend had a point.

"You didn't go back too soon and get all stalker-y. That's good," Ted said encouragingly. "You just gotta close this."

"Why did you have to say that?"

"Say what?"

"'Close this.' I don't do well with that stuff. Trust me. I subscribed to GQ for a full year. None of it *ever* worked for me."

"I see." Ted sipped his coffee. "So, I'm misremembering the part where you wandered into a bar and talked IT crap with a goddess and she remembered you, remembered your favorite beer, and wants to see you again."

"Uh…" Christian was certain this was a trap, but he didn't know how to avoid it.

"My *point* is," Ted said, "call it what you want, but you've done well. You trusted me enough to go in and talk to her, and that went great, right? Trust me one more time."

Christian heaved a deep, put-upon sigh. "You're only saying this now because you know I'm not all there after that meeting."

"Maybe." Ted grinned. "So, I ask again…are we doing this tonight?" He stared Christian down.

There was no getting out of this without agreeing. Christian sighed again and took a gulp of his coffee, delaying as long as he could. He'd been enjoying the idea that he could go into the bar again and get Kera's number.

The fantasies might not be as good as the real thing, but if he struck out, he was going to have to give up even those.

It was a good thing Ted was relentless.

Christian nodded. "Fine. We're doing this."

"Atta boy." Ted clapped him on the shoulder and stood up. "See you at six."

Johnny's Mustang crept slowly down the street. He made no particular effort to be inconspicuous, but he didn't do anything that would draw attention to himself either. This was one of the few times he *didn't* want to be noticed.

He turned into the alley and crept by slowly, seeing no one around, then turned down the main street, peering down the alley as he passed.

It was about 10:15 in the morning, not an hour when most bars were bustling. As Johnny understood it, some owners would show up early, especially on or right before the weekends to get everything ready for the peak business to come.

He didn't see anyone, but he decided to do a walk by as well. He parked a few streets away and came back, making sure not to look like he was hurrying. Under his jacket, the Beretta felt good and solid in its shoulder holster. He doubted he'd need to use it this time since using it the *first* time had made the point. Still, though the gun's existence would be presumed any time he showed up, it would be foolish *not* to have it.

He peered in the windows a couple of times, but there was no sound or light or movement from the building. If by some chance the cops, private security, or a concerned citizen popped up, he would just say he was a salesman hoping the Mermaid's proprietor was around.

But no one noticed, and no one was there.

"Lazy *chingado,*" Johnny muttered. "Who doesn't work their own bar in the morning?"

He shut up before he allowed himself to say anything more. They'd probably replaced their security cameras, he realized, and there was a chance there were some around the rest of the building that recorded audio as well as video.

Granted, there wasn't much risk now. They hadn't gotten a good look at him the last time he'd been here, and he was wearing massive sunglasses. He'd parked his car in a different lot the night he'd made his initial offer, so there was no way they could associate his Mustang with that little event.

Still, risk or not, it bothered him to have wasted a trip.

"Well," he said as he headed back to his vehicle, "let it be said that I *tried* to do this the polite way and keep it out of everyone else's hair."

He gave one last look over his shoulder at the Mermaid. For a place he'd pegged as second-tier, it had cost him a lot of trouble.

That would end tonight.

Kera's phone rang at 11:00. She saw the clock before she saw the screen, and therefore did not bother asking who it was as she sat up in bed and put the phone to her ear.

"Hello, *Mother*," she said through a mouth sticky and muffled from sleep.

"Hello, Kera." Even accounting for the time difference, the other woman sounded disgustingly energetic. "How are you doing, dear? I hope you're getting up earlier. It's not natural for human beings to wake up after noon, regardless of what work schedule they're on."

Kera rubbed crust from her eye. "Well, today I got up earlier than usual."

"Oh, good." Her mother was either oblivious to the joke or ignoring it. "Anyway, I've been waiting to hear from you about that old college flame you mentioned, but I haven't heard a peep. Has he looked you up again? It was a week ago last night, wasn't it?"

It was very like her mother to have noted the exact day, Kera thought. "Yes. As in, yes, it was a week ago. And he's not an old flame, he's an old *classmate*."

"He looked you up," her mother pointed out.

"He came into the bar. That's not the same."

"Kera, I'm not trying to pester you, and I'm sure you're trying to *pretend* it doesn't bother you, but you can't fool me. I'm your mother, and I can hear the dejection in your voice—"

"Mom…" Kera sank her head into her free hand.

"—and I bet you're doing that thing with your lip," her mother finished.

"What thing?" Kera picked her head up, her fingers fumbling around her mouth, trying to figure out what her lips were doing. "You've never mentioned that before."

"Don't worry about it, dear. But maybe it *is* time to consider working somewhere you're more likely to meet a higher caliber of man. Cleaning up after other people's drunken escapades sets a bad precedent as to what you're willing to put up with from them, after all. And men who hit on barmaids usually don't amount to much. I've seen it happen to friends of mine. You're far too smart for that. It's not who you were meant to be, Kera Lynn."

The younger woman paused, momentarily amazed at her mother's ability to bring either of Kera's main perceived failures —lack of a serious relationship and lack of a serious job—around to the other one.

It was remarkable.

"You do know," Kera said in falsely pleasant tones, "that I hate my middle name, right? Unlike this mysterious lip thing, I'm positive I've mentioned *that* before."

"Hate it all you want," her mother said, unperturbed. "It's on your birth certificate, and it's part of who you are. Besides, everyone is *supposed* to hate their middle name."

Kera stood up and did a mild stretching routine while she

spoke. "Yours is Amber. How is that bad? I could have dealt with Amber."

"I'm not everyone, I'm special." Her mother laughed. "Face it, dear, I'm older and have way more experience than you do at verbal sparring. You have no chance, you realize."

"Weird," Kera commented. "I never thought you'd be the one to admit how much older you are than I am."

"Not by *that* much," her mother said, nettled, "although I will point out that I gave up some of my prime years to chase you little terrors all over the lawn at that country home."

"I thought you loved that lawn," Kera pointed out.

Her mother laughed again. "I did, aesthetically speaking. It was nice to look at. The practice was another matter entirely. Do you know how many bugs nested in that grass? It makes me shudder to think about it."

Kera saw an opening to score a point. "Glad I don't have to deal with the hassles of a lawn, then. I'm doing great where I am."

"Nonsense," her mom retorted. "You're living in a warehouse, darling, and I'm sure you have no plans to make it a long-term thing. You just wouldn't be happy."

You mean you *wouldn't be happy.* Kera gritted her teeth. It was mostly fun and games when it came to arguing with her mother, but every now and again, the woman managed to get under her skin.

"I'm happy right now," Kera said carefully.

"Yes, maybe for now," Mrs. MacDonagh warned, "but if you could have any career and living arrangements you wanted, would they be what you have now? If the answer is no, you're selling yourself short, which means I'm right."

Kera decided it was too early to deal with this shit. She rubbed her forehead. "Okay," she said with a sigh, "fine. You win, Mom. Good job. I'll update you soon on all the things I'm required to do to meet your definition of happiness."

"You know that wasn't what I said, Kera." But the woman

knew better than to push it after the tone Kera had just used. "You're going to do great things, sweetie, I know it. I'm just trying to help you get there. Take care."

"Yeah. Bye." She hung up, planted the phone on her nightstand, and blew upward from her lower lip, the puff of air blasting a disheveled strand of black hair away from her face.

Parents, she thought morosely as she ambled to the shower. It wasn't that her mother was a *bad* parent, but nothing Kera did or said seemed to have any impact on the woman's certainty that she and she alone knew what would make Kera happy.

Maybe Kera didn't *want* to make all the right decisions. Maybe that path looked like a giant trap, and *maybe,* just maybe, she didn't want her mother to say something like, "Everyone feels that way at your age."

"Stop trying to get me to skip ahead," she muttered uselessly as she shampooed her hair. Her mother couldn't hear her, and even if she could, Kera's protest would change nothing.

Having given up on sleep, she got dressed and ate half a tub of peanut butter on a similarly insane amount of toast. When that was done, she looked at the corner and sighed.

She really should get that workout gear up. The magic had given her a false sense of her strength and speed, and even if she didn't intend to use it that way again, she wanted to know she could get out of a bad situation *without* using magic.

Plus, if her mother was going to keep calling this often, Kera was going to need to hit a punching bag on a regular basis.

She shouldn't have showered until she got everything set up. Kera put on her work shirt and began hauling things around, hopping up on chairs and oiling chains and bench joints and smashing her fingers more than once.

She was good at all the tasks relating to Zee, but she could do those from muscle memory. *This* was just hauling around huge and heavy things. Some of them were as big as she was. By the time she was done, she couldn't tell if it looked good. All she wanted was another shower. She rinsed off, put on new clothes, and contemplated whether she should try to do a load of laundry before work.

There was a knock on the door, and she frowned at it before heading over to look out.

Don't be Mom, don't be Mom, don't be Mom...

Luckily, it wasn't. "Sam," Kera said, surprised. "What brings you this way?"

There was just enough time for a spike of worry, but he blushed and held up a square box wrapped in a thick cloth. "I brought you some soup," he explained. "It's from my mom. She feels better today."

Kera closed her eyes, relief pulsing through her. "I'm happy to hear that...and thanks. Come in, and just set the soup on the table there."

Sam obeyed, then began unwrapping the package. The girl saw with mounting curiosity that in addition to a sealed plastic dish of soup, there was another box. Sam picked it up, turned, and handed it to her.

"This is from Mom, too. She said to return it when you're ready. Don't bother opening it right now. I'll, um, go. Have a good day, though."

"Sure. I appreciate it." Kera nodded. "Tell your parents I said hi."

He agreed and left, seemingly in a hurry due to embarrassment. She wasn't sure why, and with teenage boys, who knew?

The soup smelled delicious, but before tearing into it, Kera examined the box. It was clearly a reused generic packing box, with no markings. She opened one end and out slid a smaller box that was original to the product.

"What the heck?" she breathed, staring at the soft, semi-shapeless mass of gleaming gold.

It was a blonde wig—an exceedingly nice and high-quality

one, which could not possibly have been cheap. Seized with morbid curiosity, Kera studied the box for a price tag.

"Holy shit," she sputtered. "$2,750. They're lending me something that costs half as much as a fucking car."

For an instant, she felt guilty and considered politely refusing the wig, giving it back with an "Oh, I could never…" statement. But she knew the Kims trusted her and were trying to return a favor. She would accept this graciously and do all in her power to return it to them intact.

After all, this was only until she figured out how to change her hair magically.

And she hadn't realized until she held it in her hands just how much she wanted to look like herself again. Kera took the wig into the bathroom and pulled the mass of gold onto her head, then she almost teared up. The rush of pleasure was surprising in its intensity.

"I really, really screwed my hair up," she admitted. "Fine. Offer accepted, Mrs. Kim."

The girl found two halves of a plastic dummy head within the box and snapped them together to mount the wig on it, then put it on top of her wardrobe. She wouldn't be able to wear it under her helmet, of course, but she could bring it to work in her backpack.

She found her phone and looked up the number for the Kims' grocery store, then tapped it in. Mr. Kim answered.

"Hi," she greeted him. "It's Kera."

"Hello, Kera! Sam stopped by, yes?"

"Yes. I love the wig. I mean, I love the soup, but you knew that already. The wig? Absolutely *love* it. Thank you so much."

"Wonderful," he told her. "Ye-jin insisted. She said it is important to a woman to be able to present the image she wishes to present. I trust her opinion on such things."

Kera laughed. "That was very sweet of her, and she was right. I'd love to thank her in person. Could I stop by tomorrow?"

"Yes, yes, of course. She would love to see you." Mr. Kim was always gracious, almost excessively so, but Kera suspected that meant that her "reiki" treatment had been a success thus far. She wanted to cry for happiness but stopped herself.

"Well, thank you again," she told Mr. Kim. "I'll see you later. Oh, and stop feeding me. You're going to make me fat!"

The old man guffawed at that. "Not a chance. You'll eat good food until I say to stop!"

She heard the door tone in the background, and Kim excused himself. They said their goodbyes and hung up. She leaned back on her bed, sighing.

Just you wait, Mom, she thought to herself. *One of these days, I'm going to blow your mind when I tell you just how cool my career really is.*

The thought made her chuckle.

At least she had something to do on her weekends when she wasn't at work. Speaking of which...

She got ready in a hurry, deciding she wanted to be early. Her leathers went on at the end of the process, and the rest of her stuff was strapped into her pack, including the wig, which she wrapped in cloth and plastic to ensure it wouldn't get wet or damaged.

"If someone throws a drink in my face while I'm wearing that thing," she muttered while climbing astride Zee, "they're dead."

CHAPTER TWENTY-NINE

Christian marveled as Jennifer, the bartender, laughed at the latest of Ted's jokes. Incredibly, in his opinion, it sounded like Ted was on the verge of a home run. That was good because Christian didn't make much of a wingman under the best of circumstances.

And Ted's drunken jokes did not give him much to work with.

"So yeah," Ted continued, leaning over the bar with a suave smile. "I have the next couple of days off. What do you say we get a few drinks? Someplace a little...quieter than this."

She chuckled at that but shook her head. "Sorry," she said. "You're funny, but I'm already with someone."

"Huh?" Ted asked. He didn't seem to know what to do with that and looked at Christian.

All Christian could do was shrug.

"Don't want to ruin a good thing," Jennifer said, taking pity on the two of them and finishing up the conversation on her own. She gave Ted what looked like a genuine smile. "No offense!" With that, she darted off to tend to another customer who was calling for her.

Ted stared after her forlornly.

"There, there." Christian patted his shoulder and tried to keep the laughter from his voice. "It happens to the best of us."

"It doesn't happen to *me*," Ted said blankly.

"That's weird. What did I just see then?" Christian couldn't keep from laughing, and he snorted when Ted shot him a stony look. "Oh, come on. Good learning experience, huh?"

"I may never love again," Ted grumbled morosely.

"I predict that outlook will last until…oh, tomorrow at lunch." Christian grinned and drained his beer, then did a double-take. A familiar figure had appeared at the end of the bar, sending his heart rate spiking by several notches.

"Hey, guys!" Kera said as she got close. "Sorry, I didn't see you come in earlier. It's a busy-ass night. Nice to have you back."

Christian nodded and tried to remember how words worked. "It's good to be here," he said and mentally cursed himself for sounding as if he were accepting an award. "Uh, did you do something different with your hair?"

It occurred to him that maybe he shouldn't have asked that. Women sometimes got sensitive about anything that could be remotely construed as criticism of their appearance. Her hair did look like it might be a different shade of blonde, however, and the length and style had also changed.

"Oh," she said, and to his surprise, she looked evasive for a moment. "Ah, different conditioner. More, uh, body. Shiny. Refill?"

Christian nodded, and she whisked his glass around the end of the bar and took it to the appropriate tap.

"Anyway," she added as she filled the glass, "I'm glad I reached you guys before you got completely wasted."

"Hey, now." Christian pointed at his friend. "That's just him."

"Huh?" Ted looked back, having missed Kera's appearance while staring after Jennifer. "Oh. Hi. When did you…hi."

Kera followed his gaze. "Oh, Jennifer? Don't worry, man, you're in good company. She breaks hearts on the regular." She patted the bar. "Order of fries on the house to take the sting out?"

Ted grumbled good-naturedly, and Kera smiled. She could tell that unlike many guys, he was frustrated that he had struck out but wasn't going to try to change Jennifer's mind. Behind all his overdone posturing, Ted was a good guy.

She was glad she had the busy night to keep her moving since it meant she didn't linger next to Christian and possibly make a fool of herself. She backed up Jennifer when backlogs formed at the bar and took orders from the kitchen out to patrons in the booths and at the tables.

Once she glanced at Christian, but he caught her looking at him, and she felt like an idiot—even more so when she had to ask the patron she was waiting on to repeat their order.

In addition to her other duties, she also kept an eye on new customers streaming in through the front door. Around midnight, a trim, dark-haired figure who looked familiar slid in. Kera, who had just placed an order of onion rings on one of the tables, slowly straightened. Her eyes tracked the figure across the bar to a corner booth, and she looked away when his gaze moved toward her.

It was him. She might not be able to prove it in a court of law, but she knew in her gut that this man was the same asshole who had hit on her and shot up Zee after she said no. The same asshole who had threatened Cevin. Her certainty grew when she heard him give Stephanie a drink order. The voice, the way he moved—it was the same guy.

And if he was back, he was going to try to resolve one or both of his pieces of unfinished business. Strategies flashed through her head; she could lure him out into the alley, she could set a trap for him in the bathroom...

She took a deep breath and told herself not to do anything rash. She had gotten in over her head the other night and been lured into making a stupid mistake, and she *knew* this man was dangerous. A man with that temper and that sense of being owed was *always* dangerous, and this one had a gun.

And possibly backup.

As the night wore on and he didn't make any shady moves, she told herself that she had overreacted to his presence in the bar. Maybe he'd learned his lesson. Maybe he wouldn't do anything violent.

Part of her knew that wasn't going to happen, but she felt trapped. How was she going to take this guy on without getting other people caught in the crossfire?

She had done something good for Mrs. Kim. Her powers *could* do good things, but not if she got herself killed.

She came back to herself to hear Ted laughing. She smiled and set down her tray, looking over as he said, "I already got shot down by the brunette. It's *your* turn to ask someone out. Man up."

Kera's eyebrow shot up, and she busied herself by neatening up the container of cocktail umbrellas. She didn't trust her face right now.

Out of the corner of her eye, she saw Christian fidget. "That…*might* be valid."

"Yeah, exactly." Ted wiggled his fingers drunkenly as if he'd tried to make a gesture and forgotten what he was attempting halfway through. "How else would we decide it?"

He was too drunk to realize he'd made an error, but Kera knew exactly what Christian was going to do next.

"Random number," Christian asserted suddenly, holding one finger up. His voice was triumphant. "Get a random number generator running, and let chance or chaos theory or whatever be the one to select which of us goes next."

Before she had time to think, Kera turned toward them. "Hey, can anyone join in?"

They both looked at her, blinking.

Shit, shit, shit, she told herself.

"Join what?" Ted asked cautiously.

There was no way out now. Her heart was beating irregularly; she was pretty sure that was a sign of a serious health problem, but she didn't see a graceful way to call an ambulance. Kera dried her hands on her towel and cleared her throat. "Uh, determining who has to be the next one to ask someone out."

They looked at each other.

"Uh, sure," Ted said.

Beside him, Christian was doing an impression of a fish.

To make it more fun and take some of the focus off her, Kera looked over her shoulder and called to her work partner, "Hey, Jenn! Come over here. Think of a number between one and ninety-nine. Just don't tell us what it is."

Jennifer came over, frowning. "Is this a contest?"

"Kind of." Kera tried to mask her nervousness with a smile. "We're going to see who picks the number closest to yours. Let's start off with this gentleman." She pointed at Ted. "Number?"

He cleared his throat. "Forty-nine."

She gestured at Christian next.

"We'll go with fifty."

Kera shook her head in mild disappointment and crossed her arms. "You two are playing it safe, I see."

"Well, sure." Ted looked at her owlishly. "You should have gone first. Now you...hmm."

Kera smiled. Unlike the other two, she didn't need to play it safe; she knew Jennifer. She pulled over a napkin and wrote down a number before folding it up and putting one finger on it. Then she turned to her co-worker. "Okay, Jenn, what's your pick?"

The brunette smirked. "Sixty-nine." She stuck out her tongue. "Had to liven your game up a *little* bit, didn't I?"

"So, what was yours?" Ted asked Kera, gesturing at the paper.

Kera slid it over to Christian. "Open it."

Christian did so and groaned. "Sixty-nine."

Kera grinned. "I guessed you two were going to play it safe.

Meanwhile, I know Jenn, whose head is always in the goddamned gutter."

"I *heard* that," Jennifer said as she navigated behind Kera with a tray.

"It's *true*," Kera pointed out. She turned back to the two men. "Anyway, since you two accepted the terms, I win. I get to choose who asks someone out next. And I choose…"

Both men had priceless expressions on their faces.

"Myself," Kera said before she could chicken out.

Both men looked as though their brains were restarting, which made her feel a little better. She was pretty sure her stomach had just attempted to do a full somersault.

"So, Christian," she asked, "want to go out with me?"

She had just enough time to think she'd horribly misjudged the situation before Christian gulped, then stuttered, "Um, y-yes?" He shook his head. "Wait, that sounded like a question. Definitely a yes, but will you let me pay?"

She gave him a smile disguised as a cynical squint. "*I'm* the one who asked *you* out," she observed.

"Okay, how about Dutch?"

Kera grinned. "Dutch it is. Shake on it." She extended her hand.

Christian took it and sealed the deal while Ted's jaw went slack.

Before he could say anything, Kera saw Jennifer make a gesture. "Sorry, duty calls." She gave Christian a smile and slid away, silently congratulating herself.

Hopefully that meant she had used up her nervous energy and wouldn't do something stupid when it came to the asshole in the corner.

It only felt like a few minutes before she saw it was almost 2. She straightened up from clearing a table. "Last call!"

At least her voice was steady.

At the bar, Christian and Ted had sunk into silence.

Finally, Ted nudged Christian with an elbow. "You did it."

"Uh-huh." Christian looked at him and tried to figure out if he should say he *hadn't* done it.

"No offense," Ted said, "but…"

"She's out of my league?"

"Not that. I, uh, I didn't think you were going to pull it off." Ted tipped his glass up to get the last of his beer. "I have yet to see if you're going to need me. I should know soon."

"What does *that* mean?"

"You'll see," Ted said.

It was only a couple of minutes before Kera stopped by, just as Chris was putting down the cash for their tab.

"I'll, uh, I'll be back next week to set up a date and time?" he asked Kera.

"Sure." She hesitated. "I only work Monday through Friday, though."

"Oh. Right. Uh, we could…stay in touch?" Chris patted himself, longing for a pen or a piece of paper, only to see a business card appear next to his face with his cell phone number written on the back.

"I figured you wouldn't remember," Ted said. He sounded deeply pleased. "Hey, look at that! I *was* useful." He handed the card to Kera.

Kera looked as if she was trying not to laugh.

"Thanks for blowing my cover, man," Christian grumbled.

"Mmm." Kera smiled at him. "This is nice, but Chris?"

"Yes?" His stomach clenched. Had he done something wrong?

Kera's lips twisted in a subtly mischievous smile. "Don't you remember that I still have your cell from our study dates?"

Ted threw up his arms, sputtering in disbelief, then slapped his friend on the arm. "She has your number *already?*"

Kera nodded. "Mmhmm. And he has mine. I'll see you soon, Christian."

"Yeah." Christian couldn't keep from grinning at her as he

helped Ted out of the bar. His friend had been more careful this time, but he still wasn't sober by a long shot.

Just sober enough to wait until the door closed behind them to punch him on the arm again. "You could have called her this whole time!"

Christian grinned and held a hand out to keep his friend from tripping. He felt like he was walking on air. He couldn't help but think things were better this way. If he'd just texted her randomly, he didn't think she would have responded well.

"It *was* you, Ted," he admitted. "I wouldn't have said hello to her if it hadn't been for you."

Ted paused to consider that drunkenly, then nodded. "I know that," he said with great dignity. "I was just making sure you did."

"Uh-huh. Let's get you home, buddy."

Back in the bar, Jennifer finished closing down and cleaning up while Kera did a quick visual scan of the floor. Stephanie had left an hour ago.

Only one person still sat at a booth—and unfortunately, his presence ruined Kera's hopes of not having a confrontation tonight. She made sure to keep moving as she ran through her options. She was annoyed, on top of everything else, that she was focusing on *this* when all she wanted to do was do air-punches at the sky about getting the balls to ask Chris out.

Call the police, she told herself as she swept a few imaginary specks of dust off a table.

But they weren't going to help. They had been outmatched all week by what was going on in Little Tokyo. If this guy wasn't long gone by the time they got here, they'd be on the losing end of a fight.

She was delaying. You have some power, she told herself, and not winning against this guy once doesn't mean you get to duck out of confrontations forever.

If she had gotten lured into a trap by him last time, well, she would be the one to set the trap this time. She knew what the guy wanted, and she knew how he operated. She knew what she had to do, and she knew she needed to get everyone else out of here so she could do it.

She headed toward the back and ran into Cevin as he was emerging from his office to help his remaining employees.

Her boss didn't notice her; his flint-hard eyes had shot past her to fix on the dark figure lounging in the booth. "That guy," Cevin growled under his breath, "better leave soon. It's closing time. We might have to call the cops."

Shit. Kera had hoped she could do this without Cevin knowing about it. She took a deep breath. "I'm sorry, Cevin." She put a hand on his arm to urge him back toward his office and out of sight of the man in the booth.

"For what?" he asked.

"Nothing you'll remember." She met his eyes briefly before she murmured an incantation and twisted her fingers in a strange gesture.

The surrounding light dimmed oddly and sound was muffled, then it was over. Cevin stood blinking into space until Kera guided him back to his office by the arm and sat him down in his chair.

"I'll be right back," she told him. "Just start shutting the computers down and get your things, okay?"

He swallowed. "Uh, okay." He didn't seem to be aware that she was present.

Kera turned and left the office, rubbing her forehead and making a mental note to check on him before she let him leave. She hoped he remembered what day it was, at least.

And where he lived. This was the first time she had cast the spell on him, so she figured it should be safe. Safer, at any rate, than having him try to interfere in what she was doing, but she wanted to check later and make sure he was okay.

When she arrived in the bar, the final booth was empty, and the trim figure of their mysterious guest was vanishing out the front door. Kera knew where he would be in a little bit. She needed to get into position before he did.

She looked around. Jennifer still had a good ten minutes' worth of work to do. It would have gone faster if someone helped her, but...

"Hey, Jenn," Kera called. "I'm really sorry, but my mom is calling, and I gotta take it. It's important. I'll be back in fifteen. Make sure Cevin is okay, please. He wasn't feeling well."

Her co-worker nodded. She might not want to close down the bar on her own, but she wasn't going to insist that Kera help in the middle of a family emergency.

Feeling a little guilty, Kera went to the lockers and pulled on her leathers. Then she yanked her blonde wig off, allowing her shorter black hair to spill out from beneath it, and set the wig on the shelf where the leather clothing had been. Finally, she slid on her black helmet.

There was one more thing to do. Around a tight corner between the office and the hallway leading to the rear entrance was the console for the security setup, including the cameras. It only took the girl a second to find the button to put the whole system on pause until further notice.

"Right. Here we go." She slipped out the back of the bar into the darkness.

CHAPTER THIRTY

Johnny Torrez chewed his lower lip as he peered down the alley. Cevin apparently had two brain cells to rub together after all. He'd bought extra lights with which to flood the alley, meaning there was no sufficiently dark place for Johnny to park his Mustang on the Mermaid's property. Not only that but operating on foot would be more difficult.

One of the other businesses had a back lot, however, and a nice, shadowy corner where trees and a dumpster would block the sight of his car, even if someone squeezed around the Mermaid's dumpster and looked at the other side of the alley.

Perfect.

He checked to make sure the Beretta was securely in its shoulder holster and that his dark glasses and hat were on to obscure his identity. He thought about lighting a smoke just in case they were too stupid to remember who he was.

He didn't want his hands full, though.

He climbed out of the Mustang, taking a second to admire it, and locked its doors before turning toward the Mermaid. It wasn't difficult to squeeze past the dumpster, though he resented them for the necessity.

He was still in the shadows next to it when a low voice froze him in his tracks.

"You shouldn't have come back." There was a faint rasp at the edges. At first, he thought it was a woman speaking, then he thought it might be a man.

For some reason, that seemed more threatening than any woman or man he had ever met. He froze in place, his mind shifting into full alertness, and looked around. No one was visible.

He told himself not to be stupid. He knew these tricks. He *used* these tricks. "Don't fuck with me, whoever you are. I'm not the guy, you're not the one, and now is not the time. You need to get yourself someplace safe, my friend." His voice had taken on a cold, venomous edge, and anyone who wasn't a complete moron would have caught the deadly threat in it.

"*That*," the voice insinuated, seeming to come from a different direction now, "is the whole point, except you've missed it. *You* are the one who needs to leave. You're on LA Witches turf, and we don't appreciate other fucks trying to edge in on our territory."

Johnny snorted. The stealth his challenger had demonstrated so far was mildly unnerving, but in his line of work, bullshit threats weren't enough to faze him. Also, he was now pretty sure the voice was female.

That, he could handle.

He drew his pistol, grinning at the various pools of shadow. "Territories have a way of changing hands. Maybe you're too new to know that yet, but trust me, you're about to learn. This isn't going to be your bitch-ass turf, so get the hell out of here."

He began to take slow, deliberate steps, still scanning the shadows around him for a human silhouette. There was nothing. He racked the slide on his gun, allowing the distinctive metallic sound of a round being chambered to echo across the pavement.

Nothing moved, and no noises indicated that his hidden

adversary had a firearm of their own. Unless they were on a rooftop and had a rifle scope on him...

Then why would the voice be coming from his level?

A trick of sound, maybe, but people who set up little tricks had a way of crumbling when the chips were down. They couldn't handle a one-on-one fight.

He wasn't scared of them.

He wasn't.

The voice spoke again. "Stitches are for bitches, not witches."

"What?" Johnny blew out his breath in exasperation. "That doesn't even make sense. Let me tell you 'bout you kids since I've learned a lot about you this week. You're fucking weak. You been watching too many of those robot magician cartoons on YouTube, smoking weed until you think you're invincible, but you're about to get hurt for real."

Light flooded the alley—the distinctive blue-tinted light from his custom headlights. Johnny watched as it grew lighter—clearly, only one headlight had gone on at first, but now there were both—and then dimmed again, going back to one, and then off entirely.

He hadn't heard his engine.

He clenched his jaw and turned toward the Mermaid. "Great time for a malfunction," he mumbled.

His visitor wasn't done. "I bet you like that car," she offered in that strange, muffled rasp. "It's a shame the paint job is total shit."

That was the last straw. Johnny stomped toward the voice, brandishing his pistol. "You scratch my car, and I'll scratch a knife across your stomach."

"Who said scratch?" the other asked. "How about a little fire instead?"

Suddenly afraid that someone was going to start tossing Molotov cocktails, Johnny spun, seeking targets for his Beretta, and pushed out of the alley. He ran for his car, knowing it was a trap and not caring.

They'd finally be in his sights now, and if they thought he wouldn't shoot them, they were *wildly* mistaken.

He saw no one as he ran toward the shadowed corner where he'd parked, but he *did* smell something.

The godawful acrid stench of paint on fire.

Johnny skidded to a stop in front of the car to see wisps of smoke rising from it—and, undeniably, the hood glowing red like a sheet of metal in a forge.

"No. *No*. What the *fuck*!"

He strode toward it, slammed his hands down on the metal in a blind rage, and fumbled for the catch. Whatever the hell they'd done—

"Shit!" He jerked his hands off the burning metal, dropping his pistol on the pavement. It landed on one of the corners of its grip and bounced noisily in the opposite direction from where he stood.

He spun away from the car, shaking his hands out with a hiss of pain and scanning the darkness. He could hear footsteps, but they seemed to echo all around him, unmatched by any movements he could see.

"The LA Witches are *not* to be messed with," the weird voice insisted. "I'll be nice and write you a reminder note."

"Huh?"

"You won't remember any of this." He could *hear* them smiling, dammit. "Trust me."

The figure finally stepped out of the pitch-blackness into the gloom. It was a slender figure of average height, possibly female, but it was hard to tell under the leather outfit. The hands removed a glossy black helmet, and choppy black hair a little shorter than shoulder-length fell out.

Johnny edged closer to where his pistol had fallen. "Who the hell are you?"

Kera settled her helmet under one arm and tried not to laugh aloud at his fear. He didn't have any idea who she was, and his anger and confusion had combined to make him indecisive. The truth of who he really was under all that bluster was coming out.

"I'm the head bitch, shithead," she said. "And you're the one who might need stitches after this is over."

She cast the spell, speaking the incantation in a rush of words now familiar and well-practiced, and twisting her free hand behind her back in the associated gesture. Her nerves fired as her body demanded that she move—action, because now it could move faster and hit harder than any human should be able to.

She shot toward the man, and her knee connected with his stomach before he could react. The helmet in her left hand helped her balance, and she smiled at the thought of smashing him across the face with it.

She didn't think of herself as a violent person, but this man liked to hurt people. She wasn't going to lose sleep over giving him a taste of his own medicine.

From his strangled cry and the spasm in his arms, she knew he was shocked by her speed, but he clearly had been in more than a few street fights in his life. He ducked aside before she could smash him in the face with either her helmet or her fist and struck at her, hand lashing toward her back.

He had clearly learned not to freeze at the start of a fight. Apparently, there *was* something under the bluster.

There wasn't enough to change the outcome of this fight, though. Kera pivoted in time to avoid the full force of the blow, so it missed her kidney and bounced off the leather that covered her back ribs. She was already moving to her next goal, the pistol. She'd already marked where it lay and figured he would go for it.

As he did, she flash-stepped ahead of him, and his eyes bulged in shock as her boot came down on the fallen pistol a half-second before his hand could. Then she swung the helmet, catching him hard behind the ear with it.

He grunted and toppled to the pavement, shocked and moaning in pain though still conscious. "*Puta*," he spat at her. "You got no idea who you're—"

"Try to get back up," Kera warned him, seeing that he was on the verge of rising to one knee, "and I'll set your balls on fire. You saw what I did to your car. Think about all that concentrated heat focused on something a little more *delicate*. Nice thought, isn't it?"

"What do you want?" he gritted out. He was holding himself back from attacking her, and she could tell how much he hated that.

"Well," Kera said, drawing the word out, "I'd tell you, but you wouldn't remember."

She kneed him in the upper chest. The force of the blow sent him reeling back toward his vehicle, and the back of his head clunked into its front bumper. Johnny let out another groan and slumped to the ground, conscious only in the loosest sense of the word.

Kera nodded in satisfaction, then drew the necessary spells to mind: first, the charm of forgetting, and second, the enchantment for sleep. With adrenaline pumping through her, it took real effort to restrain the flow of magic. This time, after all, she didn't care as much if her spells spread out.

Once the man was oblivious, she picked him up and deposited him behind the wheel of his damaged Mustang, allowing his head to rest against the dashboard beside the wheel.

With that done, Kera wrote a note on a slip of paper she'd grabbed back in the bar.

LA WITCH TERRITORY. HANDS OFF.

She stuffed it into Johnny's pants pocket but then thought better of it. "Nah," she said, half to herself and half to him. "You won't recall any of this when you wake up, so I can't afford to be subtle." She tore a tiny hole so she could hang the piece of paper over the front of his rearview mirror. "Yeah. That works."

Hustling now that her main task was done, Kera pulled off her leathers and wrapped her helmet in them, then trotted back across the empty lot to the rear entrance of the Mermaid.

She reentered the bar, flipped the button to turn the security system back on, and strolled up to the bar to help Jenn with the last five minutes' worth of chores.

The brunette looked at her with narrowed eyes. "Are you okay? I thought I heard someone yelling out there."

"Yeah," said Kera. "I'm fine. Some guy passed by on the street, cussing out his girlfriend or something on the phone."

Jennifer was almost done sweeping the floor. She rolled her eyes and shook her head at Kera's story. They'd both seen plenty of shenanigans at this time of night.

"And your mom?" Jennifer asked a moment later.

With a jolt, Kera remembered the story she'd told her coworker. "Right. Turned out to be a false alarm. They thought my grandma was really sick, but the tests all came back fine. She just didn't want me to be awake worrying."

Once the girls finished up front, they collected Cevin from his office. He was mostly fine but spaced out. Kera decided a Jedi mind trick was in order.

"Hey, Cevin, we're closed now. Jenn and I finished cleaning up. You're done with the computer stuff, right? Anything left you can do tomorrow, on Saturday. Let's all go home."

He shook his head and pinched the bridge of his nose. "Um, yeah, sure. Sounds good." She saw him pull himself back together, which was good.

She didn't know how to do the opposite of a sleep spell on someone.

The three left the bar behind, locking up and going to their separate vehicles. Kera waved at Jennifer as she pulled away, and then at Cevin, where he was doing his usual radio-and-cigarette routine. Then she fired up Zee and headed out of the alley, looping around the block to take a glance at the back lot.

The Mustang was gone, and so was the man who'd driven it there.

Kera shook her head and looked into the darkness. "Don't come back, asshole."

She revved Zee and headed home.

CHAPTER THIRTY-ONE

Saturday afternoons at the Kims' grocery store tended to be slow, and today was no exception. When Kera came in, there weren't any other customers to get in the way.

Mr. Kim noticed her right away. "Kera! Good to see you. Come here, come here."

Kera smiled. He had sent her so much free food that she didn't need to do any shopping. She had come here today to see the family, and to buy something if he would let her. She walked over to the counter, taking heart from his contented smile. Mrs. Kim must still be doing well.

"How is work?" the old man asked. "Did you wear your new wig?"

"I did! It worked perfectly." Kera gestured at her wig-less head. "I don't wear it under my helmet, and I don't want to damage it. And work is fine. There was a little bit of excitement with some local people—the person who damaged my bike. But nothing serious. I don't think they'll be back."

"If they are, you know to call the authorities, yes?" Mr. Kim gave her an unusually sharp look. "Remember, I too was once young and thought myself indestructible."

If that asshole comes back, a lot more is going to get burned than the hood of his car, Kera thought, but she didn't want to worry her friend. "I won't get in over my head, I promise. How is Mrs. Kim?"

The man's face almost glowed, it was so happy. "She is doing well. I think she would like to see you. Would you like to come up?"

"Of course. I would love to."

Mr. Kim bustled around, locking the door and putting up a sign to say the store would be open again soon, then led Kera upstairs.

Once again, Mrs. Kim was lying on the couch, though this time she looked more normal. Her skin was a healthier shade and she was fully awake, clearly at ease instead of wracked with pain.

She looked around at the sound of footsteps and smiled when she saw Kera. "Hello," she said warmly. "I hope you liked the soup."

"I did," said Kera. "And the wig; it's beautiful. You'll get it back in the same condition I got it in. I promise."

"There's no rush." Mrs. Kim gestured at her bathrobe and the blanket over her legs, smiling. "I will be here on the couch for some time, I think, so I will not be using it." She reached over to pat the chair beside the couch. "Come, sit. I have heard things about you from my husband, but I would like to hear more from *you.*"

"Of course." Kera sat down, noting that Mrs. Kim seemed a bit winded from the minor effort of speaking. She tried to keep her story light and amusing, telling Mrs. Kim about college and her current living situation and even mentioning Christian.

After a few minutes, however, Kera could no longer ignore the exhaustion in the woman's eyes.

She hesitated but knew she could not leave without trying to help. "I don't know how you feel, but if you'll let me examine you again and maybe try a little more reiki, I might be able to help again."

Mr. and Mrs. Kim exchanged glances, then both gave the girl a nod.

This time, it didn't take as much sugar and fat and caffeine, which was a relief. Still, it took a lot out of Kera, and the old man watched her closely as she channeled subtle, carefully-directed streams of healing magic into his wife.

Kera's heart rate quickened each time she pushed against the outer edges of the cancer. She knew she was approaching her limit in each push when she grew dizzy and had to struggle not to pass out, and by the sixth attempt, she was able to pull back *before* reaching that point.

She was excited. Though she still didn't dare try to eliminate the disease at its source, she was pushing back the tumorous tissue. She was winning, and it was losing.

When it was over, Mrs. Kim needed to rest, and Kera figured she'd require the same. Strung out and drained, only a mixture of energy drinks and politeness kept her going. In fact, she found herself dreaming of the prepackaged cupcakes downstairs. She might treat herself to a pack of those before she tried to drive.

Mrs. Kim reached out to squeeze Kera's fingers. "Thank you," she said. "Tonight, I will be well enough to cook again. The smells, the textures…it is good to be able to do the simple things."

"And she has another appointment on Tuesday," Mr. Kim added. "We will see what they have to say."

"Good." Kera smiled, though she felt a stab of worry. "Uh, don't mention me, okay? Doctors can be…very dismissive of reiki." That hung together as an excuse, she was fairly sure.

"Of course," Mr. Kim assured her.

On the couch, Mrs. Kim had fallen asleep, her lips curved slightly in a gentle smile.

"Come, come." Mr. Kim offered Kera a hand to help her up and guided her back downstairs, where he offered her a candy bar. He shook his head when she pulled out her wallet. "No, no. And, Kera, you are safe with us."

She blinked at him, perplexed, though something in her core went cold with a faint premonition of dread. "Safe? How?"

The old man gave her a rueful smile. "I lied to you. Very sorry. I have studied reiki. I know what it is."

Oh, shit. Kera tried to keep her face straight. "I…see."

"Reiki," Kim went on, "doesn't make you eat so much, only to grow thinner. Don't think I don't notice this. You have lost weight, and unless you have a tapeworm, I know it's because of what you did for my wife. You have…sacrificed for her. You have done things most people cannot do."

It took Kera a second to realize that the cold numbness spreading through her was a form of shock, not magic, though her recent expenditure had likely not helped. "Mr. Kim," she murmured, "I'm…"

He raised a hand, palm outward. "No, don't worry. When you are ready, you can share with us, but you should know that no one will find out from me or my wife talking, or our son. She is my life, Kera. I was afraid for the future. Now it looks like we will make it to July."

Kera nodded wordlessly. She did not trust her voice, and her chin was trembling.

"I think we should have you over for dinner," Mr. Kim said. "Sometime after her appointment on Tuesday. You work on weekdays, right?"

She nodded again.

"How about Saturday?"

Oh, shit, she thought once more, though it was a different kind of alarm from what she'd felt a minute ago.

On the other hand, the distraction was a welcome one. She felt herself blushing. "I, uh, I have a date Saturday. I asked a guy out."

Mr. Kim's eyes widened. "Well, then. You will have to bring

him by to see if we approve of him." He reached over to pat her hand. "You think I am joking, but I am not. You have been a good daughter to us, and we owe it to your parents to look out for you. I take this seriously."

Kera laughed; she felt giddy with something like relief. "Okay, I think I can manage that. Maybe on our second date, if nothing else. Anyway, I should get going now." She gave the old man an embrace, then turned to leave.

"One more thing." His voice carried more authority than usual. He waited until she turned back, surprised, before switching into his usual tone. "Be safe, Kera. The abilities you have are unusual, but you are not the only one who has them. Playing with those forces can be dangerous, not only to your health but if others find you. That, I have some knowledge of."

"Mr. Kim…"

He shook his head. "When you are ready, come talk."

Kera nodded and headed out through the store into the warm sunlight with her head full of a jumble of thoughts. She stopped beside Zee, resting her hand on his surface, and spent a moment untangling her brain.

Mrs. Kim is getting better, she clarified to herself, *and she's going to make it to treatment. I achieved the incredible without killing myself.*

Having sorted that out, she was thrilled.

But there was still that chilly undercurrent to it, the vague, perilous sense that something might be wrong and there was more going on than she knew or could handle.

How much does Mr. Kim know? she wondered. *And who else knows?* As she swung a leg over Zee, she could only think of one person—or group.

Whoever had put out the spell-book.

Melvin's Legendary Barbecue lived up to its name so far.

More importantly, James was in the mood to appreciate it. They had located their second prospect and found her to be far more promising than the first—a young black woman with a touch of power. She'd been performing miracles of the small, unobtrusive variety, mostly gentle channelings to help plants grow, which seemed to be her passion. The full spectrum of her powers would not manifest until she was older.

Which was good. It meant the council's thaumaturgists had time to prepare.

Now he and Mother LeBlanc could have a well-earned celebratory meal.

"Ribs," James opined, "are a finer form of meat. More of a connoisseur thing. You don't get as much meat-meat as with some other cuts, yet the quality more than makes up for quantity."

He was acquainted with people among the old New England gentry who would have turned up their noses at Southern cuisine. They were fools, he felt, who didn't know what they were missing.

Across from him at their table, Mother LeBlanc simply smiled.

"What?" James asked her. "Did I say something amusing?"

"It's the advertiser in you," she told him. "Whenever you enjoy something, you cannot rest until you have described *precisely* why it is so wonderful."

James glowered. "It is a service I perform for this jaded, indifferent world—trying to reawaken the spark of their zest for life."

"That was lovely," she said courteously.

"I thought so." He dug into his food, cutting more glistening morsels off the charred rib bones, and settled into the companionable silence of a good meal.

When they were done, Mother LeBlanc produced two cloth napkins for them to clean their hands and mouths. James winced to see the streaks of barbecue sauce and grease on the white cloth and found himself wondering if she had a washing machine hidden in her gown.

Come to think of it, she must have some way of keeping the *gown* clean. He had often wondered if she had several identical gowns, but this trip had resolved that question handily. There was no way she had managed to stow other versions of *that* gown in her tiny suitcase.

"What are you thinking?" she asked. When he looked up, she was watching him.

James did not want to admit that he was trying to puzzle out the mysteries of her spells. Each thaumaturge had their own methodology and areas of expertise, but it was hard on his ego to explain that he had no idea how she made her dress work.

"I'm thinking about where we'll go next," he said. It was a white lie. It was what he *should* be thinking about, and he had been, up until the cloth napkins made him wonder about interdimensional laundry service.

"Well, what does your scrying spell say?" She raised an eyebrow and sipped her lemonade.

James pulled out his phone and accessed the web camera in the council chamber, and he and Mother LeBlanc leaned close to peer at the screen. Though they made a strange couple—both well-dressed, a white man and a black woman, her clothing hearkening back to an entirely different era—no one seemed to notice them.

Magic was useful that way.

On the screen, the image of the council chamber resolved from a mess of pixels, and James zoomed in to see the map.

There was no doubt about where they should go next. The glow, brightening and fading at intervals in multiple areas of Los Angeles, showed there was someone *very* powerful at work there.

"Los Angeles," Mother LeBlanc murmured.

"That will be…different." James rubbed his head. "I've never gotten a handle on LA."

"You don't have to," she pointed out. "You just have to get a handle on who this recruit is."

"With my luck? A movie star we can't remove from the public eye."

"Don't be pessimistic, James. It doesn't suit you." She smiled at him and pointed at one dot. "This. This is a truly impressive amount of magic. Frankly, if there weren't more recent ones, I would be worried that this person was dead. This could be our most promising recruit in more than a century. James, we thought we had hit the jackpot when we found the girl and her plants. This is even better."

James had to nod, but he was cautious. "A lot goes on in LA, and if whoever this is is involved in the upper levels of those games, they might be dangerous."

"They might." Her eyes met his. "Or they might be exactly the recruit you were looking for when you proposed this initiative."

Thank you for not only reading this story, but these Author Notes in the back!

For those who have read my story, please jump to the bottom to catch up on the latest. I am going to drop in a little "about me" up here at the top to catch up any new fans.

Who Am I?

I wrote my first book *Death Becomes Her* (*The Kurtherian Gambit*) in September/October of 2015 and released it November 2, 2015. I wrote and released the next two books that same month and had three released by the end of November 2015.

So, just at five years ago.

Since then, I've written, collaborated, concepted, and/or created hundreds more in all sorts of genres.

My most successful genre is still my first, Paranormal Sci-Fi, followed quickly by Urban Fantasy. I have multiple pen names I produce under.

Some because I can be a bit crude in my humor at times or raw in my cynicism (Michael Todd). I have one I share with Martha Carr (Judith Berens, and another (not disclosed) that we use as a marketing test pen name.

In general, I just love to tell stories, and with success comes the opportunity to mix two things I love in my life.

Business and stories.

I've wanted to be an entrepreneur since I was a teenager. I was a very *unsuccessful* entrepreneur (I tried many times) until my publishing company LMBPN signed one author in 2015.

Me.

I was the president of the company, and I was the first author published. Funny how it worked out that way.

It was late 2016 before we had additional authors join me for publishing. Now we have a few dozen authors, a few hundred audiobooks by LMBPN published, a few hundred more licensed by six audio companies, and about a thousand titles in our company.

It's been a busy five years.

What am I up to?

So, I'm presently in a restaurant called Scrambled in Henderson, NV. This is the first time I have tried the place, and the vibe is FANTASTIC.

In one week, the governor of Nevada is going to cut the number of people who can eat here by 50% (from 50% to 25% capacity.)

This will gut them financially. The owner was obvious to pick out (and since I was eating at the bar, it was easy to ask her questions), so I asked how the new expectations from the governor were going to affect their business.

It was rather heartbreaking.

I have no idea how I can help businesses like this survive when we are looking at hospitals overflowing, etc.

For me, the ability to get out and eat at a restaurant helps me emotionally. Yes, the food is nourishing, but being around people (even fairly far away from them) still helps. I am not the type of person who does well with no human interaction. I don't need much, but the first COVID ripped me up pretty well and families who suffered even worse.

There are no good answers.

Stay tough, everyone. Chins up, help someone who needs it, or put a hand up at an appropriate time and let others know if you are flagging.

There IS light at the end of the tunnel. Let's find a way to make this second wave of @#%@#% covid easier than the first.

Now, I'm going to go take my own advice and brighten a stranger's day.

(Editor's Note: I have been privileged to know Michael Anderle for over three years. When he says he's going to go brighten a stranger's day, he is not kidding! Since I met him, I have seen him perform SO many acts of kindness for total strangers, fellow authors, and anyone who just needs help that I can't even count them. He is one of the most genuine people you will ever meet, and way up there in medal position in the best human being Olympics. So glad to have met this man!)

We hope you enjoy this new series. Still assuming you have never read one of my books, I will close with my traditional sentiment from *The Kurtherian Gambit*…

Ad Aeternitatem, (to eternity)

Michael Anderle.

CONNECT WITH MICHAEL

Connect with Michael Anderle

Website: http://lmbpn.com

Email List: http://lmbpn.com/email/

Social Media:

https://www.facebook.com/LMBPNPublishing

https://twitter.com/MichaelAnderle

https://www.instagram.com/lmbpn_publishing/

https://www.bookbub.com/authors/michael-anderle

www.ingramcontent.com/pod-product-compliance
Lightning Source LLC
Chambersburg PA
CBHW060245100726
47907CB00003B/770